Kate Lagan's
Rough Guide
to *Heaven*

Marnie O'Doherty

Note for Librarians: A cataloguing record for this book is available from Library and Archives Canada at www.collectionscanada.ca/amicus/index-e.html
ISBN 1-4210-9592-1

Printed in Victoria, BC, Canada. Printed on paper with minimum 30% recycled fibre. Trafford's print shop runs on "green energy" from solar, wind and other environmentally-friendly power sources.

TRAFFORD

PUBLISHING™

Offices in Canada, USA, Ireland and UK

Book sales for North America and international:
Trafford Publishing, 6E–2333 Government St.,
Victoria, BC V8T 4P4 CANADA
phone 250 383 6864 (toll-free 1 888 232 4444)
fax 250 383 6804; email to orders@trafford.com
Book sales in Europe:
Trafford Publishing (UK) Limited, 9 Park End Street, 2nd Floor
Oxford, UK OX1 1HH UNITED KINGDOM
phone +44 (0)1865 722 113 (local rate 0845 230 9601)
facsimile +44 (0)1865 722 868; info.uk@trafford.com
Order online at:
trafford.com/06-1348

10 9 8 7 6 5 4 3 2

for

Rosaleen, Cahir Francis, Sara and Annkin

[always summer children]

"And trust me dear! Good humour can prevail
When airs, and flights, and screams, and scolding fail.
Beauties in vain their pretty eyes may roll;
Charms strike the sight, but merit wins the soul.
So spoke the Dame."
-The Rape Of The Lock, Canto V
        Alexander Pope

Kate Lagan stood as close to the edge as she dared. She was almost above the clouds on this side of the mountain and she felt the evening sun boast its warmth. Taking a deep breath she shouted her question at the universe.

"WHY AM I HERE?"

To her complete astonishment the universe answered back. This is what it said...

1

"Kate, I hope you don't mind me asking but has everyone in your family diarrhoea?"

.Patricia looked meaningfully towards the three bulging bags of toilet rolls at Kate's feet as the two friends sat in the café of their local supermarket. Kate stopped stirring the murky brown coffee and stared blankly at Patricia. Then her brain caught up with the question.

"They're on offer this week two pounds and twenty pence for a packet of nine. I bought twenty-seven rolls. You'd be surprised how many we use."

"How come I didn't see a bargain like that?"

"They're stacked ten shelves high near the delicatessen aisle"

"I don't go near that deli aisle. If I gave my Jimmy stuffed black olives with goat's cheese I'd get a delicate kick up the arse."

"You let him come back then?"

"Aye", Patricia looked slightly guilty. "Sure he had nowhere else to go. He stayed in his mate's house for a few days. On Sunday morning I opened the back door and there he was sitting on the step like a bedraggled Lassie-come-home. He was wet and miserable and panting for a cup of tea."

"I hope you gave it to him, in a bowl on the back step"

"You're terrible Kate. At least it's the other way around now. I was opening the door to let Jimmy back home. Years ago when my Susan was small I packed my bags and walked out on him."

"Where did you go?"

"Nowhere, anywhere, ended up in a hostel. It was terrible. Susan cried all the time, along with a dozen other kids. The staff were good enough but after a couple of days I decided that my own fire was better than a frying pan. I went home."

"Why didn't you rent a flat?"

"What with? I had no money, no job, no, future, a two year old kid and I'd maybe another one on the way. Oh and a black eye! I couldn't go to my ma's because she still had a houseful of children herself. Besides, I didn't want to worry her. But Kate, that was years ago. The good old days I think they were called."

Patricia lifted her cup in both hands and sipped the lukewarm coffee. She continued,

"We've survived Kate, the thirty year war of The Troubles and the eternal war of the sexes! That's the main thing. Most of the time we didn't know what we were doing. When I think of it now I don't know whether to laugh or cry. Sometimes I do both. Jimmy was seventeen when we were married and he was single-handedly set to save Ireland. I was sixteen and wobbling on my first pair of high heels. I told my ma I was pregnant and she had me up the side aisle in St. Paul's Church before anyone could say 'for better or for worse'."

"Or for richer or poorer" Kate murmured.

Patricia laughed "Aye, all I remember was the oul priest muttering words under his breath. I woke up the next day a married woman. I wasn't even a woman. I was just a wee girl. It's the wee girl in me that takes him back every time. I haven't the wit to be a woman and I'm forty-five."

Kate remembered the little girl in both of them. They had played together on the street, skips, kick the tin, red rover, hide 'n seek, german jumps, two balls. The older girls in the street had sniggered at them when they said two balls. Kate and Patricia, at ten years of age, knew the words meant something else. When they reached thirteen they had a vague vulgar notion of the meaning When Patricia was sixteen her innocence had been caught and netted.

"Do you want to know how pathetic I am Kate? Do you want to know why I keep taking him back? I feel sorry for him."

"What's wrong with that Patricia?"

"Pity! I can't build a strong foundation on pity."

"It's probably as good as anything else. Maybe that's the answer. I suppose that's why Jesus Christ made Peter the first Pope". Kate enjoyed these meanderings.

"Why?"

"He felt sorry for him Patricia. I mean, he was no great shake as an apostle was he?"

"Here, that's cheered me up. My Jimmy might become the first married pope to sit in the Vatican and I'll be his faithful wife by his side. May God and his Holy Mother take pity on us all."

Patricia finished her coffee and rose as majestically as she could from the plastic chair.

"I'm away to get some of those toilet rolls Kate. I hear the loo paper in Italy is very hard on the oul arse."

"Recycled"

"Like ourselves. See you Kate."

Kate finished her coffee, left the tray back to the counter and carried the bags out to her car. The key stuck in the boot and she wrestled with her shopping, keys and temper for two full minutes. When all was settled, she sat in the driver's seat and allowed herself a cigarette letting her mind drift with the smoke.

In contrast to Patricia's 'happiest day of her life' Kate's wedding had been a lovely affair. She was the last to leave the house and her mammy had more money by then. It was a good occasion. There had been a grand hotel, a beautiful meal, a honeymoon in Dublin and a very sexy negligee sent from a holy, but realistic, aunt in Boston. It still irritated Kate when people mentioned that her marriage had failed.

"It was not a failure" she would retort impatiently. "It just didn't last as long as I expected. It lasted ten years and I have two wonderful, talented children. How can that be a failure? It's better to have ten fair years than forty miserable ones."

Sitting in the car she coaxed the ashtray out of its hiding place and stubbed out the cigarette trying not to burn the tip of her finger. Smoking and driving were no longer complementary activities. It was too dangerous. The ashtray was in an obscure slot situated somewhere below the left kneecap. It was impossible to open without the strength of Samson. That was a difficulty for a committed smoker. If mobile phones distracted drivers then finding somewhere to flick ash was almost as mind defeating as understanding Matrix 3 or the appeal of rap music.

The car knew its way back to the house. The journey to the shops was one of the few outings Kate took these days. Petrol was becoming another bill to look at woefully and car maintenance was a luxury she could not afford. The car was getting old, like Kate. She rarely bothered to lock it hoping someone might do her a favour and steal it some night.

"Like my marriage in more ways than one," she thought.

She was home in five minutes. She opened the front door and shouted to her son,

"Charlie, are you home from school? Come downstairs and give me a hand with the shopping."

Charlie appeared at the top of the stairs, changed out of his hated uniform and wearing his baggy jeans and wise-crack tee shirt. Today's blue cotton announced in bold white letters 'this shirt looks great on my body', a message which Kate could understand. Some messages were more obscure and others downright improbable. Kate always checked the writing or symbols for innuendo when they paid a family visit to her mother. Usually her son or daughter had to explain the meanings of various slogans. Kate's mother, a devout catholic, daily communicant and staunch member of the parish choir could see immediately the rudeness, bareness or implied sexual misconduct on the breast of any garment.

Charlie shouted over the stair rail,

"Wait a minute mum I'll be down in a second."

"That's a stupid thing to say Charlie. It should be printed on a tee shirt. Unless you want a mother who has arms trailing along the ground like some urban orang-utan you'll come down right away."

Charlie responded heroically taking the stairs three at a time.

"Here take these bags with the milk and potatoes and leave the others at the bottom of the stairs. I'll sort them out later."

"I see the toilet rolls are on offer this week mum."

"All right wise guy. Bring those into the kitchen."

Kate followed him and he set the bags on the kitchen table. She looked at his back. He was now almost as tall as his father. He had the same wide shoulders, the same easy way of strolling. He walked in a way that could that only be genetic. He saw his father once a month yet he carried many of the Lagan gestures. He was fifteen and hated school but miraculously received high grades in all subjects. He loved reading and had enjoyed poetry from his first recitation of nursery rhymes. Kate was delighted but had warned him to keep those particular pleasures a secret from his friends. He had taken her advice. Nonetheless he would often sit in the evenings reading poetry aloud to her as she ironed or cooked the evening meal. His voice would lose its rough Belfast city edge and its sound tugged at her soul. Kate could not understand why other mothers talked so disparagingly about their teenage children. She thought of young people as kaleidoscopes. When they saw someone watching too closely they changed pattern. It was best to acknowledge the patterns, Kate assured herself, because then she could enjoy the complexity of their growing without trying to understand it.

Of course it was not all bright colours and glittering glass. His skin was becoming spotty but what teenage boy didn't have spots? She had treated him to a small and expensive vial of tea tree oil but he rarely used it. What teenage boy would?

"Anything else mum?" Charlie's question had a hopeful escape tone.

"Plenty. While I'm putting this stuff away run upstairs and bring down the washing."

"Okley dokley."

11

He arrived back at the kitchen door a moment later. His friends would be waiting for him at the corner of the road.

"Did you bring the toilet rolls upstairs Charlie?"

"No, you said you would sort them out later."

Kate sighed and looked at her son framed in the kitchen doorway, a young Shane at his moment of departure. She shook the thought away, asking quickly,

"Charlie, are you offering me that washing as some sort of ritualistic gift or are you going to stand there until it grows legs and walks over to the washing machine itself?"

"I thought you wanted it."

"Oh yes, I was just waiting for someone to give me a big bundle of dirty washing, nicer than flowers any day."

"What do you want me to do with it?"

"I don't mind. Marry it, if you like. Bring it to see "The Da Vinci Code." It needs a good night out by the look of it."

"Seriously mum."

"Put it into the washing machine and switch it on."

"Can't do that."

"Why not?"

"I don't know how the washing machine works. I can't read 'woman'."

"Very funny. Where did you hear that?"

"Jeremy Clarkson. Top Gear."

"Well, do you and Jeremy Clarkson think that I came out of the womb clutching a washing machine manual in my little clenched fist?"

"Oh very good mum."

He put the bundle on the floor beside the washing machine and escaped out of the kitchen calling to Kate over his shoulder,

"Back in half an hour mum. Have to meet some friends to borrow a book for homework."

It dawned on Kate that there was a serious gap in her son's education. Teenagers had created text language and understood the lyrics of Coldplay. No-one, even Charlie, could convince her it was difficult for them to understand five buttons on a washing machine. He could also master the significant fact that two cycles out of the two hundred options were the only ones needed for an average armful of laundry. Who boiled clothes these days for heaven's sake? Kate caught her errant son on his way to the front door and coaxed him back to the kitchen for a lesson in life skills. He pretended it was difficult but he managed. With the new language of "woman" safely tucked away in a hitherto unused corner of his brain he was only five minutes late as he greeted his friends with a rough edged "Hey!"

Kate began stacking toilet rolls in any conceivable space while making a mental note to teach Charlie his second lesson that evening. She called it 'how to take clothes out of a washing machine and hang them to dry in such a way that the minimum amount of ironing is required.' It had taken her years to learn that a little girl baby was not automatically born with a tiny iron attached to her big toe.

Kate was also determined to make a good dinner. It was the day she collected her family benefits from the post office and her shopping trip had reaped good bargains. She had bought a chicken for under three pounds, a bag of floury potatoes reduced to fifty pence and a harvest of green beans. She would roast the potatoes. Her daughter Roisin loved a good dinner. Roisin went straight from school three days a week to her part-time job. This helped her pay for bras, knickers, deodorant and sanitary towels. Kate did not believe in tampons and was strict about Roisin's use of them. Kate had lodged one a bit too deeply and had suffered intense embarrassment in the cubicle of the accident and emergency department of the Royal Victoria Hospital. The indignity of a doctor who looked as if he had not started shaving but was twiggling between her legs with a pair of forceps to dislodge the bloody thing still caused her to break into a sweat of menopausal proportions. The story, retold to her daughter, worked well against the temptation of celebrity advertising. Kate believed in talking sense and talking straight when it came to matters of survival.

13

The thought of the misadventure wafted into Kate's brain with the smells of crumbed bread and onions as she prepared the stuffing for the chicken. At least she could laugh about the incident now, or almost laugh anyway. For the present she allowed herself a smile. She had good faith in herself and her children and the Lagan's were having a Sunday dinner on a Tuesday so she would hope for nothing more. The washing machine whirred to a stop and forgetting Charlie's life lesson she washed her hands and began emptying the clothes from the machine. She was single. She was poor. She was not travelling along life's super highway. Her journey over the last forty five years seemed very insignificant but had required hard work. She did not pause to count the cost.

Late that night the Lagan's licked their fingers contentedly having consumed the remains of the chicken for supper. Then they went to bed. No-one, rich or poor, great or small actually knows what will happen to them in a new day. And if someone had told Kate what would happen to her she quite simply would not have believed it.

2

On Wednesday morning Kate was introduced to Mary the Mother of God.

She was sitting on one of the headstones in Milltown Cemetery and she was smoking a cigarette. Not Mary, the Mother of God, just the woman who told Kate about her.

Kate walked in the cemetery once a week. It was quiet and rather depressing. People rarely stopped to talk but it was also a place to keep material worries at bay. Those who chose to walk among the graves were alive and therein lay hope.

"Have you seen Mary?" the woman asked as Kate passed by.

"Who?"

"Mary."

"Mary who?"

"Mary, the Blessed Virgin, the Mother of God."

Kate hesitated but a response was required.

"No I haven't seen her...lately." she replied with what she hoped was respect.

"Would you like to see her?"

Kate's mind halted. Childhood nightmares screeched with the force of strobe lighting across her mind. The teacher from her primary school appeared from some dark recess asking, or rather, demanding in a sickly sweet southern Irish accent,

"Have you searched your souls girls for a vocation."

Kate had been short-sighted. She found it difficult to see the blackboard let alone search for a soul. She had gradually realised that the words meant they should all think seriously about becoming nuns. The knowledge terrified her. Nuns were big and black with whispering tight lips and chattering loose beads. They commandeered the main aisle in the parish church every Saturday morning during children's confessions. If the children dared to wriggle or giggle they would be given a look of such piercing menace that the wriggle would turn to a shiver and the childish giggle change to a racking cough. The nuns with determined zeal would shift their stares from the weakening children and direct them towards the rafters of the chapel. As the years of confessions continued and the lies rolled more easily from Kate's tongue she realised the look was a complex signal. It captured a god looking angrily down from the heavens on wicked children. This understanding brought relief. For years Kate thought it meant that the grilled priest would stride out from the confessional box and hang her from the balcony. She knew it was a venial sin to shuffle because your bum was sore on the wooden pew. It was a mortal sin to laugh or giggle because you were just an empty-headed little school girl with no worries and no future and absolutely no will to be blessed with a vocation. Kate always said a special prayer that she would not find a vocation. She did not want to dress completely in black and hide her face and hair under a winged veil of martyrdom.

Kate heard the teacher's voice again as she said quietly to one of the good girls in the front row of desks, "fetch me the black doctor." The 'black doctor' was a long yellow cane with a hooked handle kept above the blackboard and always in view. The whack of the cane was considered poor punishment. To inflict further pain black tape had been wrapped around the frayed end. This helped the children's learning to a considerable extent. They quickly learnt a fear of teachers, a fear of doctors and a fear of people of African origin from which some pupils may never have quite recovered.

Kate's mind was summoned to the present by another question. The woman sitting on the headstone asked again.

"Would you like to see Mary?"

"Okley dokley" Kate answered. She could think of nothing else to say.

"She's up there," the woman pointed, "in the tree."

Words raced through Kate's head,

"What the bloody hell is the Mother of God doing in a tree" Kate thought irreverently. Then she rebuked herself quickly and silently, "No Kate don't say that. This woman really believes what she is saying. Now don't smile, look solemn, slightly sad, a little bewildered. But whatever you do, don't laugh. And for Christ's sake, don't giggle."

The woman eased herself off the headstone and stubbed out her cigarette with the toe of her shoe. Then she bent down, lifted the butt and threw it a little way into a pile of nettles on another grave.

"This cemetery is untidy enough," she said to no-one in particular, "I don't want to be responsible for making it look even worse."

Milltown Cemetery, as with most places in west Belfast, had been neglected for years. Outsiders, or to be more precise, anyone who had not been born in west Belfast found the people who resided there - either dead or alive - very threatening. The place and the people were generally ignored.

The living population of west Belfast unanimously agreed that the cemetery was a sacrilegious disgrace. They often voiced their collective opinion in acoustic terms. There were demands at frequent intervals best summarised in the phrase 'the bishop should do something about it'. Kate was a sole, discordant echo in the background. She thought that Milltown was exactly how a cemetery should be. Grasses, ivy, hawthorn, chestnut and oak growing at random among the buried but not forgotten. It was, in her limited experience, the biggest, wildest and busiest graveyard in Europe.

Mary, the Mother of God, was in the tree. It was a huge oak tree which had guarded the main path for as long as Kate could remember. 'Mary' wasn't carved into the tree, or sitting in it.

"Thank God" thought Kate.

She was there naturally where an old branch stretched away from the main trunk. The image was worn, weather beaten and quite astonishingly beautiful.

Kate had been preparing to humour the old woman and was mentally rehearsing the words,

"Oh yes, there is a sort of likeness, in a certain light. If I turn my head, yes, yes, I see what you mean, very unusual."

She had intended to strain, screw up her eyes and nod graciously in the general direction of the woman's faith. Instead, Kate began to smile. She felt a sudden and acute happiness both with the image and with the fact that she could be honest with this woman who had stopped her in her tracks. Kate saw a true likeness, without squinting or squirming. A lifetime of icons, holy statues, May altars, rosaries and Hail Marys, doubts, misconceptions and misunderstanding did not vanish. They accumulated. Kate stood looking at the tree and witnessed what her companion witnessed. It was a pure distinct image of a woman in a long robe with arms outstretched, head bowed and a heart exposed to the elements.

"I can't believe it." Kate said.

"It's lovely, isn't it?"

"Yes. It is lovely. It's so natural. I like the way the image has been worn into the tree and by the tree. It's part of the tree. But why here?"

"Why not here? Suffering doesn't recognise borders."

"True enough." Kate replied and began to fumble in her bag for cigarettes and lighter.

"Would you like another cigarette?" she asked.

"No thanks. I'll smoke one of my own love. Those are too strong for me."

"They are strong, American or maybe Russian. I buy them in a wee shop in Macdermott Street at two pounds fifty a packet."

"I buy mine from under the counter too, great isn't it, not having to pay the taxes."

"Aye."

"Only goes on improving nuclear bombs, as if they bloody

well needed improving. People in power like to know they can kill three million people instead of two million. Progress is a wonderful thing love."

"So is saving money."

Kate was still looking at the tree. Suddenly she left the path, crossed over a few graves, touched the tree and for the first time in years blessed herself.

"Makes you think, doesn't it love."

"Yes." Kate replied solemnly, then added, "do you show everybody?"

"No."

"Why not?"

"I don't like to."

"Why?"

"Some people would laugh." The woman was realistic in many ways. Then she asked, "Is it your husband you come to visit?"

"No."

"I come to visit my husband. God rest him. Though this place needs tidied".

"I like it overgrown. It's wild and a bit restless."

"It's a disgrace. The bishop should do something about it."

Kate smiled and said,

"When we were kids my mammy and daddy used to bring us here every Sunday. We had a picnic."

"In the cemetery?"

"Not really a picnic, just a sandwich and a biscuit or an apple. It was great. We used to find all the children's graves, the ones with the little pictures on the headstone or a statue of an angel. We would say a prayer. We took the shiny stones off the posh graves and put them on the poor ones. We thought it was right."

"I come here every Wednesday that's the day he died."

"On a Wednesday?"

"Yes."

"That's nice."

"Yes."

The woman lifted her bag from the corner of the grave and began to walk towards the cemetery gates. She tilted her head as she passed the tree. Kate wondered if it was a nod of friendly recognition or a bow of reverence.

Later Kate would search for the woman who had introduced her to the Mother of God but she was destined not to find her for one woman in a cemetery looks much like another, sad, thoughtful and between worlds.

The Wednesday morning had brought a well worn image on a tree. The Wednesday evening brought another well worn image on a television screen.

Kate had made a pot of stew and it was bubbling away contentedly on the stove. Charlie was sitting at the kitchen table with homework. Roisin was painstakingly ironing the smallest pair of knickers Kate had ever seen. She had innocently remarked that one tiny triangle of cloth held together with bits of string would not cover a decent pair of nostrils never mind a backside. Roisin tried to ignore the comment but mildly hinted that she would have her toenails pulled out rather than willingly wear the knicker-bocker glories her mother preferred. Kate remarked that as far as value for money was concerned she certainly had the better bargain.

"At least I get more material for my cash Roisin."

"Mum, it's not quantity that's the issue here. It's quality."

"Tell that to the greengrocer."

"What's a greengrocer?"

Kate submitted silently in recognition of a changing world. She decided to watch the local news in the other room.

Towards the end of the programme an interview took place with the most hated man on the planet, or rather the most hated man before Osama Bin Laden was awarded the title. Kate recognised the terraced houses and the small shop fronts that were the designated media backdrop for an interview with Gerry Adams.

The presenter's tone was calm though Kate detected the usual trace of annoyance as he asked,

"And why do you think people would want to visit west Belfast Mr. Adams?"

"Well Noel," replied the leader of Sinn Fein, "there's a history here, a sense of culture, a renewal process."

"Are the public interested in that?"

"I believe they are. We are trying to move forward, bring all the people of this island into a new future. We are trying to reconcile the past with the present and look to the future."

"And how do you plan to do that, Mr. Adams?"

"One of the things we are researching in west Belfast is tourism."

"Sweet J.C. Christ." thought Kate.

"Tourism?" The reporter was as surprised as Kate.

"Now don't interrupt me Noel, let me finish." Mr. Adams rarely allowed the media to set the agenda when he was on screen. He continued,

"The people in this part of the city have much to offer. Travellers come here. They look. They listen. They try to understand our history. We appreciate their interest but they stay in leafy south Belfast. What we need here is an infrastructure. We want people to come to the Falls Road, to Ballymurphy, to Andersonstown. We want them to hear our story, understand out lives and our aspirations. They come to look but they book into the more residential areas of the city. We need guesthouses, hotels, as I said, an infrastructure."

Kate bounded into the kitchen, a woman possessed.

"A guesthouse kids. I'm going to open a guesthouse."

"Mammy! Wise up!"

Kate endured the tone for almost half a second.

"Seriously kids. I'm going to open a guesthouse offering bed and breakfast to visitors."

"Where?"

"Here."

"Where?"

"In the house."

"Oh mammy!"

21

"It would be great. Gerry Adams says we need an infrastructure."

"Oh mammy!"

"Honestly now if all three of us slept in the front room."

Roisin interrupted,

"Together?"

"Yes."

"Where?"

"On the floor. Oh please keep quiet kids and listen. It will just be for a couple of weeks. We could use a mattress and cushions and bring our clothes into the room."

"It's eight foot by ten foot," Charlie argued, "We'd suffocate."

"No we won't. We can leave the window open at night."

"Then we'll freeze to death." Roisin was quick to take advantage of Charlie's practical viewpoint.

"No, I only meant to breathe. We'll close it if it gets too cold. Now, if we hauled that old mattress down from the roof space it would fit into the room easily."

"What will we use for bedclothes?"

"Sleeping bags."

"We don't have any."

"Our Christina has a whole lot of them She used them when she went to Italy. Sure we never heard the end of it. We'll borrow hers."

"I don't like sleeping bags." Roisin almost whimpered.

"Don't be negative kids please," Kate implored. " If we sleep in the front bedroom that leaves us three rooms to rent out to our guests."

"What guests mum? And there's no carpet." It was Charlie.

"We'll buy a couple of rugs and paint the floorboards."

Once again Charlie's practical voice broke through Kate's enthusiasm.

"Mum we only have one toilet."

"Well," said Kate, undeterred, "We'll not go to the toilet when the guests are here."

"Mammy," Roisin wailed. "We have to shite!"

"I know love," Kate was gripped with enthusiasm. " We could go early in the morning and very late at night. I've always taught you regular habits thank God. You're well aware of the Lagan's heredi-tary haemorrhoids. If you do get them they won't be from my side of the family. If we're really desperate and one of the guests is using the bathroom we could run down to the supermarket and use the toilets there. We have to be positive. Look on it as a challenge."

"Oh mammy!"

"I mean it. Why with your brains and my, my, my….." Kate struggled for the right words, "my sort of womany skills, we could make it work." Then she rustled, bustled, threatened, smiled and bribed her way through the next two hours.

Roisin and Charlie had calmed down by the morning and ad-mitted that it might be worth a try. They knew in their hearts that their mother could do with some extra cash. They also knew in their connected sibling wisdom that she was mad as a hatter. As soon as they set off to school Kate made the telephone call.

"Hello. Is that the Northern Ireland Tourist Board?"

"Yes."

"Could I speak to someone about guesthouse accommodation?"

"Certainly madam. Where would you like to stay?"

"Oh no, I don't want to stay. I live here. I want to find out about opening an establishment in west Belfast offering bed and break-fast for tourists."

There was a pause. Mechanical music filtered down the tele-phone line. Kate recognised the tune as Butch Cassidy and the Sundance Kid or maybe The Sting.

"Typical" Kate's thoughts ran along stereotypical lines, "play-ing When Irish Eyes Are Smiling would be beyond them."

"Hello Madam."

"Yes. I'm still here."

"I'm afraid Mr. Collins is not in the office at the moment."

"Who's Mr. Collins?"

"The man who deals with the Bed and Breakfast process."

A process. Kate's heart sank.

"When will he be back?"

"This afternoon."

"If I ring back about three o'clock then?"

"Yes. Would you like to leave your name and telephone number?"

Something clicked inside Kate's head. She rang enough agencies to know the telltale signs of which calls were being recorded for 'training purposes'.

"On second thoughts", she responded quickly and politely, perhaps you could just send the information in the post. It's not actually for me. I'm ringing on behalf of a friend who is travelling abroad at present. But you could send the information to my address and I'll make sure she receives it."

"And what is the name and address Madam?"

"Oh yes - just send it care of, I'll repeat, care of Ms. Kate Lagan, 72 St. Francis' Road, Belfast. When my friend returns from abroad she will be delighted I already have the information she requires. Then she can contact Mr....what was his name again?"

"Mr. Collins."

"Yes. Mr. Collins. She can contact him herself. Thanks again."

Two days later the 'Starting Your Own Business' pack arrived. It was glossy and attractive with big ideas in small print. The pack also included fire certificate forms, insurance advice forms, rules and regulations , registration details and the cost of inspection fees.

Kate threw them all in the bin.

"Fuck that kids."

"What's wrong mum?"

"I don't want to start getting involved in all that."

"All what?"

"A process."

"What process?"

"Any frigging process. Too much red tape. Too much negotiation. Believe me it will only end in misery."

"But mum, you can't start a business just like that!" Roisin clicked her fingers.

"Why not?"

"What if there was a fire or somebody fell and broke a leg?"

"Where?"

"Here or on the stairs, maybe."

"They won't fall."

"How do you know?"

"I'll take the risk. That's what the politicians keep telling us. It's all about taking risks. Anyway I don't want my family tax credits to stop. I need that money to feed you."

"They'll find out."

"Who?"

"The Tourist Board."

"Sure they can fine me and I'll pay them back at a pound a week. That's what my Uncle Andy did when he ran up that one thousand pounds electricity bill during the Troubles."

· "What!"

"The electricity company brought him to court and he promised to pay them back a pound a week for that was all he could afford. He was working though, never took a day off in his life. But he had seven kids and a wife who always seemed a bit sickly."

"Did he pay them back?"

Kate could not decide whether the question was Roisin's genuine curiosity or moral honesty.

"How should I know?" was her sound parental reply. "You can't take money from people if they don't have it. I was wondering if the innkeeper charged."

"What innkeeper?" Charlie and Roisin exchanged knowing looks. Kate was off on a tangent and they knew they had to humour her.

"You know, Mary and Joseph and the baby in the manger. I wonder did he charge them for the stable - a reasonable rate."

"Mum, what are you talking about?"

"Nothing, just thinking about honest business ventures and giving unto Caesar that which is Caesar's and unto God that which is God's. I'm bloody sure of one thing though. When Caesar called for that census he had a substantial interest in the tourism trade - hotels, inns, stables and such like. All those travellers heading to their birthplace and not a room to be rented. Did you ask your Aunt Christina about the sleeping bags?"

"Yes, she has three. She said they're not great for our weather but we can borrow them."

"Did you tell her why you wanted them?"

"I just said me and Charlie were thinking of going camping with a few friends."

"Good girl. Honesty is the best policy as I have always taught you."

Kate Lagan knew she had a good idea, inspired or otherwise and one thing was certain she was going to give it a try. Roisin typed out an advertisement in school during lunchtime. Then Kate paid to have it photocopied forty times. She walked up and down her leafless territory taking a new interest in the familiar hairdressers, bars and shops. She thought of her dwindling finances and her complete lack of business acumen. But she went into battle as most warriors do, with a brave heart and absolutely no idea of what was going to happen. Armed with her A4 posters and a roll of sticky tape she asked each proprietor for a small square of window space to display her wares.

Four days later the telephone rang.

"Hello is that Lagan's Bed and Breakfast? There's a poster here in the window of the bar with your telephone number on it".

"Who wants to know?"

"This is Seamus. I'm the doorman in the Gravedigger's Arms, the pub beside the cemetery"

"Yes Seamus. How can I help you?" Kate's voice shifted from nervous apprehension to excitement. She hoped Seamus could not tell the difference.

"Would you have a couple of rooms for tonight? There are three American cops here looking for somewhere local to stay just for one night. Could I send them up to you?"

"Certainly Seamus. What time will they arrive?"

"Hold on, I'll ask them. About seven o'clock?"

"Certainly Seamus. Do you know where the Bed and Breakfast is situated?"

26

"On the main road, near the supermarket."

"Yes, that's right, above the Kennedy Centre, they'll like that."

"Who?"

"The American cops. You know, J.F. Kennedy."

"Is that right, very good, I'll send them up to you at seven."

"Lovely. I look forward to meeting them."

Kate replaced the telephone on the receiver and began to pace up and down the hall. "Oh fuck, oh fuck, oh fuck," she muttered in a voice of pure panic.

She checked the rooms at least ten times. The beds had clean, crisp linen. Fresh towels adorned the bathroom and surfaces gleamed. Everything was aired, welcoming and ready.

"But" Kate thought, "am I?"

Kate was indeed ready and everything went well. Over the next ten weeks she accommodated many people visiting west Belfast. She had not imagined people would be so interested in the place where she lived. The cops from New York were followed by a Dutch couple from Amsterdam. She noticed a peculiar smell lingering in the room for a day or two after they left. Then an English family arrived for a funeral. Kate felt she could not possibly charge them the full rate though it was reasonable. They took very little breakfast and cried, Kate thought, a bit more than was good for them. When they left she went up to service the rooms and found a five pound note on each pillow.

Kate tucked the welcome and unexpected tips into the pocket of her apron and smiled.

She had at least one guest every night and sometimes two or three. Despite Charlie's fears the three Lagan's did not suffocate in the small back room. They also managed their bowel movements reasonably well.

Kate resisted the urge to spend the money on luxuries. It went back into her fledgling business. She bought a new dinner set, fluffy white towels, expensive soap and shampoo. She put a hairdryer and kettle in each room. She employed a handyman to fix two wonky cupboard doors in her kitchen. He also painted the shelves bluebell blue.

Arthur arrived from Sydney and stayed a week. Initially Kate though he was a spoilt priest. She liked chatting as she served breakfast so she soon discovered that he was a retired engineer. He told her of his two failed marriages, his problem with alcohol and a democratic vision that helped keep him off the drink. On his last day he asked Kate out to lunch and sent her postcards from his travels in England and Scotland. He wrote her an endearing letter on his return to Australia. She decided not to reply. She was on the wrong side of forty for a holiday romance.

Two lovely girls from Argentina insisted on sharing one double room although Kate offered them a room each. They spoke good English laughed a great deal together and left a lesbian magazine behind, Kate realised, on purpose. She enjoyed flicking through it when she had a moment to spare and was quite surprised at the information. Her knowledge, her skills and her horizons were certainly broadening. Her enthusiasm and interest in her guests was growing with each new day as she learnt to give time and energy to every detail.

Nothing went to waste and the steady flow of visitors proved two things. The service and accommodation Kate was providing, albeit clandestinely, was appreciated and Gerry Adams had been right.

Then Thunderhawk arrived.

3

Thunderhawk was a Native American accompanied by a native of Belfast who was guiding him through the intricacies of the Irish peace process.

"Did he bring his peace pipe?" Charlie asked, always interested in each new arrival. Kate gave her son a sharp rap on the arm and suggested he did not make racist comments. Something he vehemently denied.

Kate serving breakfast learnt that Thunderhawk was chief of his tribe. His people were experiencing difficulties with official administrators. He liked the look and sound of words such as self-determination and cultural equality. "Like most displaced people," thought Kate, as she turned the eggs on the pan, " he needs those words and phrases."

He stayed for four days, ate with care, made his bed, and tended meticulously to his dark flowing hair. He thanked Kate courteously before leaving to catch his early morning flight back across the Atlantic. There was no problem with Thunderhawk. The problem occurred when he returned to his own land. From there, he emailed the Northern Ireland Tourist Board to express his thanks for the welcome he had received from the Irish people and his warm gratitude for the hospitable and friendly accommodation at Lagan's Guesthouse in west Belfast.

The telephone rang just before five o'clock.

"Hello is that Lagan's Bed and Breakfast?"

"Yes." Kate replied politely, "how may I help you?"

"Do you have any rooms available for tonight?"

"Just let me check my bookings. Yes I can offer you accommodation for tonight."

"Can I ask what rooms are available and what is the cost for each room please?"

Kate should have smelt a rat.

"Certainly, I have three rooms available this evening; two doubles and a single. Will you be requiring breakfast as well?"

"What is the charge for each room please?"

"Sorry?"

"What rates do you charge?"

She smelt the rat.

"Could I ask who is calling please?"

"You certainly can ask Mrs Lagan, this is Mr. Collins from the Northern Ireland Tourist Board. I have reason to believe that you may be offering accommodation in west Belfast without having officially registered with us, had an inspection or paid registration fees. Would that be the case Mrs. Lagan?"

"Well, Mrs Lagan is not actually here at the moment." Kate's mind raced. She had always felt slightly guilty about telephone lies to her mother over the years. At least now the practice proved a life skill.

"This is her sister. Can I tell her to telephone you when she comes home?"

"No that won't be necessary. Would you be kind enough to give a message to your sister?"

"Certainly."

"Could you tell her that I will be calling tomorrow to speak to her and inspect the premises?"

"Certainly, what time?"

"I'm not sure but possibly it will be early morning. Would you tell your, er, sister to be at home tomorrow?"

"I'll give her the message, an inspection tomorrow morning by the tourist board officer, Mister...what did you say your name was?"

"Collins."

"Mr. Collins, right he ho!"

Kate looked woefully at Roisin who had been listening at the hall door and then called Charlie from the kitchen. Roisin made a cut-throat sign to Charlie as their mother placed the telephone quietly on its cradle.

Kate faced her children,

"Jesus, Mary and St. Joseph kids, what am I going to do?"

"Mum, they could have you in court." Roisin was worried.

"No they won't."

"Yes they will."

"They can't prove anything."

"That's not the point mum. They obviously do have proof." Charlie's voice sounded deep and authoritive with a warning tone which Kate found unduly upsetting.

Fear began to steal over her, fear and nausea.

"I need some fresh air kids. I need to get out of the house and let's look on the bright side at least we've no guests tonight".

Roisin and Charlie made no response so Kate continued,

"I'll go for a walk."

"Where?"

"I don't know. I just need to clear my head. Will you peel the potatoes Roisin love and take those frigging kettles and cups out of the bedrooms."

"Don't worry mum." Roisin got Kate's coat from the hook under the stairs.

"And Charlie will you shove those sleeping bags up into the roof space and cram our clothes into any empty drawers, Mr. 'I know it all' Collins will wonder why the three of us are sleeping in a cupboard in a four bed-roomed house.

"The craic's good mum you could tell him that." Charlie's voice was calm again. He sounded helpful and reassuring. Kate needed that tone and reminded herself that Charlie had inherited her genes too.

"I know love, but still, put the sleeping bags away somewhere."

She slipped on her coat, left the house and began to walk towards the local park. Her mind held a two-way conversation. For the first time in years she had a bit of extra money. Would Mr. Collins understand that? For the first time in years she had bought herself a pair of trousers in a real shop instead of a charity shop. Would he understand that? For the first time... her brain began to scream that he would not understand. He had a job and a wife probably. He had credit cards. He had a boss and a management team and a secretary. He had rules and procedures. He had all the things Kate had rejected to allow her to spend time with her children outside the very system which now threatened. She had just wanted to learn how to think for herself and manage by herself. Currently her thinking was simply

"Mr. Collins has me by the balls."

She walked past the supermarket car park and glancing towards it saw Patricia struggling as usual. There were bags of shopping, a double buggy and two tearful toddlers gathered around Patricia. Kate put aside her own panic and crossed the road to give a helping hand. In moments of crisis the ordinary is profoundly comforting.

"Are you alright Patricia? I think you might be losing the battle"

Her friend turned and put one of the twins' hands into Kate's saying,

"Here, hold onto this for a minute while I sort out the shopping bags."

She began looping bags over the handles of the double buggy simultaneously explaining her new set of challenges.

"I've had my Susan's twins for weeks now Kate. If I see Winnie the Pooh one more time I'll go stir crazy."

"Is Susan working again?"

"Yep. The money's good but the hours are not exactly child friendly. I like to give her a hand minding these two. You know what it's like Kate. It's no joke trying to rear twins and a husband with asthma."

"Chronic."

"Yep"

"I told her I'd mind the little monster's during the day." Patricia leaned down and producing a tattered piece of kitchen roll from her pocket wiped one delicate little snotty nose. Following the swipe with a kiss she continued talking.

"God love Susan she gives me fifty quid a week out of her wages though I haven't spent any of it."

"Why not?"

"I'm keeping it to give back to her when she needs it. Maybe she'll get away for a long weekend or buy a new carpet for her front room."

"Patricia you're a laugh." Her friend's generosity never failed to amaze Kate. "You could do with the money yourself and a long weekend away."

"I'm fine, what about you?"

Without waiting for an answer Patricia manoeuvred the two little girls, five bags and the double buggy into Kate's temporary care as she pushed the shopping trolley into a holding bay.

Kate watched the second battle as Patricia fought heroically to get her one pound coin from the handle of the trolley.

"And they expect us to believe that they've landed men on the Moon," she shouted across her shoulder, "they can't design a frigging shopping trolley that goes around corners and gives you your money back without a fight. It's my bloody pound," she shouted at the trolley. "Ah, got it. I'll do the lottery with that pound, now it's bound to be lucky."

She took charge once more of her belongings and Kate releasing the grip of two small sticky hands lifted the girls and reined them into the buggy hoping that shopping, grandchildren and granny would all survive though she imagined them toppling in one untidy heap to the ground.

"Heavy load." said Patricia, "but at least it's balanced." She began to push her burdens out of the car park asking as she went,

"So how are you Kate?"

"Okay."

"That doesn't sound too good."

"What?"

"The way you said okay."

"Have you second-sight Patricia?"

"What's wrong?"

"Well you know I've been taking in guests, tourists mostly for a bit of extra cash?"

"Know? The whole frigging road knows Kate. Our Susan noticed two suspicious looking characters standing in your driveway last week and she was going to phone the police. She thought they were burglars."

"Lawyers, from Oaklahoma. They were here observing a trial. They were lovely and said they really enjoyed the ethnicity."

"Good for them. So did Bill Clinton."

"They left a bottle of wine and a ten pound tip."

"More than Bill Clinton then. Sounds as if it's all going well Kate."

"That's the trouble Patricia. It's going too bloody well. I hadn't a clue so many people came to west Belfast, wanted to come to Belfast. But the Tourist Board have found out."

"Are you not legitimate?"

"Wise up Patricia."

"I know it's too much hassle. I haven't had my windows cleaned for over a year. A great wee man used to come once a fortnight until somebody reported him."

"Doing the double? Income support and income?"

"Naturally."

"I met a guy years ago who bragged that he knew every tax loophole that existed. Even his clothes were tax expenses. He would boast that his accountant told him to buy a new and bigger car. He was making too much money that couldn't be hidden in the accounts."

"Huh, my window cleaner could hardly afford a new bucket never mind an accountant. He was caught and had his money stopped. He was only trying to scrape a living, scraping the dirt off other people windows. Tell that to the British Chancellor," Patricia continued, "he wants the system to find us all a proper job. Every god-damn mother one of us. Let him mind our Susan's kids for a couple of days and push this lot back to the house without the chauffeur-driven car. He'd soon find out about real work. What are you going to do about the Tourist Board?"

"Some inspector is calling to see me tomorrow. I'll have to brazen it out or act as if I'm stupid."

"You haven't a stupid bone in your body Kate."

"I don't know about that, I've done so many stupid things in my time."

"Haven't we all but remember my maxim Kate, in the event of a breakdown stay where you are and wait till help arrives."

"Thanks Patricia," Kate smiled, "I'm going to walk on down the road to the park. I need the fresh air to clear my head. Give me a ring when you get a minute to yourself we deserve a night out sometime."

Kate crossed the road as Patricia shouted her farewells.

"Good luck tomorrow when the inspector calls Kate. Don't forget to keep your hazard lights on, or failing that, wear a low cut blouse."

Moments later Kate was in the park walking by the edge of the muddy stream which bordered the railings. Her mind wandered backwards as it tended to do when the future held further worries. She tried to plan for the next day but her mind rejected her concerns and filled instead with window cleaners and buckets. She remembered her own mother sitting precariously on the ledge of the bedroom window trying to clean the glass thereby risking her life to save a few pennies and she had needed to save every penny. Kate Lagan had then been Kate Conlon, the second youngest of five children. Her father worked hard but work for men in west Belfast was often temporary and always unforgiving. The Conlon's were considered a small family by Irish standards. Most of Kate's friends had nine or ten brothers and sisters. The Conlon's lived in a small terraced house with an outside lavatory. They had a plastic bucket for household cleaning and a tin bucket which was carried upstairs every night for household convenience. Kate used it more than anyone else. A particular night crept stealthily into her head as she walked through the park. A neighbour had been visiting for a chat and a cup of tea. Kate and the youngest child, Ralph, had already been sent to bed when Kate realised that the bucket had not been brought upstairs. Her mind unwrapped the scene once more.

"Mummy!"

"What is it?"

"Mammy!"

"What is it Kate? Can't you hear I'm talking to Mrs. O'Neill? She just called in for a chat. I get no peace in this house."

"Can you bring it up mammy?"

"Bring what up?"

"It."

"What?"

Kate's young mind and filling bladder stretched for the right words.

"The silver bucket."

"God almighty!" It was Mrs. O'Neill's voice beating its way upstairs.

"Everybody else in the street has a tin bucket on the landing but the Conlon's pee into a silver one. Wait 'til I tell that when I'm out and about."

Kate could hear and feel the laughter.

"Mammy!"

"Alright, I'll be up in a minute. I just have to polish the bucket."

More laughter.

It had not occurred to Kate that every house in the street used the same method for comfortable nocturnal activities. No one had an upstairs bathroom, or a downstairs one either. Kate was six years old and not quite sure what constituted a bathroom. Her granny's house, a few streets away, had a bath in the kitchen. It was used as a seat when all the cousins gathered there on Sunday evenings. She remembered sitting on the edge herself but had no recollection of the taps ever being used. Kate's family had a big tin bath. It hung on a hook in the whitewashed yard. Every Saturday night the bath was carried into the kitchen by her daddy and her big brother Paddy Joe. It was quarter-filled with warm water. Kate, her older sister Maggie and baby Ralph were put in it together and scrubbed with sunlight soap. When their mother had the three of them wrapped in towels in front of the fire Kate's oldest sister Christina would carry mysterious sachets and her own small bars of soap into the kitchen, shut the door and do in the bath whatever really big sisters did. Kate was usually in bed before it was Paddy Joe's turn to wash, or her mammy and daddy's. She did not think of how they kept clean. Sometimes, lying awake upstairs, she would hear the sounds of the bath being carried out to the yard and the dirty water emptied. It was poured over the flowers in the small back garden which her mother insisted would grow big and beautiful if they had a bit more sunlight and a bit more attention.

That was her childhood home. The front room, the scullery, the yard and the outside toilet. Between the yard and the toilet was the coal shed. It was a dark mysterious place and was inhabited by a family of vicious rats, or so the older ones said. Between the three small bedrooms and the roof was an attic, an equally dark place. It was also inhabited, or so the older ones said, by an old lady who came out at night to stare at little children to see if they were worth kidnapping. Kate's childhood was full of ghosts and fears and mad stories and the unexplained laughter of adults. Kate had survived. She wondered why she was worrying about Mr. Collins from the Tourist Board.

"Wait 'til he sees my bathroom," she said aloud and turned to take the short walk home. She spent the rest of the evening making the house look as presentable as possible. It was a challenge. It was spotlessly clean but like Kate, rather too careworn round the edges and in desperate need of a make-over.

Mr. Collins arrived at ten o'clock the following morning. He was duly shocked and gave Kate a duly shocked warning.

"You must not operate without a legitimate license from us, Mrs. Lagan."

"Ms. Lagan." Kate responded quietly.

"Ms. Lagan. I have every reason to bring you to court and you could receive a hefty fine. However, under the circumstances we will not take that route. I am here to give you a verbal warning."

"Really?" Kate tried to keep the tone of relief from her voice.

"Yes really. There are two adequate reasons for this decision."

"May I ask what they are?"

"The email from Mr. Hawk, ah, Mr. Thunderhawk."

"I think it's just Thunderhawk Mr. Collins. Native Americans don't use titles. Their names describe aspects of their character not their status. At least that's what he told me when I asked him about it."

"Really?"

"It's a bit like the Irish language. In Irish there are no titles. I am referred to as béan an tí, the woman of the house. There isn't a hierarchy."

"I didn't know that." Mr. Collins sounded slightly annoyed and Kate made a mental note to keep her mouth shut, at least until she was off the hook.

"I'm sorry, you were saying Mr. Collins?"

"Yes, the email from Thunderhawk was indeed complimentary. You may like to know that it was his correspondence which began this investigation in the first place. He was in fact praising your facilities not castigating them."

"That's nice."

"Please let me finish. The second reason for not prosecuting,"

Kate winced and stayed silent. Mr. Collins continued,

"The second reason is because we are very short of low priced, suitable and respectable accommodation in this area of the city. The Troubles have left their mark on west Belfast."

Kate thought, "Only someone in tourism could make the comment left their mark with a straight face. It was more a shattering blow."

"You seem to have a flair Ms Lagan for this business," the inspector continued, "I was wondering if you could possibly consider it as an appropriate and legitimate venture?"

"Seriously?"

"Yes, seriously."

"What would I need to do?"

"Cosmetically, a considerable amount, new carpets, rooms painted, better quality curtains or drapes, a proper shower over the bath, not a hand held plastic tube."

"Some guests thought that very ethnic." Kate could never learn to hold her tongue.

"And I'm sure some thought it very annoying as I would, Mrs, Ms. Lagan."

"What else?"

"The front door and the window frames painted, better lighting in the hall and on the stairs, a modern cooker, a microwave oven and a large fridge freezer. We are talking in the region of three to four thousand pounds."

"You must be joking Mr. Collins. Where would I get that sort of money?"

"That's up to you Ms. Lagan."

"As usual."

Kate sighed. It was long, weary, relieved and agitated. It was a sigh all women recognised and most men ignored.

"Well I'll leave you to think about it."

"Okay I will," Kate walked the inspector to the front door and added, "thanks, Mr. Collins."

"What for?"

"For not bringing me to court."

"Court is a very expensive business Ms. Lagan. We cannot afford it."

"Neither can I Mr. Collins."

"A pity."

"Yes."

"It's a good location, becoming quite popular with visitors if you can believe the local papers."

"I know."

Kate stood at the open front door and watched as he reversed his car out of the driveway and drove south to the city centre and his comfortable office. The telephone rang behind her.

"Hello is that Lagan's Bed and Breakfast?"

"Yes may I ask who is calling?"

"My name is Padraig Morgan. I'm from Dublin. I was wondering if you had accommodation as a friend recommended you. I'm involved in a documentary and we're filming in Belfast next week."

"Certainly, would you like a single room or a double?"

"Oh, a single will do fine."

"How long will you be staying?"

"Four, five nights, maybe all week it depends on the filming schedule. Would that be alright?"

"Certainly. If you are staying a week then we can come to some arrangement about the rates. Now, coming from Dublin you need to leave the motorway at exit four, turn left and then second left. The house is on the right just past a supermarket. My gates are painted white with a green top. You'll find it very easily."

"Is there a sign?"

"No, not yet."

"Okay I'll look out for the white and green gates. No orange stripe in them yet then?"

"No," Kate smiled, "not yet."

"Thanks. I'll be there about seven o' clock on Sunday night. See you then."

"I'm not running a bed and breakfast Roisin." Kate had described her meeting with the tourist board official when Charlie and Roisin arrived home from school. She had quietly tacked on the information about the film guest when she thought they had stopped listening.

"I'm just renting a room for the week and giving him a bit of breakfast. That's a completely different situation"

Despite her bravado Kate had been shaken. An inconsiderate fear of the establishment was engrained in her as it was with many who existed on low incomes. It was comparatively easy to understand systems and procedures and decision making if you sat at the top of a pyramid whether you had some intelligence or none. Those working at the bottom layer who tried to look up often got grit in their eyes. It made things hard to see and understand. Furthermore intelligence was considered a dangerous rather than useful commodity for those nearer the foundations.

Kate often wondered how it might be possible to rise through the guarded steps of modern pyramids. She thought that being photogenic would be a desirable gift. Perhaps long legs and luscious hair might help. The ability to say 'yes sir no sir three bags full sir' was also essential and perhaps the view would be better and the scrabbling about in the rubble could stop. Kate was five foot two inches tall. She had brown hair and though she had been told she had shapely legs they were not catwalk long. She was not considered pretty having inherited her father's dark complexion and his sombre brown eyes. Her mother, brothers and sister had fair skin which did not seem to wrinkle in exact proportion to fiscal or marital tensions.

Kate had listened to the same nursery rhymes, the same fairy stories, the same legends and myths as her sisters and brothers. She had attended the same school to be fed and watered to the shape that made the world go round.

Somehow it had not worked. She had attempted numerous jobs in various places. She was unable to keep quiet when she disagreed with the fundamental principles of what was required. This had resulted in no promotions. As one door closed another door was locked along the next institutional corridor. There was one bright moment of triumph. It ended the prospect of any career but she recalled with pride how she had finally walked out of the system and slammed the door firmly shut behind her.

She had been working for eighteen months as a contract secretary for an education trust. The team had successfully managed a series of government initiatives for primary schools and managers were basking in the 'glossy brochure' stage of completion. The educationalists bartered and dictated. Kate typed and edited policy procedures, new learning strategies and lists of criteria which were to be the benchmarks for excellence. Occasionally she thought of the little mites in the classroom and wondered if four year old's could take the onslaught. She prepared the new documents meeting printing deadlines and her manager's promotional prospects. Her personal views remained unchanged and simple. She believed if children were nourished properly and felt happy and secure then they would learn in spite of being taught. These thoughts stayed inside her head until the fanfare launch of the brand new procedures. The brochure proclaimed that the task of "creating new educational horizons" had been accomplished.

Kate flicked through the pages noticing that the centre fold could be removed to display in classrooms and staff rooms. She thought of smiling children busily engaged in creating huge wobbly robots from toilet rolls and cereal packets. Unfortunately, staring from the centrefold was the remarkably unengaging face of the education trust's chief executive. It was rumoured he had a 'bit of a problem'. His rather purple face was the focal point from which pointed black arrows extended. These drew the reader's attention to regulations, financial expenditure, and legislative requirements.

"And," Kate asked aloud as she followed the arrows, "Does it tell the teachers how to get an oak tree back into an acorn?"

"Well frig that ladies and gentlemen," she announced to the office staff as she threw the brochure into the bin "I thought extra money was going to be used to help children. Now I know it is spent on pumped-up old farts having their photographs taken. No doubt they are currently treating themselves to a corporate lunch, patting each other on the back and wondering about new year honours lists."

Everyone in the office seemed extremely busy but Kate continued unabashed.

"I can't believe I have just spent eighteen bloody months of my time helping to promote that ugly face. I'm off to look at the sky."

She walked out of the office stopping briefly to inform her line manager that she would leave at the end of the week. She spent ten minutes standing outside the dull office block, smoking a cigarette and staring up at clouds drifting across a grey horizon.

That afternoon Kate signed her resignation letter. She left the following Friday evening having finally decided that the regular pittance of a weekly wage was not worth her soul.

She had expected white feathers to drift down from the heavens. The only white that gravitated towards her over the next few years were bills. Her meagre savings vanished quickly but she shuddered sometimes when she remembered the face of the chief executive staring blindly from the pages. She hoped he had not been displayed where young children could see his beady eyes glaring out from the centre-fold of his own peculiar mind map.

4

Chapters of life, like fairytales, should end with the possibility of good conquering all. As a child Kate had not fitted neatly into a role of little princess. She thought beautiful princesses lacked vigour. She had shrugged at the idea of their overwhelming sense of victmhood. Kate knew, even as a child, that the link between stories and experience was virtual.

She had left her job because she was principled but she knew she had also left because she was bored. Now her business venture had failed at the first hurdle. She began to wonder if she was just a scared old nag for whom no fairy godmother would ever exist. But then she did not believe in tales.

Her latest guest and film personality Padraig Morgan turned out to be a self-employed sound engineer. He was hired by a company who contracted workers on a temporary basis for minor television productions. The pay was not good and cheap accommodation was one of Padraig's priorities. Kate dutifully dismissed the slight expectation that he was going to be a handsome prince and the niggling concern returned that she was desperately in need of a life. Padraig stayed a week and apart from wisps of shaving cream around his ears at breakfast each morning he was a pleasant guest. He was quiet, for a Dubliner, and at the end of his stay he thanked Kate kindly and paid his dues. She watched him drive off into the jaws of the Celtic Tiger.

"God love him." Kate said as she closed the front door.

Within an hour of his departure she had paid her electricity bill at the post office. She then walked to the local chemist's shop and bought herself the small present she had wanted for some time. It was a disposable camera. There was ten pounds left and this was placed in an envelope and put in the kitchen drawer underneath the tea-towels. It was enough spare cash to develop the film.

Kate tidied the house and gave the single bedroom a thorough cleaning as therapy for her soul. She would take no more guests. Roisin's warning had indeed borne fruit. Kate explained courteously to callers,

"Please accept my apology but we are currently unable to provide accommodation as structural work is being carried out to keep abreast of new regulations."

One bright but cold morning a few weeks later her brother arrived and found her trying to retrieve lumps of coal from the wheelie bin.

"What in God's name are you doing Kate?" He asked.

"Fuck all." She replied, then realised that Paddy Joe was not referring to her life experiences, merely to her search in the bin.

"I always said you had the skills to make it as a bag lady. I knew I was right."

"What do you want anyway Paddy Joe?" Kate ignored her brother's sense of humour.

"I came to leave the dog. Don't tell me you forgot Kate. You promised to keep him. We're going to Donegal for the week. Kate tell me you didn't forget. We've managed the time off work and the hotel is booked. I really need this break."

"Of course I didn't forget," Kate lied "Did you bring the lead, and his bowl and some dog food?"

"Yes. they're in the car. Can I bring him in?"

"Well, I'm just waiting for an officer and a gentleman to carry me off to paradise but in the meantime the dog can keep me company."

"The guests won't mind?" Paddy Joe was worried. The dog had been taught to be a growler.

"No worries. I don't have any guests this week so you're in luck."

Kate did not believe that a problem shared was a problem halved. She thought a problem shared was rubbing salt into her own wounds.

She walked down to her brother's car and greeted the small black and tan terrier. It was a good enough cross mongrel but sometimes had ideas above its station.

"Come on Rebel," she said, "let's be having you."

She waved goodbye to Paddy Joe and the dog trotted at her heels around to the back garden. Kate continued her rummaging for lumps of coal thrown out by mistake with the fire ashes. She looked as though she had the natural instinct of an urban fox. Kate convinced herself it was a purely environmental concern but she knew it was a pagan action. Despite her Catholic upbringing, or perhaps because of it, she had a deep and respectful awe of any superstition. She knew them all, the misfortune of spilling salt, the bad luck of placing a new hat on the bed or shoes on the table and the good luck of saving coal. She followed each with religious zeal. They had been passed from generation to generation and meandered around in the part of her brain that remembered the recipe for fish and milk, the Latin verses of the Tantum Ergo and all the words of the Hail Holy Queen.

"Got it." She announced to no-one in particular and the dog barked in a gleeful response to her tone.

The coal was safely returned to the bucket. Kate manoeuvred the wheelie bin to the front gate ready for collection. The collection was at nine o'clock and god help the woman who left her bin a centimetre short of the exact spot where it could be emptied. If it was placed a fraction outside the gate it was delivered to a house fourteen miles away. If it was left a fraction inside the gate a note was stuck on it proclaiming that bins could only be collected if left outside the property. A bin with grass and hedge cuttings sticking from the lid was left unattended. A bin with explosives wrapped neatly in a bin liner and tied at the top would be emptied without a second thought.

The dog growled at a man disembarking from a black taxi. The taxis were one of west Belfast's better answers to the thirty year conflict. During the 1970's council policy meant that bus services were suspended at the first sign of a riot. The community devised a good-will method of transport which simply involved car owners stopping and picking up people left standing at bus stops. Grateful passengers tipped the car owners for their kindness. Then a few local entrepreneurs had an idea. As it happened it was a very good idea. The men, quite possibly, did not know the word entrepreneur, nor would they use it as an occupation on their passports. Most of them did not have a passport or had a passport withheld. They made their way to London and brought back five black taxis. Others followed and a much needed service was born. Perhaps due to some reconstructed socialist thinking the service did not become the property of the few. It remains co-owned by the two hundred and fifty drivers and works on the principles of efficiency, value for money and a decent gossip with other passengers sharing the journey and the cost. Management gurus would do well to throw the business manuals in a handy bin and take a 'black hack' down to Castle Street car park to witness circle management at its best. They would find a fleet of black taxis neatly filling up with passengers and witness driver-owners sharing cups of tea, hamburgers and the news of the world with conversations ranging from the price of vineyards to the war in Iraq. They would listen to decisions being taken in good humour with information relayed from driver to driver. They would see a safe convenient system that paid an honest wage and kept many families in west Belfast from the stigma of state benefits. There was a long waiting list to become self-employed driver-owners. The workers managed their schedules to balance customer demands, parenting and leisure time. Holidays are taken with regard to the needs of passengers. Drivers were encouraged during their breaks to make good use of local sports facilities. All rather like Microsoft.

The dog growled again.

"Rebel, come here you bloody nuisance."

"Good name missus." the man commented as he paid the driver and nodded a goodbye to the four other occupants of the taxi.

"I'm thinking of putting him forward for the next election", Kate joked, "with the state of this place he stands a good chance of winning a majority vote. He already has the skills of some of our local politicians. He growls at everybody and doesn't listen to a decent word. In fact," she continued, "you might just be looking at the next minister for social development."

"He would do a better job missus. He couldn't do much worse, that's for frigging sure!"

Kate laughed, checked the position of the bin and went back round to the kitchen to defrost the fridge. It had belonged to an old lady who was found dead in her flat. She had not meant to die. When Paddy Joe was summoned to take the lock off the door he found her in bed with her hair in curlers. It was a sure sign that she fully intended waking up again. She did not though. She had lived alone and died alone. Kate was deeply saddened and helped to clear the council flat for the next occupant. She had reflected that something like this would not have occurred when she was a child. People had frequently checked on elderly neighbours in the small terraced streets. Five barred locks were something vaguely associated with gates on country fields.

Now box rooms in the terraced houses were converted to en-suite bathrooms and the whitewashed yards decked with timber and decorated with patio sets. The close-knit community was replaced with individual urban living. Care of the elderly was an institutionalised system beyond the responsibility of family and friends. Large housing estates had gradually crept outward claiming the lower slopes of the Belfast Hills and Divis Mountain. Kate imagined modern houses and apartments were wilfully designed to separate rather than unite. They had grand anonymous names such as Laurel Mews and Cherryvale Grove but they often concealed lone parents in lonely apartments or elderly people too frightened to knock on a thin wall for help.

Kate knelt down with her thoughts and began to scrape the ice from the freezer compartment at the top of the fridge. She often thought she expended more energy on scraping away ice than she did on rearing her children. The fridge would be used until she could afford a new one. When she finally purchased a bright new fridge freezer she worshipped it for weeks and gained a tiny flow of pleasure every time she filled a glass of ice cold water from the little pump located in the door. For the present however she cursed Mr. Collins and his legal requirements.

"He doesn't know his own backside from Joe McKibbons." She informed Rebel as he sat expectantly near the fridge door hoping for the odd scrap.

"Oh god Rebel," Kate was exasperated as her day grinded grudgingly on, "do you know what is happening. Oh god, Oh god, I am turning into my mother. My forty something birthday barely past and I have spent my day rummaging around in bins, talking cheap politicals with complete strangers and shedding tears for a lonely old woman. Now I'm scraping ice and talking to myself, muttering expressions I swore I would never use as long as I lived."

In Kate's teenage years she had the frightful vision of Joe McKibbon's backside when her mother uttered the words. As a married woman she had plucked up courage and asked how the expression had evolved. Having assumed for her entire life that Joe McKibbon was a fictitious character she stared in horror when her mother said,

"He lived down the street from us when we were kids. Your granny said it all the time. She would also yell it at anyone who annoyed her including Joe McKibbon."

"Was he not angry?"

"No. He was no match for your granny. There were few men who would face her when she was in a temper. She had a hard old life with ten of us to rear. Women had it very hard in those days, not like young ones now."

Kate gave her mind a mental shake. It was just before noon and she rose from her knees as she heard the post dropping through the letter box. She reckoned there had been a policy decision a quarter of a century before which stated 'few people work in west Belfast so there is no need to send a postman out at dawn to deliver their letters. Their correspondence is irrelevant in the grand scheme of things. They will be lying in bed, smoking or recovering from the consumption of ten cans of cheap beer. They have no work. They do not want work. There is no work for them. Leave west Belfast to the last' Wolves in blue suits writing policies in stone.

In the hall lay a brown envelope and a supermarket brochure. The brown envelope contained a letter signed by a Mrs. Pamela Fitzpatrick. It informed Kate that her income support benefits would rise by one pound and thirty six pence. She was told in starched conservative tones that she could feed, clothe, house, educate and entertain herself and her family on this new royal sum.

"Might even join a croquet club with the money that's left over," she announced.

Calculations had been made taking into account her family allowance and child tax credits but not considering petrol, mortgage, electricity, or credit payments. Kate wondered why rich people had the impression that poor people had everything paid for them and only wanted to stare at the television. Marie Jones play "A Night in November" was being revived at the Lyric Theatre. Tickets were expensive. This required Kate to juggle furiously with her finances. She knew Charlie would enjoy the play. He would also learn more from it about the history and politics of his city than would ever be disclosed in the carefully constructed school curriculum. Kate was determined that Mrs. Pamela Fitzpatrick and her commander-in-chief would have as limited an influence as possible in her life.

The supermarket brochure had better news. The previous weeks offers concentrated on yellow and orange peppers, aubergines and jars of chicken tikka sauce. Kate thought these offers useless. This week promised cereals, apples, butter and shampoo all reduced and a sensible choice of savings ahead.

"Sod Mrs. Pamela Fitzpatrick anyway," thought Kate, "I bet her kids are given the obligatory five pieces of fruit a day by the childminder." Kate wondered vaguely if the signature belonged to a Catholic or a Protestant.

"Probably a mixed marriage." she said aloud as she threw the correspondence into the cold grate.

When Charlie came home from school that afternoon she told him about the play they would soon be going to see and then asked her favour.

"I see you were in Iceland again." he laughed pointing to the defrosted fridge.

"Yeah, the aurora borealis was lovely. Charlie will you come with me to take some photographs."

Kate knew the answer.

"You're mad, mum! You can't take proper photographs with a cheap disposable camera."

"It'll have to do."

"Okay. I'll go with you. What do you want me to do?"

"Not much. Just keep a lookout in case anyone comes along. I don't want to look daft."

Charlie called the dog and the three set off at a brisk pace for Milltown Cemetary. It was late but the gates were open and they marched through with Rebel in the lead.

Kate checked the light filtering through the top of the trees though she had no idea how that would help. She asked Charlie to hold her bag. Then stepping back carefully she focussed the camera and began taking pictures of the virgin image in the oak tree.

They were not disturbed by passers-by or mourners and soon Kate tucked the camera back into her bag.

She hoped the photographs would look nice when they were developed. After all, with photography, as with religion, she was no professional.

5

That night Kate somewhat remarkably slept the sound and dreamless sleep usually reserved for the newly born or the newly blessed.

She was up bright and early next morning and waved Charlie and Roisin off to school. She gave the dog one half of her biscuit and felt that once again she could face anything the world could throw at her. Anything but a phone-call from her mother. That was exactly what the morning brought.

It was chilly and Kate was pulling on an extra pair of socks when the telephone rang.

"Hello Lagan's...hello Kate here."

"Are you only up out of bed?"

No matter what time of day or night Kate's mother rang this was her first question.

"No mammy. I was up to see the kids off to school."

"Sure they're old enough to see themselves out."

If Kate had said 'yes mammy, I'm only up,' the response would have been 'why were you not up to see your children out to school?' It was the same repeated pattern. Rib one, purl one, rib one, purl one. Her mother often talked but rarely conversed and her main hobby as she grew older was the dedicated art of preaching. She went to daily mass to pray for sinners though always considered herself more sinned against than sinning. Kate loved her but was totally frustrated by her in almost equal measures. She knew her mother had put cardboard inside her shoes to save the soles and had worn the same dull brown coat for ten years when her family needed food not style. She had taken pride in her childrens school achievements and all had won places at the grammar school. Money for the annual fees and bus fares had been paid promptly from god -knows-what-savings. There was an old tin money box kept on the ledge above the front door. Every week Kate remembered the sound of a chair scraping across the floor as her mother pushed it into place to reach up to the box. The scraping was followed by the clink clink of coins being carefully deposited. The money box had one small slit and when cash was required her mother would stand at the old Belfast sink in the kitchen and fish out coins with a knife. She trusted a tin money box above the front door more than any bank and there were no charges.

There were five Conlon children and Kate cringed when her mother proudly proclaimed "I had all my children and I never once saw your father naked, not like the dirt you see on the television nowadays." Kate had had two conversations about sex with her mother. The first was when she was eleven years old. Her mother talked to her one night in quick and quiet whispers sitting uncomfortably on the edge of the bed. Kate was told that something was going to happen and if it did she was to take off her vest and use that. For the next few months Kate wondered seriously what she was to do with the vest, or where she was to put it. She finally decided that she would have to wear it round her neck if it happened, whatever it was, in school. She took her first period one night when her mother was at a novena. Kate thought her insides were leaking out and called Christina upstairs to make a final confession. Christina checked the back of Kate's pyjamas and gave her a sanitary towel. It was a huge bulk of a thing. She told Kate to put it in her knickers and not to say anything to daddy or Paddy Joe. The next morning Kate's mother took her by the hand, opened the door of the hot press, lifted aside a few old blankets and pointed at a nest of white towels saying,

"I keep them in there. When you take the old one off wrap it in newspaper and throw it in the fire then take another one when you need it and don't say anything to your daddy or Paddy Joe."

It was the last time Kate remembered holding her mother's hand.

The second time Kate talked about sex with her mother was on her forty-third birthday. The sweat had begun in the pit of her stomach and worked its way out like a huge wave to every part of her body. Her face flushed, the back of her legs burned and perspiration found its way mysteriously to the tips of her ears. Six sheets of kitchen roll later and moisture was still pouring from her like a holy well.

"Oh," her mother said when Kate had broached the subject, "so 'it's' started. Well, every sweat is worth a guinea. That's what your granny used to say and she never spoke a truer word."

Kate suddenly muttered "Jesus, the phone call!"

"Catherine," her mother always used a queenly tone at the beginning of every telephone conversation, "I was wondering if you knew that there is a meat sale at the supermarket."

"Yes mammy."

"Have you been yet?"

"No."

"I'll have to get a few things for I haven't much bread."

Kate pictured her mother's breadbin. It was likely to contain three plain loaves, two Ballymena scones, a fruit loaf and a bag of crusty rolls.

"Do you want me to pick you up mammy?"

"Not if you're busy. What are you doing?"

"Ironing." A lie.

"There's no ironing these days. I just fold the sheets when I take them out of the machine. I only iron a few things. Everything's drip dry."

"The kids school shirts. I have to iron those."

"Sure it's Monday. Did you not get everything ready for them over the weekend? I had all your school blouses washed and

54

pressed every Sunday night (a lie). And your daddy had every shoe in the house whitened or polished."

"I know mammy."

"There's no housework now. It was different when I was rearing all of you."

"I suppose that's true."

"And then you just have to jump into the car and get your groceries."

"Do you want to go?"

"Where?"

"To the supermarket."

"Have you to get anything?"

"Not really."

"Well, I'll just go down for a few things. I can get a taxi."

"No. I'll pick you up."

"I suppose you're still in your dressing gown."

"No." [a lie.]

"What time will you pick me up then?"

"About two o'clock."

"Okay. Don't be late. We can do our shopping and then I may as well go with you to pick up the kids from school."

"They don't like me picking them...okay I'll see you at two o'clock"

Kate finished clearing the ashes and set the fire. Though the morning was cold she would not light it until later.

Christina was calling to collect the sleeping bags. She needed them for the Easter holidays. The Lagans did not. Christina was good at planning and reclaiming borrowed property. It did not matter. The Lagans had reverted to normal sleeping arrangements. Kate had enjoyed the indoor camping and had managed a couple of cosy chats with Roisin. She smiled as she stuffed the sleeping bags into their packs recalling one conversation.

"Never smoke Roisin."

"Why not? I know it's unhealthy mum. You don't have to explain"

55

"That's not the reason Roisin" Kate was undeterred.

"The reason is that you will find yourself choosing between a good leg of lamb and a pound of mince steak."

"Why?"

"The mince gives you enough money to buy the cigarettes. They always win when it comes to choices. Mind you I've learnt how to make a pound of mince taste like almost anything, except a leg of lamb."

"Can I drink?"

"Yes."

"How come I can drink but I can't smoke?"

"Even Jesus changed water into wine love."

"I suppose so."

"And do you know why he did it?"

"Why?"

"Because his mother asked him to. Good for her. Fruit of the vine and work of human hands."

"I forgot to wash my teeth." Roisin had wriggled out of her sleeping bag ready to tiptoe to the bathroom saying quietly "Suppose you'll be asleep when I get back mum."

"Probably."

....

Kate carried the sleeping bags downstairs and left them in the hall. Christina arrived an hour later her coat buttoned to her neck, a scarf muffled around her chin and wearing a pair of woolly gloves.

She always came prepared.

"I don't know how you stand this house Kate. It's freezing. Did you not light the fire or put the heating on?"

"I only use the heating early in the morning and late at night Chrissie you know we're warm blooded."

"You'd need to be. What about the guests?" The gossip about Kate's latest venture had travelled quickly as bad news invariably does.

"They didn't complain."

"Have you any of them around the place today?" Christina

56

could make paying guests sound like vermin. "I don't know why you would want to do it, strangers wandering in and out of your house, rumpling the cushions, using the bathroom."

"I'm taking a break for a while. I'm thinking of putting a fresh coat of paint in the bedrooms," Kate lied. "Do you want a cup of coffee?"

"Is it that cheap stuff?"

"Yes."

"No thanks, I'll have a cup of tea instead."

"I don't have any sugar."

"I don't take sugar. You know that."

Kate went into the kitchen and shivered. Christina had a good job. She believed that some were born poor but could rise above it and some had poverty thrust upon them and therefore needed charity. She also believed that some people achieved poverty.

In Christina's opinion her youngest sister fell into the last category. Christina could not understand why Kate was without a man, without a job or without sugar in the cupboard. When Kate returned with the tea Christina asked about the future. She always knew when Kate lied.

Kate cupped her hands round the mug as she answered,

"I don't know Chrissie. I'm doing nothing at the moment. I need time."

"What for?"

"To think."

"To think what?"

"I don't know."

"Jesus, Kate." Christina was exasperated. She worried about Kate but treated her sometimes as if she was five years old. "You have two kids to think of you know."

"I know."

"They shouldn't be poor."

"They're alright. It's good for them. It helps them appreciate things a bit more. Anyway we have a good laugh."

"That's not what it's about."

"How do you know?"

"What?"

"How do you know that that's not what it's about?"

"What what's about?" Christina was confused.

"Life, just enjoying it as it is."

"You talk crap sometimes Kate do you know that?"

"Yes. I laugh therefore I am."

"You see what I mean, crap. If I had put my children into this situation I could not live with myself."

"That's because you take the idea of rearing children so seriously Chrissie. The problem with most mothers nowadays is the fact that they love their children but they just don't happen to like them. I consider myself lucky. I like my kids, that's the easy bit. It's loving them properly that takes all the hard work."

"That's a disgraceful thing to say Kate."

"No, it isn't Christina. Unconditional love is something very difficult to attain. I mean think about those pancakes advertisements."

"What?"

"You see Christina. You didn't even notice them, never mind taking time to think about them."

"Too busy working Kate, which is something you should be thinking about."

"But we have to notice Chrissie. We have to think. I mean I'd hardly digested my frigging Christmas dinner when some media monster decided it was time to stick a big red heart in my face for St. Valentine's Day."

"You're annoyed because you didn't get a card."

"Or a forty quid teddy bear with 'I love you' stuck on its arse. Wise up Christina. I suppose your Harry got you the biggest card in the shop."

"Yes actually. And flowers. There's nothing wrong with that. All the young ones in the office got presents and I just wanted to show them that there can still be romance even after years of marriage."

"Romance Christina, romance - at your age?" Kate could feel the heat beginning in her stomach.

"Love isn't romantic. Love is bloody hard work. Love is making someone a wee cup of tea when you are dog tired. Love is washing the dishes at twelve o'clock at night with no hot water. Love is being free and allowing others to be free. I don't want my kids to have my worries my doubts my pain. Look at Mary for Christ's sake. She probably fretted and worried and fussed about clean underwear and teenage spots and what happened to her son. Murdered by self-righteous men who feared unconditional love. Love, Christina is making sure there is no cruxifixion."

"That's blasphemy Kate. You ought to be ashamed of yourself."

"It's common sense Christina. Unlike pancakes."

"Christ, are we back to the pancakes?"

"Yes, there they were, in between Christmas and St. Valentine's Day on a billboard. There were two men in suits and one of them was showing off his bloody big pancake."

"There's no need to be rude."

"He was holding it in his hand."

"Just stop Kate."

"His pancake. His enormous big round pancake. For pancake Tuesday."

"Oh I see. What's wrong with that?"

"Everything. There has to be more to celebrate in life than pancake bloody Tuesday. We're just being programmed Christina. Thoughts put into our heads and sprinkled with sugar or lemon. But they are not our thoughts. They belong to someone else. There are people who want us to be slaves. Why do you think kings built palaces, and pharaohs built pyramids and cardinals built cathedrals? Why do you think presidents and prime ministers start wars? It is to keep us working so that we don't think. They keep us from original thought. Someone even invented original fucking sin just to keep us in our place. May God forgive them Christina."

"And you too Kate. I hate when you use bad language."

"It isn't bad. There's no such thing as a bad word for heaven's sake. Just a wrong word in a wrong place."

"And stop shouting. I came to collect a couple of sleeping bags Kate not to receive a lecture."

"I'm sorry. I wasn't shouting at you. I just get so exasperated sometimes. Anyway I have made a decision. I will not be programmed. I don't want their thoughts, their ideas, their sins or their bloody pancakes. Kate paused then said lowly "Do you want a digestive biscuit?"

"Chocolate?"

"Only plain I'm afraid."

"No thanks. I'll have to go soon."

Christina lifted the sleeping bags from the hall. She put them into the boot of the car and called to her sister.

"Cheerio Kate. Try not to be a martyr will you. And look for a decent job. I worry about you honestly, trying to sort out the world. You know what Maggie Thatcher said about the good Samaritan."

"I didn't know you were a follower."

"I'm not. But she said that no-one would remember the good Samaritan if he only had good intentions he had money too."

Kate smiled. As her well-meaning sister reversed the car Kate mentally reversed what she had just heard and murmured to herself,

"If he only had money no-one would bloody well remember him either. He was not going to be told how to think. He refused the programming. That is what the story is about Chrissie" But Chrissie was already turning the car onto the main road.

Kate closed the door and thought back to the day Christina had started work. She remembered how startled she had been not recognising her eldest sister. Chrissie usually wore flowered frocks and brown sandals. The first day she started work she wore a straight black skirt and high-heeled shoes. Her hair was lacquered and layered on top of her head. She was taller. She seemed to be looking out for herself where before she had always looked out for Kate and Ralph. She was a surrogate mother bridging the gap between Kate and a strange adult world. But Christina's speedy transition from home life to work life brought benefits as well as confusion. Kate and Ralph had had strict borders for playing on the street. They were allowed three doors down as far as Toner's and five doors up to Smith's. On Friday evenings the borders were relaxed and they could race hand in hand to where the next street criss-crossed their own. Here they waited patiently for Christina and her Friday night gift. It was usually a packet of rolos or fruit pastilles and a sixpence from the owner of the factory where she worked. The pleasure was not in the sweets or the money. The pleasure was not having to share. Kate and Ralph could eat the whole packet of sweets themselves or spend the sixpence entirely as they wished over the weekend. It was Christina who first introduced them to individual consumption. They did not know why this was important and at that age they did not much care. She would hold their hands and walk towards home telling stories of her day helping her to overcome her fear of this new world. She described the huge ovens and the smells. She told them about her office and how she worked directly for the owner. She talked of the owner's kindness. It was years before it dawned on Kate that the sixpence was from Christina's own allowance saved from the previous week. She always handed her brown wage packet to her mother unopened and waited to be given her dues. Kate and Ralph would also wait until Christina brushed the tallness out of her hair then they would barter with pastilles for a place on her knee. She would continue the story:

"The rich owner once lived on a street," she told them, "in a house just like ours. And he had a little brother and a little sister just like both of you. They were very hungry so one day he decided to bake some bread. He got up very early and baked ten loaves. He them put them in a huge tray which he balanced on top of his head. He went out early and sold all the bread to people who were going to work. The next day he did the same and the same the day after that. He carried the tray around the street winter and summer. Soon he had enough money to buy a handcart, then a van, then a huge factory and his little sister and brother were never hungry again."

Kate and Ralph loved this story until the night Paddy Joe informed them that a woman had found a fly in one of the factory's currants buns. They listened mouths open as Paddy Joe described how the woman brought it round to the office to claim some fresh compensation. The owner insisted it was not a fly and to prove his point promptly ate it. The woman, Paddy Joe insisted, left the office empty handed but with a story that was priceless. Kate never quite believed what Christina told her again about work. Ralph continued to think the owner was great and secretly wondered how the fly had tasted.

Christina was a good big sister. Kate knew that. She just did not left the mantle fall when it was no longer needed. Families and religions are expert at this and are often armed with a barrel load of good intentions as well. Both institutions shape lives and thoughts. Both curtail and limit emotion. Both keep people in their place according to an established hierarchy. Both name escape betrayal. Two thousand years later very few people want the name of Judas.

Three main things tied Kate, her sisters and her brothers together as they grew. They were Catholic. They were Irish. They were poor. They lived in a small house in a small street, one of the many capillaries from which the Falls Road later drew its blood.

Their mother's fear of borders was unprecedented and mostly unwarranted. Her rules were a maze of bad wolves and nasty strangers. She knew of water that could drown and heights that could kill, boys who could main and girls who knew things 'not worth knowing'. So the family were raised, sometimes afraid of what lay inside the house more often afraid of what lay outside it.

In the summers when Kate's skin darkened like her father's the others would tease her with an old photograph of their grandmother dead a long time before any of them were born.

"You'll look like that when you grow up Kate." The older ones would laugh.

"You look like that now." Ralph echoed, anxious to join in the fun.

Kate's temper would erupt. She would scream and kick and sulk and swear.

62

"We're going to tell mammy you said a bad word."

"No I didn't."

"Yes you did. You said two bad words, bloody and shite."

"You just said them as well."

"We were only saying them because you said them."

"It doesn't matter, you still said them."

"But you said them in a bad temper. And that's a sin."

Kate would sit solemn, scowling and scared in case the others would tell mammy when she got back from the novena.

They never did tell about the tantrums or the teasing but Kate sometimes wet the bed in spite of the bucket on the landing. She was beaten for that so everything was fine.

The order and chaos of the home had weaved itself in and out of Kate's consciousness all her life. She grew but often felt stunted. Sometimes she pulled viciously away from her brothers and sisters. At other times she clung to them. There were many fruitless attempts to free herself from the religion and poverty that were her birthrights.

The Conlon children had been forbidden by their time and their culture to perceive their parents as people and they were unable to see each other as individual or separate. Every child needs something different or at least something else. They were led to believe, like many others, that if one branch of the family broke away then the tree would rot. And as they grew they twisted and turned around each other in shyness, in confusion and in silence. They learnt to live among and between and because each other existed. They gave this living a name. They called it love.

But Kate was beginning to think about things differently. New ideas were edging their way into her thoughts in exact correlation to the developing photographs she had taken with the cheap disposable camera.

6

Modern life coaches might suggest that what happened next had three distinct elements; faith, hope and opportunity. Realists would agree with Kate that the distinct elements were three rather arthritic old aunts. They lived in Boston, blown there by the last great exodus from Ireland in the 1940's and 1950s.

Kate was pleased with the developed photographs. The tree looked beautiful. A headstone complete with cross was visible in the background and 'miraculously' thought Kate the light had been just right. It shone through the branches and onto the image which was clear and defined.

"It's clear enough to me," Kate said as she studied the photograhs, "maybe because I know what I'm looking for."

She had taken five photographs of the tree and had used the rest of the film on family shots. There were two of Roisin in her baggy pyjamas and some of Charlie asleep on the couch in his bobble hat looking positively sheepish. There was one of Rebel guarding his bowl with all the authority of a land agent and one of Kate standing arms folded at the front door. She tore it up. It reminded her of her grandmother. Most were thrown in the kitchen drawer but Kate propped three of the cemetery ones behind the tea cannister. She wrote only occasionally to her aunts but she thought they might like a photograph to remind them of home and the burial place of their parents. At least it gave her something to write about.

The major excitement of her childhood had not been Christmas. Those mornings did not live up to anyone's dreams. But waiting for a parcel from her aunts in America brought excitement beyond the boundaries of expectation. It was a feeling she was to experience only twice in adulthood on the births of her daughter and son.

The letter from her aunts in Boston would always arrive before the parcel. It was usually a collective correspondence from her mother's three youngest sisters, Martha, Maggie and Ellen. Dreams of what the box might contain filled Kate's days at school. She would imagine it in the hold of the ship with labels stuck on it proclaiming to the world that the Conlon Family were to receive gifts from across the wide Atlantic Ocean. Kate's father would collect the heavy cardboard box from the main post office and the sorting began as soon as it was opened. Big brown shoes were taken out and put aside. They would do some-one else. Pollyanna dresses were hastily pulled on over ordinary frocks with a silent prayer that they would fit. One parcel had contained corderouy trousers for Paddy Joe, and another one a bathing costume for Kate. Until that day Kate had thought everyone tucked their dresses into their knickers before paddling in the sea. There was usually a polka dot dress and a pillbox hat for Christina and romper suits for Ralph, blouses for Mammy and coloured short sleeved shirts for Daddy. The young aunts remembered their homeland and what they had left behind with a theatrical presence of mind. The box when emptied was left to dampen in the back yard and used to stoke the fire when coal was scarce. After the day's excitement Kate's mother would become quieter that usual, more permeable. She had torn up emigration papers years before unable to leave what she knew for what she feared. Most days and nights her children cocooned her but when parcels or letters arrived she missed her own little sisters with a broken ache that heal.

The parcels stopped as the children grew older and telephone calls replaced hand written correspondence. The planet shrunk as travel and communication became cheaper and no longer special. Kate still liked to write to her aunts and Martha,

Maggie and Ellen, now all in their seventies, each received a short letter and a photograph the following week.

Martha smiled and popped letter and photograph into the kitchen drawer. Maggie read the letter, pleased that things in Belfast were brightening up at last and glad that everyone seemed happy. She took out the newest of her family albums and securely placed the photograph on the last page. Ellen popped the photograph behind a jar of coffee, read the letter quickly and went to attend to her ailing husband. Later that morning when his medication had induced grateful sleep she remembered her niece's words on the back of the card and followed her instructions. She lifted the photograph from the shelf, held it up to the morning light filtering in through the kitchen blind and really looked at the image. Then she did what she did every morning of her life. She blessed herself. She left a note on the bedside table in case her husband should waken. She reversed her car out of the driveway and headed to St. Veronica's Church a few blocks away for ten o'clock mass. The photograph was placed carefully on the passenger seat beside her.

As with most people who have chosen a religious career, the parish priest of St. Veronica's was highly suspicions of miracles. He said goodbye to his parishioners after ten o'clock mass, walked back past the church, into his office and put the photograph into his out-tray. He was a busy man and it was the next morning before his secretary had the chance to ask him what she was to do with it.

"Oh, I don't know, file it somewhere will you Abby."

"Of course Father Gasannio. I'll do it later. I'm just working on the final layout for this month's parish newsletter. Do you want to check it before it goes out?"

"No, fire ahead Abby. I have a meeting this morning and God knows what the afternoon will bring. Well, God does know doesn't he. It's just that I don't! He! He!"

"Very good Father, very funny."

The secretary lifted the photograph again and looked at it.

"What is it Father? Has it some significance?"

"No, I just glanced at it myself. A parishioner gave it to me after yesterday morning's mass Ellen McDonnell I think. She sometimes helps out with the dinners for the elderly and the childrens Christmas concert. She is very good at turning the little devils into angels and shepherds with a bit of tinsel and a few yards of material. Wonderful what these women can do. She has been a parishioner here for years. Her children went to the Catholic school B.V.M. She lives on Rosedale Avenue now. She mentioned something about Milltown Cemetary in Belfast. Her parents are buried there I think she said. She was in a bit of a rush, something about her husband's wake. That's an Irish tradition I believe. To tell you the truth I was in a bit of a rush myself. The bishops are pulling out all the stops about our stance on the war. We have to make sure we hold a united front, no trouble in the ranks.

Father Gasannio lifted a pile of business papers from his desk and walked briskly out of the office. Abby typed up the last article for the parish newsletter. As she cut and pasted the various items on the computer screen she made a mental list of what she needed to buy in the shopping mall during her lunch hour. It was the Lenten season in the Christian calendar which meant that the monthly newsletter was sparse. With a flash of inspiration Abby scanned the photograph and placed the image neatly onto the last page. She typed some text underneath to fill the last space:

'Milltown Cemetary, Belfast. Photograph courtesy of Mrs. Ellen McDonnell, Rosedale Ave. Boston, USA.'

She emailed the finished newsletter to the Diocesan head office for printing, made nine telephone calls, typed up and corrected Fr Gasannio's sermon for Sunday and arrived at the shopping mall just before noon.

Kate, unaware of secretarial thrift across the Atlantic was completely shocked when she received the call three weeks later.

"Hi. My name is Dolores O'Reilly. I got your telephone number through St Veronica's Church newsletter. It took a while for them to give me your aunt's number. I almost had to produce my baptism certificate. You know what it's like these days with data protection and all that. But anyway your aunt gave me your telephone number so I figured it was okay to call. It's 11.30 am here. I hope I haven't called at an inconvenient time for you. I'm ringing from Boston."

Kate listened politely to the meaningless American monologue and when there was a pause for breath she jumped in.

"I'm sorry. Dolores did you say? I think you may have the wrong number."

"Oh, I can't believe it! I thought this was the number for Lagan's Guesthouse. Is that not right?"

Kate hesitated for a second but the voice sounded genuinely disappointed and it was after all three thousand miles away.

"Yes, this is Lagan's. I'm Kate. I'm not sure how I can help."

"My husband and I are travelling to Ireland just before Easter. We've been planning the trip for months so I just couldn't believe it when your aunt told me that you had a guest house right next to the cemetery. We'll only be in Belfast for four days and it just sounded so perfect right next to Mill Town. Isn't that the right name, Mill Town?"

"Yes, but I don't live next door to it."

"Oh I see." The tone of disappointment returned.

"My home is a few minutes walk away."

"Oh great then you can book us in for four nights. Wait till I tell my husband. Thank you so much Mrs Lagan, may I call you Kate? By the way I'm a vegetarian so I won't take a cooked breakfast, and I'll bring my own soya milk. Do you take credit cards? I guess we'll need to pack raincoats and will that give us enough time to see the vision?"

"The what?"

"The vision."

"Sweet Christ."

"No, not Christ. His mother, The Blessed Virgin Mary."

"Dolores, this is a very bad line." Kate paused, then said, "Can I hang up and would you mind terribly ringing back in exactly ten minutes. I'll be here."

Kate put the receiver down. The swift action followed by a swift proclamation.

"Jesus, Mary and St. Joseph kids what am I going to do?"

Roisin's response, when Kate explained the telephone call was more realistic.

"Jesus, Mary and St. Joseph mum, what have you done?"

The three Lagan's looked at each other for a moment in astonished silence then Charlie said,

"Cool mum, we're back in business big time then? When do we add the disabled parking spaces?"

Dolores rang back in exactly ten minutes. Kate took a deep breath, told her the double room was fifty pounds a night and she would provide fresh fruit, cereal and the soya milk. Credit card facilities were not available as yet Kate explained, but cash on departure would be fine.

Dolores made the booking and Roisin found herself down at Millet's that afternoon purchasing three cheap but comfortable sleeping bags. The Lagan's were 'on tour' again.

And the resurrected business went crazy. Two double rooms at fifty pounds per room per night helped Kate deposit an incredible £500 in the local credit union by the middle of May. On the strength of that she plucked up the courage to apply for a £2000 loan to fit a new shower, order a fridge freezer, choose new carpet for the hall and stairs, install new lights on the stairs and landing and phone Mr. Collins at the tourist board to ask for an application form to register as a guesthouse.

Six weeks later Nigel arrived to erect her signage at the front gate. "Lagan's Town House. Tourist Board Approved."

By the end of the summer Kate was exhausted.

"You'll need to get help mum." Charlie suggested. "Roisin's going to need somewhere decent to sleep and study. She'll need a bit of peace and quiet and you need a bloody good rest."

Kate looked at her son with pride. No other man in her life had ever said that to her.

"I know you're right Charlie." Kate had never said that to any man in her life. "What should I do?" Or that either.

"Phone Patricia mum. She could give you a hand. And don't take so many bookings. Give Roisin the small front bedroom. She needs space. We all do. The business is there. You don't have to kill yourself. And if Mary and Joseph turn up we can always put them up in the stable, I mean the garage."

"Don't knock it Charlie. How was I to know a photograph would bring this much business."

"It isn't just the photograph mum. It's you. You're good at this sort of thing. People like you. They tell other people. You give good value for money.There's no mystery in that."

"Maybe a wee miracle though!"

Charlie grinned. " I start school again next week mum. You need help. Phone Patricia."

On Charlie's adolescent but sensitive advice Kate reached out to her perpetual succour feeling guilty and tired.

"Patricia, are you still looking after your Susan's kids?"

"Oh is that Ms Lagan, Lagan's Townhouse?" Patricia's tone was curt. "I died three months ago. Haven't you heard? Or are you too busy making your first million?"

"Sorry Patricia. I really am." Kate actually bit her tongue.

"I saw the sign going up at the front gate. It looks well Kate. I thought you might have had a champagne opening and invite all your old friends."

"You're the only old friend I've got Patricia. You know that. Anyway, I haven't had time for an opening. I'm too busy. That's why I'm ringing you. Patricia, honestly, I'm sorry. I can hardly tell you what my kids look like, or my mother. It's been bacon and eggs and cornflakes and toilet rolls and laundry all summer. Bloody hard work."

"Are you making any money Kate. There's no point in killing yourself."

"Not yet, not really, but for the first time in my life Patricia I'm in charge of myself. And that's the difference. I love it."

"So what do you want from your old impoverished friend?"

If Kate had considered herself a business woman she would have offered Patricia employment there and then, negotiated an hourly rate, drawn up a contract and had self-satisfied thoughts about expanding her business and taking on employees. She would have thought, in capital letters, the word Boss. And things would have gone from strength to strength. She could have made a million. She may even have been awarded business woman of the year.

"Well Kate, what do you want?" Patricia asked again her tone softened and concerned.

"Help. I need help Patricia. Can you help me?" Kate burst into tears.

"I'll be over in ten minutes Kate, with a box of tissues."

"What about your Susan's kids?" Kate blew her nose.

"I don't have them anymore. The job didn't work out so she's off the treadmill and back to the Disney films. Switch the kettle on."

There is no business manual in the world which suggests that the owner of a successful business, no matter how large or small should, in a crisis, cry. Strengths, weaknesses, opportunities and threats should be handled constructively with essential reference to a business plan.

Kate had never heard of a SWOT analysis, didn't have a business plan and wrote down all her bookings and the money she received and spent in an old blue exercise book belonging to Roisin. The first two pages had lists of French verbs but the rest had been blank. Her management system was the one she knew best, working day to day, bargain to bargain and spending less than she received and thanking the universe for the difference. Kate had always appreciated value and that had become the unwritten principle of her business. She tried to give more in value than she received. She did not know it yet but it was also what she would give to her best friend.

Patricia arrived with a packet of chocolate digestives and a promise to help.

"Anyway," she told her exhausted friend, "what's so complicated about cooking bacon and eggs? Even Mrs. Blair could manage that."

Patricia's help proved to be the best business decision Kate could have made. The friends agreed that five pounds an hour was reasonable and would not embarrass either of them. As Kate cooked Patricia served and chatted to the guests. Her easy manner and handsome looks blended well with a natural gift for storytelling. She talked about the history of the Troubles and the history of the area. Kate was convinced she was adding frills as she went along. She reminisced about her childhood in the Lower Falls but most importantly of all she asked guests quietly and with true sincerity about themselves and the reasons for their visits. Guests opened to her and spoke of their fears, their beliefs, their tensions and their curiosity. A young woman, accompanied by her mother looked up eagerly as Patricia announced, "The more I see the more I wonder what it all means."

"I think like that too." The young woman's voice was troubled slightly. Patricia gave her time to explain.

"I mean, sometimes I try to make sense of it all and I think I have the answer but then I realise that I haven't even asked the right questions. I mean, what are we doing here?" the young woman asked sincerely.

"Having a morning meal." Patricia said, "breaking bread."

"We came up from Athlone to have a look at the tree." the girl's mother explained. "A friend told us about it. My daughter believes in the tree. She's not quite sure about God though."

"Oh that doesn't matter" Patricia said briskly. "God doesn't care whether we believe or not. No use worrying about things like that."

"What do you mean?" the young woman enquired hastily.

"Well love, put it this way. I'm not God, I'm Patricia. I know I'm standing here at eight thirty on a Thursday morning serving breakfasts. It doesn't matter whether you believe that or not. I know I exist. If you don't believe it that doesn't mean I'll disappear in a puff of smoke."

"I never really thought about it like that." the young woman spoke quietly, "I mean, I've spent so much time worrying, debating, not believing, believing."

Patricia poured the golden tea into the young woman's cup and patted her on the shoulder.

"Stop worrying love it never helped anybody. You just start living."

"I feel like a bloody missionary." Patricia whispered to Kate in the kitchen as she popped four slices of bread into the toaster and filled another teapot in a synchronised movement.

"You would have made a good nun Patricia." Kate whispered back lifting the pan from the sink and rinsing off the suds. "If this was fifty years ago, or even thirty, that young woman would have been whisked off to a convent. She's just the sort to be kidnapped. Quiet, intense, taught to think too much about god and not enough about herself."

"It's not even an option now entering the convent." Patricia answered.

"Too much television."

"Too much bloody sense. Did you know Kate that nuns all take their periods at the same time?"

"Wise up Patricia."

"Honest to God. It's something to do with hormones. When women live together they can sense each others menstrual cycles and they tune in."

"Christ, I wouldn't like to be in the convent that week of the month."

"Can you imagine it? Twenty or thirty women all tensing up to each other."

"A holy war"

After breakfast Kate suggested to the woman and her daughter that they might enjoy the long route around the cemetery. It was a cold bright morning and a breath of fresh air would do them no harm.

"Turn right at the big Celtic cross and follow the path past the republican plot. Head down towards the bog meadow keeping the wire fence to your right. You'll realise you are walking in a huge rectangle. Turn left at the bottom and then left again. You'll pass an old red brick building the remains of a home for wayward boys. Just above that you'll notice a grave near the path with two angels "O'Kane" the name is. Stop there and look straight ahead at the old tree. You'll see it, or her, if you walk slowly. You'll notice the silence and maybe a sense of peace. That's all there is." Kate smiled encouragingly, "And sure maybe that's enough." she added with conviction. "Wrap up well though, the wind comes straight off the motorway and onto the graves. Funny, I always think it should be the other way around."

"Sometimes Patricia," Kate pronounced as they changed the linen in the front bedroom for the next set of guests, "sometimes, life blossoms. Did you feel like that when you were pregnant?"

"No," Patricia replied, fluffing up the pillows, "unless you mean the blossoming of a large purple balloon. What's brought on the sunshine?"

"Lack of worry Patricia."

"Seriously?"

"Yes, seriously."

"Can I make a confession?"

"Certainly my child I shall do my best to absolve you from your sins."

"Thanks Patricia. I confess that I think my brain is getting bigger."

"That's daft Kate"

"I don't mean actually bigger. I mean there seems to be more space in it for other things."

"Like money and how to spend it?"

"No. Questions mainly."

"What sort of questions? What is the answer to 6times7?"

"Forty two, the number of my granny's house. But not those sort of questions Patricia. My mind was always full of worry about how much milk cost and were sugar puffs dearer than cornflakes or was it just the packaging. Or did cheap brands work out cheaper in the end because I threw them out if they were tasteless or else they went stale."

"When they go stale I pour hot milk over them. That way Jimmy doesn't notice."

"Now that I have good, honest, steady money coming in I don't need those questions any more. That's what I mean about the space. Instead of staying as space it keeps filling up with other things."

"What other things?"

"You'll laugh"

"Go on"

"Okay. Will the next messiah be a woman!"

"What's 8times8?"

"Sixty-four, the year our Ralph was born."

"Will it be a woman?"

"It'll be a right bloody surprise if it is."

"You don't let your mind dwell on the wee niggly questions, do you Kate?"

Despite the hint of sarcasm Patricia was interested and Kate went further.

"What do you want for your family Patricia?"

"More than I had."

"Exactly. That's what any mother wants. That's the key to creation. It can't be about rules and regulations and suffering and starvation. It must be about abundance, joy, freedom, life in all its beauty. We have to do something Patricia."

"Preach?"

"No, practice" Kate added thoughtfully, "I don't want money for the freedom of spending it. I want money for the freedom it gives me to think."

"Wait till your a millionaire."

"I'm not sure that's what I want."

"I thought that was what everybody wanted. Look at the quiz shows on television, the lottery."

"I've known two millionaires Patricia. And both of them were sad bastards. One bought me a really expensive bag for a Christmas present once. He was so rich he thought he could leave the price tag on to impress me."

"Did it?"

"No, it insulted me. And the bag was no bloody use anyway.

75

Little titchy thing. Too small to hold anything except a designer lighter and a packet of condoms. Neither of which I've purchased in my life. I'm used to celibacy and a box of swan matches.

"After our Susan was born me and Jimmy sent away for condoms. We saw this add in a magazine. They arrived in a plain brown parcel. Can you believe that? Now if you go into a chemist for a packet of mint tic-tacs you're likely to lift a packet of minted condoms by mistake."

"I used to work with a woman whose husband was a bank manager."

"Did they use condoms?"

"No. How should I know! I was just thinking about the way people spend their money. She was working so she could send her daughter for etiquette lessons."

"She was not."

"She was."

"What did they teach her?"

"How to get in and out of a car properly."

"I don't believe you. Did it stand by her?"

"What?"

"Knowing how to get in and out of a car properly."

"No. The daughter ended up marrying an unemployed builder from Strabane, with a drink problem."

"That's terrible."

"Last time I saw the family the daughter was about fifteen stone. Her dress would have sheltered a teacher's family in a camp site in Provence for a fortnight."

"Did you know the French are giving away vineyards?"

"Why?"

"Because nobody wants them anymore. They're too much hard work."

"We could get one Patricia. Learn how to crush grapes in a tin bath with our bare feet."

"My da used to do that."

"What, crush grapes with his feet?"

76

"No, wash the blankets in the tin bath. The first good day in summer my ma would strip all the blankets off the beds and put them to soak in the big tin bath in the yard. Then when my da came home he'd roll up his trousers, take off his boots and socks and walk up and down on the blankets to clean them. He would sing Protestant marching songs."

"I'm sure your ma loved that?"

"She'd yell at him. Keep your voice down. No one wants to hear that on the Falls Road. He'd just laugh and go on singing and marching up and down the blankets. He'd a good voice too God rest him. Sure he meant no harm. He was a Belfast man born and bred. When he first got a wee car and him and ma went out in it on Sundays they thought they were the royal family. We used to shout after them, 'if you get past Stormont Da, send us a postcard'"

"Did he ever send the postcard?"

"He was a Catholic from the Falls Road Kate. He didn't even know where Stormont was, never mind drive past it. Why would he want to send a postcard anyway? Bloody ugly place Belfast was, still is."

"I think it's beautiful in its own way."

"It's full of despair Kate."

"There's hope in the air Patricia. I can sense it."

"Death, misery and enough tears to drown Ireland."

"Birth and rebirth and imaginings and dreams."

"A bloody swamp."

"A turf bog with layers of history."

"Every one of us a sinner."

"And everyone sinned against."

"Huge bloody walls to separate people."

"There's cracks in the walls Patricia. People have planted flowers. Belfast isn't a city. It's a concept. I keep getting these bloody glossy brochures for guests. The first time I got them I didn't even know the photographs were Belfast. I've lived here all my life and I had to read the small type. I hate it when Belfast is promoted that way, photocopied, reproduced as if it were the entertainment capital of the world. It's people like us who make this city not air-brushed photography."

"Tell that to the Chamber of Commerce."

"I will if I ever get an invitation to one of their business lunches. If they invite me I'll send you a postcard."

Some time later when Kate was invited to Belfast City Hall she wrote a postcard with the words 'weather beautiful glad you are here'. She didn't need to post it. She popped it into Patricia's bag just before they set up the power point presentation for the meeting.

But that would come later, with wine and canapés. At this moment in time they were changing the bedlinen and chatting. They were still, albeit metaphorically, crushing grapes with their bare feet

7

It would be convenient to suggest that Belfast became a Mecca for pilgrims. Imagine Kate's humble home developed into a tourist attraction. Think of the house, then a row of houses together in a series of design breakthroughs. Add a jacuzzi, a private swimming pool, massage and aromatherapy rooms, a French chef and a souvenir shop. Then forget it all. Kate was not destined to find heaven in the virtual world of consumerism. She wanted the sort of happiness that appealed to her basic sense of reality. The God she would look for would have his, or her, feet firmly planted on the ground and would know the price of potatoes.

The words Heaven and hell are as misused as most of the people on the earth.They are words used negligently by those who should know better, religious leaders, fundamentalists, politicians, journalists and prophets. Heaven and Hell are supposedly democratic words, people words, powerful words. They are very misleading. The simplicity of their meaning has been lost in the complex matrix of a blue green planet that has become too big for its own boots.

Heaven is to see. Hell is not to see.

It is that simple. Eventually Kate began to see. She would realise in spite of religion that God had not gone. She would find Heaven where it always had been, inside her and all around her. Meanwhile there was work to do.

"Hello Kate, Mr Collins here, Northern Ireland Tourist Board."

"Hi Mr Collins. How are you?"

"Fine, fine. And you?"

"Busy, busy, busy."

"That's what I like to hear Kate. I was just phoning to see when you are going to link into our website?"

"What website?"

"The Belfast one. It's very good isn't it?"

"Yep! Great. How do I link in?"

"Well just phone our technician Wesley on extension 356. Give him your email address and website domain. He'll do the rest."

"Right-he-ho, except there may be a slight problem."

"What's that?"

I don't have a website. I don't have an email address. To be downright truthful Mr Collins, I don't even have a computer."

"Tut tut. I can hardly believe that in this day and age?"

"Mr Collins, half the world's population have not used a telephone."

"Ah, but that's not the issue here Kate you will have to get a computer. I mean you cannot really run a business these days without one. How do you control your finances, keep spreadsheets, devise your business plan?"

"I use a blue exercise book."

"Ha ha! Very good. Well, let me know as soon as you're up and running with the broadband and I'll get Wesley to contact you. Okay?"

"Okay."

Kate put the telephone down and went out into the garden. She stood quietly breathing for ten minutes. She was teaching herself to treat problems in a new way. In the past problems had always been hurdles in a race. She saw the hurdle on the track and took a running jump at it and had often ended up tangled, bruised, battered and merely grateful that she had not broken her own neck. But then she had been taught that life was an obstacle race taking place inside a maze. Now she was beginning to allow herself the luxury of looking at life from the inside. Trees did not move. Their roots went down. Flowers did not run around like demented idiots. She knew that if a bulb was planted the wrong way in the soil it gradually turned itself the right way up to grow.

"If a frigging daffodil has that much intuition" she thought "then where did I go wrong?"

So she stood in the garden and allowed her feet to go down and further down. She breathed slowly. She had always been instructed to take deep breaths. She threw that idea away and did exactly the opposite. She inhaled a little air and then slowly released it making a soft "wooooing" sound as the stale air passed out of her body. She counted as she exhaled. She could count up to twenty now before taking another breath inwards.

"Problems," she thought, "are seeds. Plant the problem and it will gradually turn itself the right way up."

She counted slowly again to twenty then went into the house. That evening the seed showed a tiny green shoot.

"Charlie I'm going to start doing evening meals for guests."

"Oh mum, it's enough doing breakfasts."

"I'm quite a good cook and I can ask our Christina for a few extra recipes. It can't that difficult. I'll offer a traditional menu, stews, casseroles, poisson au lait, fish and milk to me and you. I'm thinking of charging ten pounds for two courses. Does that sound reasonable to you?"

"Mum, it's too much work as it is."

"Not really Charlie. If I do four meals a night I'll have a profit of thirty pounds a day. Five nights a week would mean one hundred and fifty pounds. In a few weeks I'll have enough money to buy a computer. What's broadband?"

"Good idea mum. I can peel the spuds if you like if I'm not too busy with homework. Broadband connects the computer to the internet through the telephone line."

"Do I have to pay for it?"

"About fifteen pounds a month."

"Okay, I'll throw in an Irish coffee at the end of the meal for two pounds each. That should cover it."

"Cool mum. Have you a license to sell whiskey?"

"No, just the coffee, but we entrepreneurs are renowned for taking risks."

The tourist board officials were taking no risks. There had been a corporate decision to ignore the small flow of pilgrimage enquiries to their reception desk and the rumours of visions. They did not wash their hands of the affair they just turned the other cheek and pretended not to notice. It was no longer in the nature of such institutions to battle with the growing confidence awakened in Catholic ghettos. For half a century west Belfast had been labelled an area of social deprivation. Civil servants had poked about but had generally kept their distance. Money was thrown, occasionally from the safe distance of a London office as one might throw a string of sausages at a pack of snarling dogs. Some of those in power genuinely thought that the area was ruled by the twenty-first century equivalents of Madam and Monsieur Defarge.

Surprisingly, the people from west Belfast, deprived of normal childhoods, normal adolescence and often labelled as "savages" had grown quietly strong and quietly professional. The worthless, the misguided, the harbourers of terrorism had become nurses, doctors, accountants, publicans, builders, joiners, artists, musicians, dentists journalists and comedians. Throw strong threads of inequality, discrimination, prejudice and injustice at any group of creative human beings and they will eventually weave a strong, if rebellious, community. Thus the children of the 1960's televised throughout the world as flared rioters and then as gun crazed maniacs were now forty, now fifty years of age.

They discarded the label of social deprivation . They said they lived in an area of increased social development. It was to them an area of historical reference, a cultural experience, a feile an phobail, a festival of the people.

Meanwhile the city airport was renamed The George Best Airport. Sight seeing tours were organised to the empty dock which had spawned the Titanic. Safari walks were arranged through east Belfast and the city centre. The republican and mainly catholic Wild West was left to take care of itself and its visions.

Rome, unlike the local city guardians, did see fit to take action. File 27356/06/BVM was opened. Fr. Gasiannno's bishop in Boston received a call from The Vatican to ask what the hell was going on. The Vatican had enough on its plate, the bishop was told in no uncertain terms. There was the Middle East conflict, Iraq, the nuclear capabilities of North Korea, The U.S. foreign policy, gay marriage, sex scandals, poverty in Africa and dwindling church congregations. The last thing the Pope needed was a new sighting of the Mother of God. A few more sermons on the nobility of suffering and less pontificating about visions was to be the message for the masses.

This activity in Rome was unknown to Kate. Visions were reported to the special investigation team housed in a small rather dingy office near St. Peter's Square. The team of priests, chosen more for their foreign languages acumen than their investigative prowess considered themselves overworked and underpaid. They could do little with the material resources at their disposal. Consequently their powers and resources were limited unlike the God they presumed to represent. Two of the more elderly members of the four strong team were currently pouring over dusty maps of Ireland trying to locate Milltown Cemetery. The third priest was on the telephone booking a flight to Lisbon and a connecting flight to George Best Airport, tourist class, while the fourth and youngest member of the team was using Google Earth to get a satellite picture of the town, the cemetery and god willing the tree which was causing the controversy. It was an impossible task as he soon discovered but he was young and keen to impress his superiors.

Meanwhile Kate was busy preparing nourishing meals for seven people. She soon realised that adding a few more potatoes and extra meat or fish meant that she, Roisin and Charlie could have the two course meal in the kitchen while the paying guests were sitting down to their Irish coffees at the dining room table.

The evening meals were a success and the extra work worthwhile. Within four weeks Kate had ordered a computer. Paddy Joe had left Rebel for another week with the promise of a computer desk in payment for dog sitting. Charlie was as excited as a five year old on Christmas Eve.

When the pack arrived Kate was astounded at her son's grasp of new technology. She left the assembly entirely to him and a few days later she was staring over his shoulder at the computer screen and a mock-up website.

Charlie was his usual confident self.

"You see mum," he was explaining, "there are bound to be hitches until I get the whole thing up and running. After all, if there's such a thing as artificial intelligence then there must be artificial stupidity."

"Very funny," Kate replied and added, "source please."

"Homer Simpson."

"Charlie, will you ever say something original?"

"Yes."

"When?"

"When I'm a barrister, defending some hooligan for vandalising property or robbing some old granny. I'll have to think of something original then."

"You'll probably go for the prosecution side of the justice system then not the defence?"

Charlie went on typing – and moving the mouse.

"You might just be right mum. I don't really mind. It's the stripy suit I fancy not the legal debate."

"Not a very good reason for choosing a career though."

"As good as any." Charlie replied. "and the money too of course."

"I thought that might have a certain appeal."

"Don't worry mum. I'll come and collect you from the nursing home every so often and take you for a burn down the motorway in my Porsche."

"Will there be room in the boot for my zimmer frame?"

"I didn't think of that. Probably not."

"Oh well that's life." Kate peered at the computer screen with her hands resting on Charlie's shoulders.

"You'd never put me into a home would you?"

"No I'm just kidding. I'll bring you over to Amsterdam and inject you with something. It would be peaceful and straight to the pearly gates with everything in working order."

"Good lad," Kate patted his broad shoulders, "wait till I'm very old though, won't you? I don't want to be whisked off on that final journey suffering from a slight summer cold."

"Don't worry mum I'll get a second opinion. If Roisin makes it to medical school I'll ask her for a diagnosis so that everything is proper and correct. After all she's due too inherit half of your accumulated fortune."

"Or half of my accumulated debts."

"I didn't think of that either, best to keep you healthy and working then."

"Do you want a cup of tea?"

"Love one."

"And a chocolate club biscuit?"

"Love one."

"Love you."

"Love you too."

He had the web page designed and ready to go live by lunch time. He spent the rest of the day trying to explain it to Kate.

Patricia arrived to do breakfasts the next morning and was duly impressed.

"How much did it all cost?" she asked hoping her anxious tone did not upset Kate. Patricia was worried that her friend was taking on more than she could comfortably chew.

"Thirty plates of Irish stew, ten gallons of home made vegetable soup, five bottles of whiskey and fifteen roast chickens" Kate replied.

"Of course we're not 'live' yet but Charlie's going to sort that out tomorrow. He's trying to think of a domain name and an email address. Do you know Patricia it's not that hard once someone explains it. When Charlie was going through it all with me I felt like my granny when she first had electricity installed. She would sit in the dark until grandad came home from work because she was scared of switching on the electric light. She thought it could harm her. She kept a gas light in the kitchen for years just in case the electricity thing didn't catch on. I was fascinated when she told me when I was just a kid. Now I know how she felt.

"I got mine for nothing." Patricia said as nonchalantly as she dared.

"What?"

"My computer."

Kate almost screamed but Patricia rambled innocently ahead in explanation of her coup.

"You know our Susan's twins started nursery school. Well the school was collecting computers for schools tokens. They were snowed under. They ordered five new computers and decided they didn't need the old one in the office. The caretaker was throwing it in the bin when Susan reclaimed it. She gave it to me. It's not very good but it's all I really need."

"What do you need a computer for?" Kate was intrigued.

Patricia looked sheepish but replied "I wasn't going to tell you."

"Have you joined a secret cult or something? Are you writing the tenth gospel? Tell me for goodness sake."

"I joined a class up in the community centre."

"Good for you Patricia," Kate smiled, "what do you do?"

"Nothing as yet. We're just reading different things and discussing them. Some of the stuff I ignored when I was at school and now I'm fascinated. I didn't know it was all so interesting. I might not stay though."

"Why not?"

"You know my Jimmy, he doesn't like me going out at night. He says he's lonely."

"He sits and watches television Patricia. What does he expect you to do? Cheer every time there's a goal?"

"He says learning at my age is a lot of shite."

"He talks a lot of shite Patricia. You stick at it."

" I'll see. It's early days. I liked school but then this aul bitch of a teacher put me right off."

"How?"

"Because of our Joey."

"You haven't a brother called Joey."

"He wasn't my brother he was my budgie."

"What's that got to do with a teacher."

"Well, we had this teacher for English and a right bitch she was. She had a dead posh accent and walked as if she had a pole up her arse. She told us we had to write a story and I wanted to write about the day our budgie exploded. When I suggested it she got all fussed and told me I had to write about something else instead. I couldn't think of anything else so I just have her a blank sheet of paper and she pronounced me a failure. It put me right off school."

"I didn't know you were in a bomb."

"What?"

"The day your budgie exploded. I don't remember you ever being that close to a bomb."

"Fuck it had nothing to do with The Troubles Kate. Joey exploded because my ma gave it a paracodal. The aul thing wasn't looking too well. It kept falling off it's wee perch and I was dead worried about it. I wanted to bring it to the vet. My ma said when she had enough frigging money to bring a frigging budgie to the vet she'd go out and but herself a frigging fur coat. I started to cry and she said she would give it something. She took one of her paracodal tablets you know those big ones everybody took during The Troubles. They were like horse tablets. She dissolved one in water and put it into Joey's wee drinking dish. She said it would cure him or kill him. I don't think she meant it like that mind you. My ma wouldn't have hurt a fly. Then I heard this funny noise when I was in bed. Remember the old Model lemonade bottles you used to get Kate. They had screw-on tops. When you shook them the brown lemonade fizzed up and when fuzzzzzzzz and then a big loud pop. Well that's what it sounded like. And when I came downstairs our Joey was all over the cage. There were bits everywhere."

"That's awful."

"Do you know Kate I was fascinated. Imagine a tablet doing

that to you. I kept looking at my ma to see if she would explode. She used to swallow about six a day. There wasn't enough budgie to bury so we just cleaned out the cage and left it in the back yard. It went rusty and my da threw it out. About a week after it happened I found this wee bluey green feather underneath the cabinet when I was looking for my pencil. I brought it upstairs and put it under my pillow and that night I said a wee prayer and had a good cry. I felt great."

"And that's what you wanted to write about?"

"Aye, except that aul bitch of a teacher didn't let me. She gave me a list of things I could write about, like 'my day at the gymkhana' or 'a letter to my newspaper advertising the summer fete.' She may as well have been talking Swahili. I just switched off and thought about nail polish."

"Maybe the teacher thought you were going to write something about a bomb. Maybe she didn't want to go down that route."

"Maybe she did, silly cow."

Patricia began setting the table for breakfasts and singing quietly, "There'll be blue budgies over the white cliffs of Dover tomorrow just you wait and see."

Kate linked into the Belfast web site and waited patiently for her first email booking. When it came a few weeks later she replied and confirmed. Charlie issued the commands while keeping a steady watch over her shoulder. Occasionally he manoeuvered the mouse then let Kate click contentedly on 'send'.

She was unbelievably excited. One week later she received a booking for the following month. The email was from someone in Rome to inform her that the traveller for whom the booking was being made intended visiting his grandmother's birth place in Tyrone. Then he would drive to Belfast to visit her final resting place. She was buried in Milltown Cemetary.

"Ah, the Irish diaspora." Kate said as she handed the controls back to Charlie. She wondered vaguely how she knew such a phrase.

8

Kate was beginning to have new ideas and new thoughts. She realised there was a significant difference between working hard and hard work. She felt as though she had never worked so hard in her life. Currently, with breakfasts, laundry, individual guests with individual demands, evening meals and new technologies she was clocking up an incredible eighteen hours a day. Her bank balance was healthy but she wondered if her body was strong enough to keep it all running smoothly. She knew it was not hard work though. Hard work was doing a job you did not like for eight hours a day. Hard work was meeting someone else's deadlines. Hard work was a week-end spent dreading Monday morning and an office silently filling with silent desperate screams. The screams could be muffled by carpets, workstations, fancy toilets and faded pot pourri. Air conditioning and smoke free atmospheres now brought healthier environments. Kate was more inclined to think that they actually brought the rarified atmosphere of an ancient tomb. She knew people who worked in offices where it was against company policy to allow employees to open a window. She had once worked in an office [for six weeks] where the manager had not allowed staff to use their own coffee mugs because it made the place look untidy. The Thatcher years had closed the mines.

"Maybe" Kate thought, "the Blair years have simply reopened them above ground. Workers no longer get coal dust in their lungs but what about coal dust in their minds?"

Kate knew wealthy people who slaved away in these modern tombs. On a thin surface they seemed to enjoy such mind grilling activities as non-uniform days and team lunches. As evening came they might be self-congratulatory on reaching a corporate target, on the way to an elusive goal. Targets reminded Kate of little black squiggly things which float dark and annoying in front of closed eyes. There was no satisfactory reason for them and she found them mildly threatening, like corporate goals.

Ideas tugged at the edges of her mind and somewhat mysteriously at the pit of her gut. She did not know yet that it was the awakening of her subconscious awareness. When she did eventually embrace it she did so with all the love at her disposal.

As her body cooked and cleaned and welcomed guests she visualised her mind as a fridge in need of defrosting. She was finding things there perhaps nutritious long ago but now tainted. She began the slow but satisfying process of reaching in and discarding the mould. She knew it was an unpleasant job but somebody had to do it. Somewhere in a subconscious reality there was understanding. There was a deepening knowledge that working hard for oneself was not hard work and that having money was not the same as being rich.

Kate worked on and treated her guests with utmost respect. Once or twice however a guest would push her patience to the edge. One family were an absolute pain in the ass. They had seemed a lovely family from Cork, the parents pretty and educated, their two little daughters solemn and immaculately dressed. But their first morning was a signal that all was not well. Kate heard the wails and had gone upstairs to see what the fuss was about. The mother was standing outside the bathroom door addressing her shivering two-year-old. The little girl did not want to dress. She had been showered and was now standing cold and miserable at the top of the stairs dejectedly crying as her mother talked.

"Why are you behaving like this? Daddy and I are ready for breakfast. Why won't you co-operate? Can you tell me why you refuse to help mummy? We're going to the museum, do you want to spoil that too?"

Kate realised that she could not have attempted to answer such complex conceptual questions.

The child shivered. Kate wanted to say,

"Please dress the child and stop asking difficult rhetorical questions. Why expect answers from a baby. Children don't understand yesterday or later they just understand now and now she is freezing to death"

Instead she said, "breakfast almost ready," and disappeared downstairs.

"Thank God," she thought, "that I was allowed to give my kids a quick slap on the bottom, pull on their woolly tracksuits and get to hell out of wherever we were. There shouldn't be a law against smacking, there should be a bloody law against trying to have philosophical arguments with babies who are just out of nappies"

At the breakfast table daddy took responsibilty. The four year old daughter was given a lecture on the nutritional value of the yolk of an egg. She was told how she had to grow up strong and healthy because one day her daddy and mummy would be old and frail and she would have to look after them.

"Sweet Jesus Christ." moaned Kate in the kitchen.

She entered the room and carefully lowered the teapot on the end of the table furthest from the children.

"I don't like your hair." the four year old announced to Kate "It's a funny colour, and I don't like your jumper, it's a funny colour too. I think it's called mauve. It's got a pluck on the sleeve."

"Very pass-remarkable isn't she?" Kate said as pleasantly as she could to the parents.

"I have always taught my children to be honest." Daddy's reply was as smug as it was swift.

"Oh,"said Kate as she retreated to the kitchen, "I taught mine to be well-mannered first. Honesty was well down the list."

As soon as they left for an educational visit to the museum Kate went to the supermarket and bought a 750 grams packet of Coco Pops. Next morning she heard no remarks from the little girls and hardly any from the parents if she ignored the crunch snap and crackle. Kate had long ago learnt a primary lesson of parenting when in public, keep a chocolate treat handy and blackmail the little sweethearts.

She reckoned it was the first peaceful breakfast the family had had since their second daughter was weaned. Charlie arrived in the kitchen and Kate was not one to miss a classic ending.

"Have you met Charlie then?" she announced bending her head round the kitchen door. "He's doing eleven exams this year and he's going to be a barrister."

Charlie grinned and walked into the dining room cueing in perfectly,

"Mum fed me on rusks, rice and digestive biscuits until I was seven. I wouldn't eat anything else and it hasn't done me a button of harm. Now I love green brocilli, sushi and blue cheese."

The parents smiled patronisingly.

"You've never eaten sushi in your life." Kate whispered when he escaped to the kitchen.

"Any extra coco pops?"

"No but there's a box of Frosties on top of the fridge. It's the home supply. Don't eat them all."

"Yes, oh great one." Charlie lifted the box and disappeared into the garden munching handfuls of cereal as he went.

"Saturday." thought Kate then she too had a moment of matronly panic.

"Where's Roisin?" she whispered then remembered that her own daughter was staying with a friend for the week-end. She had packed extra clothes into her schoolbag announcing that weekends at home were not conducive to study.

"Neither are five bacardi breezers "Kate had called after her, "don't drink too much".

She had then made a mental note to have a talk with her on Sunday evening. Kate knew that Roisin was determined to go to medical school but she had no idea how her daughter's ambition matched her ability. Still, there was no point in asking seventeen year olds rhetorical questions either.

The new age family from Cork left the following day and Kate breathed a sigh of relief. Her mother had maintained peace if not tranquillity by the use of a straight forward rule. If one of the children misbehaved and the definition of misbehaviour was never questioned by them or their mother, then one pronouncement was made.

"Right, I'll slap all of you and then I'll be sure to get the right one."

Sometimes each child received a slap. Sometimes one child admitted guilt but more often they all suddenly decided that the back yard needed cleaning and industriously scrubbed and washed until their children's antennae told them that their mother's mood had changed for the better. Then Ralph, the youngest, was sent in to ask what was cooking for dinner.

Kate had also kept her discipline to a minimum. She told Roisin and Charlie that she would slap them once a year whether it was needed or not. She remembered smacking Charlie twice in his life though he insisted it was at least five times a year. Roisin suggested that as a child she had been black and blue from various ferocious beatings but when pressed actually only recalled one incident about having her hair braided. She refused to wear the satin ribbons on the end of the two ridiculous looking plaits. Kate gave her a sharp slap on the leg. She had run up to the bathroom and repeated over and over again. "I hate you, I hate you, I hate you."

Kate was impressed when Roisin recalled the incident and quite pleased when her daughter added

"I didn't know what I hated, you, the pigtails, myself or the bloody ridiculous ribbons."

"They were to match that lovely red and white dress,."

"I hated that too." Roisin had replied. "You were always trying to dress me like something out of fucking Enid Blyton."

"I loved those books when I was a kid." Kate said nostalgically.

"How come Charlie wasn't dressed in sailor suits or short trousers and blue knee length socks then?"

"His shins would have been kicked off him if I had sent him out to play like that. I wasn't that daft Roisin."

Kate wondered if Irish parenting skills were decreasing in exact proportion to Ireland's increasing wealth. She thought of the Cork family. Cork was the richest county in Ireland.

"Well if that's what the celtic tiger cubs are like," she thought, "I'll have nothing to do with it, republic or no republic."

Kate thought of Ireland as a paediatric society in direct contrast to the geriatric society which England was quickly becoming. Ireland was comparatively new as a free state. It had embraced the twentieth century a little later than most other states. It's people behaved at times like unruly spoilt children. But it was not a colonial mind set and its children had escaped the ideas of empire which hung like wisps of cannon smoke around the great British way of life. Certainly Ireland's population were more confident Irish politics more peaceful. Kate hoped Irish children would be as nice as they ought to be.

She tried out her thoughts on Patricia always a willing listener and more increasingly a willing disciple which worried Kate more than she was prepared to admit.

"Do you think people have stopped being nice Patricia?"

"Remember in primary school Kate. Mrs Black would always put a big red pen through the word nice whenever we used it in our writing. She used to give us those blue books for comprehension exercises. I loved doing those in primary school. Then she would say 'Now girls you have to think of an interesting word instead of nice'. We could think of loads of interesting words couldn't we? But at ten years of age we were just started to say them inside our heads. I couldn't have written them. I didn't how to spell them."

"Mind you," Kate laughed, "we were nice enough to know not to write them in our jotters or poor Mrs. Black would have had a fit."

"That's true."

"I can think of hundreds of people Patricia that I couldn't in all honestly apply nice to and it's such a simple wee word."

"Who?"

"Most personalities on Saturday night television shows, some politicians and"

Patricia interrupted.

"When we were kids my ma would say 'be nice now up in your granny's'. It was funny because we always knew what she meant though she never explained it."

"I know," Kate agreed, "being nice was not asking for more sugar in your tea or making remarks about the ornaments on the mantelpiece or the stains on your grandad's jumper. I suppose we grew up knowing that nice was important and that being kind was saying things that would not hurt. Nice and kind," Kate mused, "two small words that couldn't be applied to some of the most powerful men and women in the world."

Patricia added, " I could think of a lot of other four letter words that might apply. I can spell them all too! Remember that old rhyme Kate? What's the time Mr. wolf?"

"One o'clock."

"What's the time Mr. wolf?"

"Two o'clock."

"What's the time Mr. wolf?"

"Three o'clock."

"What's the time Mr. wolf?"

"Four o'clock."

"What's the time Mr. Bush?"

"Dinner time – oblivion."

"No." Kate almost shouted

"Why?"

"Because of people like us who are intelligent and loving. We are stronger and better. We are nice and we are kind. We know how to make stone soup."

"Don't worry about it Kate" Patricia said softly, "We're not that important in the grand scheme of things".

"Yes we are Patricia. I think that's the point"

Kate knew she needed to clear her mind. She left Patricia to do the dishes and service the rooms. Charlie would help as well. She knew where she wanted to go. It would be chilly in the cemetery and she wrapped herself in a warm scarf and put on her gloves.

The image was much the same as when she had first seen it. Though people had started peeling away bits of bark from the trunk of the tree. She'd noticed the damage a few weeks previously and had realised that if that practice continued the tree itself would be severely damaged. She put up a little sign on the edge of the grass. It read simply

'Take a small pebble home' On her walks she made sure to sprinkle plenty of new pebbles around the spot. She felt somewhat silly but pilgrims could be selfish in their own way.

Kate stopped. There was no-one around so she then emptied a bag of pebbles on the ground. She had bought a sack of granite pepples from a builders merchant and scattered a pile of them in what she hoped was a random fashion every time she came to the tree. They were always gone by her next visit.

"So why did he not go home to Nazareth when you asked him to?"

The question formed in her mind. In her mind the answer materialised.

"I did all I could. I sent his two brothers you know when I thought things were getting out of hand. They were to tell him to stop all that nonsense and come home."

"Did he listen?"

"Yes but he didn't come back. He pointed to all the people gathered in the house and said 'these are my brothers'. Then he pointed to a random woman and said 'this is my mother'."

"Did it hurt?"

"Yes."

"When our Ralph left for university mammy mourned him for three years. He was only in Liverpool. The rest of us seemed to disappear. She yearned for him, ached for him. She couldn't let the mother thing go."

"I know. Then James and Jude followed him. They didn't come back either."

"What did you do?"

"I put up with it. What else can you do? I had a houseful to look after on my own. If only I'd known what would happen"

"I know."

"I knew he was right. He was always as bright as a button but he didn't deserve that. He didn't deserve political crucifixion."

"For telling people they should be nice to each other."

"Exactly."

" I hope I can let my Charlie go when the time comes. I don't want him thinking he has to stay to look after me"

"I know."

"I have other things to ask you."

"Ask away."

"They can wait for another day."

"Okay. See you."

"See you."

Kate smiled to herself. She didn't believe in voices or visions. But it was nice to talk to a mother with a bit of sense. She walked on down the path to her father's grave and settled herself on the side of the granite surround. She lit a cigarette. Her dad had loved a woodbine. She thought having a smoke was as good a prayer to his memory than any Latin incantation. She allowed herself to go slowly back in time. Was she strong enough now to touch another mother's pain. Maybe not. The least she could do was try to understand it.

She had always blamed Maggie. Maggie was the sensible one, not as old or grand as Christina and not as young and stupid as Kate. Maggie had been the in-between sister. For Kate she had always been there young but older, older but still young. Mammy had trusted Maggie and Maggie was teaching Kate about looking after babies. Maggie knew how to be a mother and she was practising now because she was nearly ten and Kate was six and they had been given Responsibility. They felt very grown-up sitting there on the grass in the local park staring adoringly at their little brother Ralph. His head was crowned with a shock of curls. His sparkling eyes sometimes took notice of his two big sisters but now they searched this new world out of the pram. They had been allowed to take him to the park and were supposed to wheel him straight home again. But the responsibility had made them braver and older in just one bright summer afternoon. They could do anything. They had taken the blanket from the pram and laid it on the grass. They had taken the baby from the pram and were teaching him about the park. It was big and bright and green and blue and white. Ralph's other world, inside the cream walls of the house, was smaller The faces were always close and always noisy. Two of the faces were watching him now. They laughed at him. They echoed his name, Ralph. That was his name. He knew but he did not know how he knew. He was their master. If he smiled they giggled. If he cried they frowned. If he made sounds they gave sounds back. If he toddled towards them they danced with delighted laughter. When he fell into their arms he smelt their love. He did not know it was love. They tasted like warm milk and chocolate. He could make these faces do whatever he desired. He ate the grass. They laughed. He tugged at his hat. They laughed. He picked the head of a little white daisy and held it in his chubby fist. They sighed. He reached over to pull more daisies from the side of the riverbank. They screamed. He felt the grass rolling around him. He saw green then blue as the sky turned towards him, then green again. He felt the cold water rushing over his head and still he heard their screams.

"Ralph! Ralph!"

His two sisters stumbled down the bank. Terrified and sobbing they pulled the soaking baby from the stream. It was only inches deep. He could not have drowned but they were too young to know. They suffocated him with kisses. They stripped off his clothes. He felt, rather than knew, the indignity.

"Mammy is going to kill us Maggie," Kate was still crying, "what are we going to do? He's soaking wet."

Maggie pulled off her cardigan.

"Kate," she said, "give me yours as well. We can wrap him up in them to keep him warm and then we can dry his clothes before we go home. Nobody will know."

Kate held the struggling damp baby to her chest and swaddled him with the two cardigans while Maggie lit a small fire.

Where did the matches come from? She did not know
Where did the twigs come from? She did not know.
Where did the survival instinct come from? Every child who has had sudden adult fear knows.

They lit the fire and dried his clothes. They unwrapped their precious dirty bundle from their cardigans and whispered love and promises to him. They dressed him as well as any nine year old and six year old can dress a small, struggling, unhappy, damp baby. They laid him carefully in his pram and walked home. They had already been out too long and their mother knew it. When she saw them at the door her worry and fear were immediately replaced with annoyance and anger.

"What happened?"

"Nothing." Maggie said, as confidently as she could.

"Don't tell me lies, is Ralph all right?"

"Nothing happened, Ralph's fine, he's going to sleep."

Ralph was pulled from his smoky slumber.

"What's that smell?"

"Nothing."

"It's smoke! Where you smoking Maggie? If I catch you smoking I'll kill you!"

"I wasn't smoking."

"Where's the smell coming from? It is smoke. His clothes are all smoky. Where you two at a fire? And they're damp, how are his clothes damp? Jesus, Mary and St. Joseph will you answer me?"

Kate remembered the terror. She raced past her mother and into the little pantry behind the scullery. She locked the door. Maggie was older and took the blame and the crack of the cane across her legs. Ralph, hungry and tired, cried for boiled milk and buttered potato. He was the only one in the house for the rest of the evening who dared utter a noise. Kate stayed in the pantry until dark, then crept quietly to bed. She was immediately comforted by her bed-sister, Maggie. Maggie had taken the punishment but in doing so had also withstood the terror.

"He's alright isn't he Maggie?" Kate voice trembled.

"Of course he is, he ate a great dinner, more than I did."

"He didn't drown Maggie. We saved him didn't we?"

"Yes Kate we saved him, we're heroes. Now go to sleep."

"Are we really heroes Maggie?"

"Of course we are."

"I didn't think heroes could feel this scared."

"Of course they do, that's part of being a hero."

"The part they don't tell you about?"

"Yes, they part they don't tell you about."

Maggie moved gently in the small bed as Kate lay as close to her as she could. Kate did not realise until much later how the burns of the cane on Maggie's leg must have smarted again with the heat of her young body pressed against her older guardian.

"Don't move away Maggie, I'm still scared."

"Okay, cuddle up to me, that's right, hush now, go to sleep."

What happened next had only now allowed itself to touch Kate's mind. She saw what lay beyond herself and Maggie all those years ago. Late that night Ralph snuggled contentedly up to his mother. The mother lay on the bed her arm wrapped around him and tears pierced her cheeks. The child beside her was alive. Perhaps Maggie and Kate had been too young to look after him. But she had needed the break if only for an hour for the child inside her was dead. She did not need a doctor to tell her what she already knew. She had not felt life for nearly two weeks. She was seven months gone and had treated herself secretly to little vests, a beautiful small white woollen suit, three tiny pairs of socks and a set of flannel nappies. She thought she would need both sets with the two in nappies. But now she was not sure she would ever be nursing again. She had not told her husband of her fears. What would be the use? She closed her eyes and prayed. "God, if you can't spare the little one inside me then please spare me for the sake of the other children What would happen to them if anything happened to me?" She tried not to think about the birth, or complications, or her age. She fell into a kind of sleeping in the early hours of a new day.

The baby was still-born three days later. There were no complications and no hospital procedures. He was born in the front bedroom, unknown to the younger children, as they sat in the room below. While Christina changed the sheets and talked quietly to the mid-wife, Paddy Joe helped his father wrap his little blood brother in a small blanket. They placed the tiny body carefully into a box and just as carefully left the house and began the walk to the cemetery. There they placed their tiny burden into the hands of a caretaker. It was his job to bury infants who had died before baptism, their little souls not deemed pure enough for a proper burial by a proper priest. Souls still stained, according the theologians of the Catholic Church, with the terrible mark of original sin. The old caretaker respectfully accepted the homemade crucible, fruit of the vine and work of human hands. He dug an opening near the boundary wall and placed the sacred contents into the earth. The grave was unmarked and consequently unvisited.

In the bedroom the nurse bandaged the mother's breasts with a tight cloth. Fever could start and the unneeded milk had to be dispersed within a few days. The adults and teenagers in the home carried their new-born grief as quietly as they could. Kate talked in whispers and remembered being told by someone, possibly a neighbour, that her little brother had been dark and looked like her. She hugged this knowledge to her and once or twice thought she noticed the others looking at her in a funny way.

Their mother rested for two weeks, until the bleeding became lighter. Then she came back downstairs and slowly returned to the running of the house and the rearing of her family. She spoke to Ralph in soft tones and nursed him more than ever. She silently thanked God for saving her but equally silently rebelled with anger against him. Why did she have to bear the pain of holding an angel.? Why should she be blessed with the grief of one tiny ever lasting kiss?

9

Kate drew a damp glove over her eyes, stubbed out her cigarette and threw it into the long grass. She had more things to unwrap of course. But not now. She was learning how easy it was to go forward. The difficult lesson was going backwards, downwards, readjusting memories, testing beliefs. Or was belief too grand a word? Small beginnings, the unravelling of her true self was, she realised, a series of endings. She wondered if touching someone else's pain was altruistic or patronising. And dying for someone else's mistakes. Was that martyrdom or ecstasy? She did not have answers. She was not sure she wanted answers. She was thankful however, to have time to form the questions. She wondered too why we allow ourselves to be layered with a consciousness that belittles our sense of being and our sense of others.

This new existence she was experiencing demanded that she embrace her mother, connect with unspoken, unshared emotions. She knew at once that this was impossible. Her mother's attitudes were now set in stone. Kate decided honestly that a practical step towards her mother would be more appreciated than an emotional one.

"I'll bring her a bunch of flowers," she decided, "and take her to afternoon mass in St. Mary's in Chapel Lane. I'll even stay behind and we can do the Stations of the Cross together – mammy would much prefer that." She smiled thinking of the Stations of the Cross – an outmoded bolt-on ceremony practised mostly by older church goers. There were always fourteen paintings placed at regular intervals around the walls of most Catholic chapels. They depicted Christ's journey to the hill at Calvary. The devotees stopped at each iconic image. They had been directed in their youth to reflect on each suffering moment. The idea was to imagine the physical and spiritual torture and the weight of the cross Jesus was to bear. The lesson, presumably was to realise the insignificance of one's own suffering, by comparison. Kate thought of an old saying her mother often quoted, "sure if everybody threw their troubles on the table, wouldn't you pick your own back out again." There was some truth in it but when she heard it she always imagined one of these dreadful parties when the husbands threw their car keys in a bowl and everyone went home with everyone else's wife. She wondered briefly if things like that really did happen in suburbia but she did not dwell on the matter. What was the point? She wanted to connect with her mother but it had to a connection her mother could also make. It had to be, on Kate's part, nice and kind and safe. Kate decided on flowers and the stations of the cross. Perhaps patronising but very practical. She had walked the long way back around the cemetery, avoiding one section. There would be time and time again when she was stronger. For now she was fairly content to feel her mind opening and her spirit come out of hiding. "Yes," she told herself as she reached the gates of the graveyard, "you're definitely moving Kate. You're wealthier, you're stronger, you're keener, you're shedding old programmed behaviour, you're..." she stopped. A man who had been bending over the grass verge near the entrance looked up sharply at her.

"Frig," she thought I was talking out loud, he must think I'm mad." She felt herself swaying slightly with acute embarrassment and was about to give an explanation when it dawned on her what the man was doing. She had presumed he was bending down to lay flowers on a grave. To her disbelief she stared as he bent down again over a little designer dog and continued to wipe its arse with a moist tissue. She straightened her shoulders, commanded her head to face the right direction and marched briskly towards the exit.

As she made the brief journey home she purposefully filled her mind with lists. The first column eggs, bacon, dishcloths, washing up liquid. The second column, Roisin's haircut and Charlie's eighteen pound deposit for a school fieldtrip. The third column, new pillowcases and towels and the grill needed replacing. The fourth column, flowers for her mum, a new rug for the hall and a pair of tracksuit bottoms. It had taken Kate's mind to reach the fourth list and her own front door to finally admit that she was also fatter. She was in fact rapidly expanding in more ways than one. With the resolution it would take to start a minor battle she opened the front door, removed her scarf and gloves and lifted the telephone directory from the shelf below the hall table. Roisin and Charlie had said they were worried. They had told her she was putting on weight. They had encouraged her to 'take time out' and they had finally suggested the idea of joining a gym. Kate had been appalled. The idea was equivalent to walking off the edge of a cliff. She was sure she would not be allowed to smoke and she had watched, in complete horror one afternoon young gym-goers on cross walkers. Roisin had insisted that she looked at a gym and they had driven to one in a nearby industrial estate. Kate had sat in the car mesmerised at what she saw through the huge glass window. She finally asked Roisin breathlessly,

"What are those things?"

"Fit men and women mum." Roisin had replied keeping the sarcasm firmly in her voice.

"No, I mean those machines. I thought torture was outlawed under the Geneva Convention." Kate said.

"They're called cross-walkers mum. They exercise numerous muscles in one go."

Kate watched. The men stepping onto the machines were turning before her eyes into gorillas.

"I can understand the men using them," Kate said quietly, "after all the machine looks as if it's bringing them back to their original state but those young women stretching their arms and legs like that in some inhuman way."

"It makes them feel good mum."

"Not by the look on their faces Roisin. Do you think it's a substitute for sex?"

Kate shook the image from her mind and counted the number of gyms listed in the directory. There were sixty-seven. She had no idea the people of Belfast were so health-conscious. She chose one at random and telephoned. Later that day she brought her mother to pray at the stations of the cross after explaining why she had arrived with a huge bunch of flowers,

"They were on offer mammy, two for the price of one and I know you like a bargain."

That night she voiced her concerns about joining a gym to Roisin in a last desperate attempt to avoid healthy exercise. She had decided it was too expensive,

"Thirty pounds a month Roisin I can't afford that."

"Yes you can mum. It's one pound a day, look at it that way. You'll love it. It'll give you a break from guests. And at least you can enjoy a relaxing shower and I think it has an aromatherapy room you'll like that."

Roisin's voice became firmer. "And you've made the appointment to see the personal trainer at two o'clock tomorrow. The receptionist telephoned when you were out! Make sure you go. I can't wait to hear all about it."

Kate found the gym and read the 'thought for the day' chalked on the blackboard in the window. She suffered the tour given by the fitness coach who explained how each machine worked, called everyone by a jolly nickname and couldn't mask his delight at his commission fee when she dutifully filled in the direct debit form.

The following afternoon Kate spent one full hour at the gym. She was pleased with her progress. The first thirty minutes had been spent pestering staff for her free bag and fitness towel. She then had her eyebrows waxed, enjoyed a 'free' cup of coffee in reception and read the papers.

However, that night doubts crept in. The bag failed to hold anything larger than a very small bikini and the huge towel had covered her entire body with baubles of dark blue cotton. It was so big it would threaten to break the drum of the washing machine and could possibly take four weeks in the heat of an Arabian desert to dry. She stuffed both bag and towel in a cupboard and vowed to get her thirty pounds worth of fitness if it killed her.

Her second visit was equally disturbing. Holding her head and a rather bulky but more practical old bag aloft she negotiated her way past the dreaded machines and entered the female changing room. Rows of lockers prompted memories of school cloakrooms and the words of the school anthem rose mysteriously in her brain. She hummed the words:

"Home of learning and of prayer where we hold the torch of truth."

Kate had sung the song dutifully every morning at assembly then returned to her locker one day to find someone had stolen her gym kit. It was impossible to ask her mother for extra money for a new kit. She had to decide what to do and thought of stealing someone else's. Instead she had forged excuse notes for the rest of the year.

Kate chose a locker near the shower cubicles and deposited her coin and bag. She squeezed herself quickly into a ten year old bathing costume and tried to find the way out. After two failed attempts to find a door beyond the showers she doubled back and discovered another door leading to the steam room. She took a deep breath, stepped in and sat down. Twenty seconds later the sweat of a thousand hours of work was pouring from her body. She slouched down further dripping and gasping for air. After sixty seconds for she was counting, she began to breathe again. Alone, allowing the sweat and the steam to engulf her she gradually began to relax. Five minutes later she could already feel the exercise was doing her some good.

"Ahhhh," she said aloud, and exhaled a long deep satisfying sigh, "I'm glad no-one else is here. I'd die if somebody saw me like this." She 'ahhed' again and slunk further down in the seat, her legs apart.

"It's hot isn't it? Do you come here often?"

Kate bolted upright and glared through the steam. For the first time she realised there was a vague shape up at the 'hot end'. She tried, as calmly as she could, to reply sensibly. She meant to say "Yes it is hot isn't it?" But the words that hissed grotesquely from her lips were,

"Is there anybody there?"

"Oh fuck, oh fuck, oh fuck", her silent voice beat at the few remaining brain cells not immersed in sweat and steam and panic. "Of course there's somebody there", she thought, "unless the place is haunted by a disembodied voice."

The voice, as if sensing her confusion, ignored the question and began again, rationally enough,

"It's good for the lungs you know, all this steam."

Kate was about to reply when it continued,

"And it gets rid of many of the toxins in the body. There are other methods, colonic irrigation for one, but this is more relaxing. I try to come here two or three times a week at least. It's modern living you know." The Voice continued. "And the lack of food nutrients, that's the cause of many of the toxins."

Kate was no longer listening. She was frantically trying to remember which way the door opened. Did she push it in or out? She was also realising that, if necessary, she could break it down with her bare hands if the voice got any closer. It was a male voice, possibly in it's forties.

She had already thought,

"It isn't the fucking genie in the lamp," and visions of the headlines in the evening paper were flashing through her head.

"Woman hacked to pieces [and raped?] in steam room of city gym." Her hand reached for the door as she rose squelching from the seat.

"That's enough toxins for me." she heard herself say lightly as she screamed inside her head "Oh god, oh god the door won't open. It's locked. I'll never get out alive. I'll never see my grandchildren."

"You have to give it a hefty push," the voice said calmly, "and be careful as drops of hot water tend to hit your shoulders as the door opens."

"Oh oh," Kate practically squeaked, "thank you. I'm just going to change and try the cross- treadly- walky- thingy. Bye then."

Two minutes later Kate was peeling her bathing costume off in the shower cubicle.

"Healthy living," she thought, "this is a fucking nightmare."

She stepped out of the shower and back to the lockers. It felt as though she was surrounded by sleek, tall, tanned nineteen year olds who had just arrived into the gym for a quick work-out between photo-shoots. She fumbled beneath her washed out towel holding the top closed over her breasts with her left hand while trying to struggle into an old pair of knickers using her right hand.

She was old enough to be embarrassed semi-naked amongst other women. Especially when those women wore thongs which exposed pert little bums and had breasts that were designed to be witnessed, not supported. She felt old and wrinkled and flabby and cheap. She pulled on her trousers and jumper, dried her hair without much effort or style, grabbed her bag and retreated. She sat in the car, lit a cigarette and felt hot tears. To induce further self-inflicting dullness she adjusted the rear view mirror and looked into a face she hardly wanted to know.

"You're worn and tired and lined and surely you're not the face I deserved. I never did steal a gym kit after all. I just kept forging the excuse notes." She let tears roll down her cheeks and was startled from her moment of victimhood by a sudden remark close to her ear.

"How's it going then? I didn't recognise you with your clothes on."

She turned. The dullness in her eyes suddenly disappearing as blessed anger overtook pity. But the speaker had already walked away towards another car. Kate shouted at the retreating back.

"How dare you. I said how dare you. That's a terrible thing to say to anyone. I've never seen you before in my life."

She rolled the car window up, took a last angry draw on her cigarette, started the car and put on the music tape. It stuck, as always. She began fiddling with the stupid tiny controls on the music deck and in doing so missed the man's wave and broad grin as he turned to acknowledge what effect his remark had had before getting into his jeep. Kate swept the car indignantly onto the main road. She was at the fourth set of traffic lights when she connected the remark to the voice and the voice to the retreating figure. The Voice was tall. She liked tall men. It's jacket had a certain appeal, well-worn but not unfashionable. It looked healthy and obviously had a certain sense of humour. Perhaps there was something in this fitness stuff after all. Despite the salty dregs of a few tears on her cheeks Kate felt the beginnings of a smile.

When Charlie asked later the evening how the health and fitness training was going, she answered truthfully.

"Not bad love, not bad at all. It may even become part of my daily routine."

"Wow mum – you're a quick convert." he replied.

"Well," Kate responded, "I'll give it a try and see how it all works out."

It was three days before she saw him again. She was going past the training area after an uneventful steam and quick shower when she recognised the back. It had a slight stoop to the shoulder. She let her eyes casually observe the old teeshirt, now with sweat marks along the spine. The shorts revealed little for they were long and baggy. Nonchalantly she changed direction and headed towards the front of the treadmills. She glanced up. He wore glasses and was not bad looking, not bad looking at all for a fifty-something. She gave a cautious wave but he seemed not to notice. She walked towards reception trying to look as if she had spent the last decade in and out of gyms and bought a tanning sachet.

"I'll call in for a sunbed tomorrow," she thought, "no harm in that."

Meanwhile the steady flow of visitors passed through her home. Some for wakes, some for weddings and some to write research papers on the politics of Ireland. Some had travelled eastwards across the Atlantic looking for a key to the past. Others had travelled westward looking for a key to their future. Kate was learning from everyone. She could see patterns among the individuals and individuality among the patterns. It was for Kate a worthwhile, honest and blossoming endeavour. She encountered thinkers who had never written a thought, philosophers who had never seen the inside of a university. There were couples who did not have children and were worried and couples who had children and were worried. And pilgrims looking for paradise. Some were holy people who could not find god because they could not find themselves. And there were one or two fanatics who thought they were god. But Milltown Cemetery was not on the road to Damascus. Brendan Murphy arrived and took some beautiful photographs which appeared in the Irish News. The story of the tree generated interest on a local lunchtime radio discussion programme. Patricia had a good laugh telephoning to lodge a complaint. Kate was listening in the kitchen and almost fell off the stool at Patricia's feigned accent as she announced grandly "Protestant Lady, East Belfast" and rambled on at length about blasphemy and idolatry.

"There are three things I don't want to happen." Patricia announced when she came back into the kitchen.

"You're a rascal Patricia." Kate was still laughing. "You wouldn't know how too get to east Belfast but the accent was brilliant."

"These callers really annoy me," Patricia said, "what is wrong with this place? Five years of comparative peace and people are still defining themselves in terms of religion and territory. If it's not Murial from Clandeboye -"

"Protestant, middle class, retired." murmured Kate.

"- it's Seamus from Derry -"

"Catholic, unemployed, thirty something." echoed Kate

"- or Janice, Crumlin -"

"Single or with partner and young family on the first rung of the property ladder."

"- Norman, Katesbridge -"

"Protestant farmer, small holding, phoning to complain bitterly about the shape of EU bananas and not too worried about the war in Iraq as long as our boys get on with the job they were sent out to do."

Kate took over.

"Who's Angie, Newtonabbey?"

Patricia was quick - "Mixed marriage, commenting on the latest blunder by the Arts Council."

"Tasmin, North Belfast?"

"Brick through the window, interface area, those immigrants coming over to take our jobs."

"We live such contradictory lives Patricia." Kate gave a bit of a sigh and continued. "All searching for our uniqueness and continually layering ourselves with labels, our religions, our locations, our jobs, our salaries, our cars, where we shop, what we buy, whether we play rugby or football, our size, our shape."

"I heard you've joined a gym," Patricia interrupted, "all that sweat and testosterone must be great."

"Just sweat at the moment," Kate replied, "but I'll keep you informed. Anyway what three things do you not want to happen."

Patricia looked thoughtful and serious, an unusual stance for her and Kate listened carefully as her friend spoke.

"First of all," she said, "I don't want the tree damaged or cut down, simply because it's a tree and has as much right to be there as anything else. Secondly I don't want Milltown to become a tourist attraction or pilgrim venue, after all it's a living cemetery. People go there to bury their dead and visit their memories. They don't want coach loads of tourists playing happy-snappy with cameras while mourners are trying to bear the burden of a funeral. That would be a disgrace. And thirdly," she hesitated though Kate had been nodding in silent agreement with all she had thus far said, "and finally," she began again, "I don't want a great big miracle. That's about the last thing this place needs. Remember when people used to talk about peace as if it was something that would drop on us, like snow."

"I know what you mean," Kate caught Patricia's train of thought, "people were always demanding peace as if somehow it was an end."

There was a pause when neither woman spoke and then Kate continued,

"Anyone could achieve that sort of static state. There are too many people who think that peace is the absence of war, a final frigging resting place. God help them. Achieving peace is a matter of negotiation but maintaining peace is when the struggle really begins. It's the big battle Patricia because it's no longer a war in human terms, tribe against tribe. It is a war on universal terms, good against evil, justice instead of injustice, truth against falsehood. It is light against darkness, freedom instead of slavery, riches for all rather than wealth for the few. You are right Patricia, we don't need a big miracle. We need lots of little ones though, miracles of our own making. Remember that old expression, 'she who bakes her own bread is warmed twice', Maybe we should add another. 'Those who perform their own miracles are blessed twice. Once by the fruits of their labour and then by the fruits of their love".

"Kate where is all this coming from?" Patricia asked quietly. "Six months ago I was wondering if I had a clean pair of knickers in the drawer."

"Our minds are getting bigger Patricia," Kate smiled, "now that we're a knicker-day ahead of ourselves."

10

The two women also had to turn their minds to more mundane matters. Patricia had offered to stay an extra two hours, to help with rooms. Kate was now paying her six pounds an hour and the extra money was adding a little spring to Patricia's step. She realised she smiled more often. Her daughter had coaxed her into getting her hair styled in a proper hairdressers. For Patricia it had meant letting go of a long held belief that a haircut was a waste of money. She felt her hair looked fine pulled resolutely back from her forehead and tied with one of her grandchildren's bobbles. The pink elastic bands sporting tiny cartoon characters or ladybirds were handed guiltily back to the twins. The packet of hair clips was designated to the bin. The new cut and highlights made Patricia look ten years younger. Susan then pushed her into a beautician' shops and demanded that the frightened young assistant waxed her mother's eyebrows and upper lip. When Patricia unharnessed two twenty pound notes from her purse Susan quickly purchased an expensive tub of moisturising cream with the change. Two days later Patricia went back to the beautician and after a consultation bought herself lipstick, mascara and creamy foundation. She was glad when Jimmy noted the difference. He remarked that he preferred her hair the way it always had been and added sullenly,

"I don't know why your putting that muck on your face you're only going over to work in a local guesthouse not run Ryanair."

"It makes me feel better about myself." Patricia had retorted, "and Kate's joined a gym."

"Huh, money doesn't grow on trees." Jimmy was uncomfortable. His part-time work was not paying much. Patricia had extra money now and she was beginning to take herself more seriously. He was worried. She had told him she did not enjoy sitting like a zombie in front of the television every night. She had taken to going to bed early with a book. It was 'A Tale of Two Cities' last week. He told her he knew the story because he had seen the film years ago. She had coughed, put down the book and said,

"The film doesn't capture the numerous themes interwoven in the text."

He didn't know what she was talking about and he was damned sure she didn't know what she was talking about either. He had climbed into bed and thought the conversation was over when he said as haughtily as he could,

"And don't be getting mascara all over the pillow cases again. Bits of it are getting into my eyes and irritating them something shocking." She had told him to drop dead and plunged the bedroom into darkness. This week she was reading 'The Woman in White' and 'Veronica Decides to Die'. After he had examined the covers of both books he had asked, reasonably he thought, why she wanted to read about weddings and wakes when she had enough of that in real life. She had remained silent as she took the duvet off the double bed and left him cold and uncomfortable as she went to sleep in the spare room.

. . . .

"Anybody down for breakfast yet?" Patricia called quietly as she closed the front door behind her. Kate came out of the kitchen.

"Not yet but they're early risers."

"Who's here?"

"Two Canadian spinsters and a spoilt priest from Tyrone."

"How do you know he's a spoilt priest?" Patricia asked putting on her apron.

"That stage-Irish accent and the tone of voice as if he was absolving my sins instead of asking for a toilet roll for the bathroom."

"Is he gay?"

"I don't think so but it's none of my business if he is though. He's in the back room."

"What about the builder? Did he ring back?"

"No and that's the third one. It'll be a bloody miracle if I get anybody to build this extension. It's either too big a job or too small. The bank says I can have the loan okay but I don't want to sign for it until I'm sure the work can be done."

"Are you sure you're doing the right thing Kate, extending and all that? It's going to cost money."

"I'm turning ten people away every week Patricia. I need more room. You know Roisin's gone to stay with her da for a while, at least until her exams are over. He's hardly there anyway. She said it's a bit lonely but she needs the peace and quiet to study properly. She's determined to do well so I don't mind, but I miss her."

"Charlie will be moving out next." Patricia said.

"I hope not." Kate replied fervently. "He's too young and I don't know what I'd do without him about the place. He sleeps on the couch most nights god love him but he seems happy enough so far. Mind you Patricia I certainly didn't set about this business to lose my kids, to feed them yes, but not to lose them. How was I to know it was going to take off like a rocket?"

"No point in looking back now." Patricia said in a hopeful tone, "let's get the bacon sizzling shall we?"

When she served breakfast Patricia decided Kate was probably right about Peter being a spoilt priest. There was something about how he ordered bacon and eggs in the tone of a celibate addressing an elderly housekeeper. Or perhaps it was the way he kept his eyes averted and of course the 'just one slice of toast please, waste not, want not' comment clinched it.

Kate reckoned he was about thirty eight though he seemed ancient,

"A cross between an undertaker and a computer software engineer," she said. He had an unworldly manner more concerned with the virtual than the real. He asked the usual questions of course, who she was, how long had she been in business, was her husband at work etc. but Kate had the funny feeling that she was being interrogated. She kept her answers brief and noted with rising uneasiness that he used a similar interrogatory manner with the other guests as they came downstairs to share breakfast. After the morning meal he asked could he use the computer and offered to pay. Kate nodded, took the one pound coin from him and popped it in the tin on the kitchen shelf. When the other guests had left she made various excuses to hover near the computer and noticed he had begun to type up a document headed "Day One: Personal Accounts & Anecdotal Evidence". Kate left Patricia doing the dishes and went out into the garden to breath and relax. It was now a morning routine. As she slowly exhaled the first breath she decided he was definitely not a secret shopper from the tourist board. The second breath assured her he could not be there to award her a Michelin star. By the tenth breath she had also excluded a rival entrepreneur, a local councillor, someone from the drinks licensing trade and the taxman.

"A spoilt priest he is then." she whispered with the last breath. Then sucked the oxygen in again as realisation dawned on her. "He's not a spoilt priest. He hasn't side-stepped the priesthood, he's side-stepped the parish. That boy's further up the hierarchy than he knows what's good for him." Kate had never heard of the Vatican's special investigations team but she was always willing to accept a conspiracy theory.

She knew what had to be done.

"Would you like to visit the cemetery Peter once you've finished that document? It's a lovely walk. The fresh air will do you good for you look a bit pale. The paths are overgrown but there's a good variety of wild life and some lovely old trees. I'll be going there myself shortly, for a walk I mean, not for the final sleep. Didn't you say in the email your grandmother's buried there. It's a big place. I might be able to help you find the grave if you've got a reference number. Though it looks higgelty piggeldy the place is laid out in a huge grid and cross-referenced. Everyone in their place and unfortunately, a place for everyone. We can have a look at Mary the Mother of God while we're there. It would be a shame to miss her after you coming all the way from Rome and Tyrone."

Peter dealt in concepts and beliefs. He spent his vocational calling falsifying visions and negating miracles. He was not at home with ordinary common sense language. Neither did he feel comfortable with the direct approach of a woman who was learning that she could not abide fools, preachers or prophets who always seemed to be arrogant and male. Kate Lagan had had enough and she was about to tell the emissary from Rome, in no uncertain terms what she thought.

"Get your coat Peter," she said. "we'll be leaving in five minutes."

Peter, beneath the academic excellence and investigatory techniques was suddenly as uncertain as his namesake had been two thousand years before. He collected his coat from the bedroom and waited at the front door for Kate. He used the few minutes wisely, offering a silent prayer to the Holy Spirit for guidance and protection and the wisdom to know the difference.

"Have you your camera Peter?" Kate asked as she pulled the front door closed. "You can take a few photographs and email them to the pope. He'd be delighted I'm sure. This way." she said, heading him off at the gate and directing him south towards the graveyard.

"Do you know Peter," she began a new conversation, "I love walking especially when it's as far away from shops as I can manage in my free time. There's no need to think about buying today paying nothing for a year when you are meandering around the dead. Walking makes me think far more than praying ever did. I used to feel guilty about that until I read a lovely phrase recently. Would you like to hear it?"

"Go ahead," Peter tried and failed to keep the tone of resignation out of his voice. He wanted to add, "if it makes you happy." but bit his tongue as the unchristian thought entered his head.

Kate began again, "It makes me happy when I come across something that really catches the eye." Peter wondered briefly if this terrible woman was actually reading his mind then hurriedly dismissed the idea as nonsense.

'Tripe' Kate would have called it but she said thoughtfully

"'Never walk anywhere to preach. Your walking is your preaching'. Isn't that a good phrase Father?"

Peter was on the point of denying the title then thought better of it. He tried evasion instead.

"Do you read a lot Mrs. Lagan?"

"Mainly people, and it's Ms. Lagan but I'd prefer if you would call me Kate. Here we are then. Isn't this what you came to check out?" Kate stopped on the path beside the tree. Peter looked and saw nothing.

"It might help if you walked around the other side. The image is on the front of the tree." Kate said encouragingly.

It was the first time in his life Peter had been told that trees had fronts and backs. He had always assumed circular. But this was not the moment for metaphysical pondering.

He dutifully walked round to the 'front' of the tree.

Kate stood her ground and called,

"Step back a bit. You'll get a better view if you're not too close to it."

Peter shaded his eyes with his hand.

"A bit further back," Kate instructed, "and try not to squint. It's a natural image not hieroglyphics or Hebrew" she added under her breath.

Peter took the advice and stopped shading his eyes. Then he saw what all the fuss was about. "She's right" he thought, "I can see an image." He knew in his heart, as Kate did, that it was the image we all see in the dancing flames of a fire or the sudden pattern unveiled in a piece of marble or the shadow of a pattered curtain that suddenly reveals a face. It was an image encountered by everyone, everywhere. His mind hurled itself back to a bedroom in early childhood. It had been Christmas Eve and he remembered

118

the guarded guilty excitement. The wallpaper in his bedroom was old and yellowed and had been there for ever. But on that night, because it was the first Christmas without his father, his mother had lit a small fire in the usually cold grate. She had kissed him goodnight and in the strange light he had seen him in the wallpaper, Santa Claus on his sleigh moving across the room in tiny childsized detail. It was an image locked in his mind for over thirty years. He had waited and watched again until he was twelve but the mystery never returned.

Suddenly he felt stupid and childish. "Why do you believe it's the Mother of Christ?" he called harshly to Kate as she stepped towards him.

"Did you believe in Father Christmas when you were small?" she asked.

He suddenly could not trust words so he nodded.

"It's the same thing we're witnessing now. A collection of images stored in our minds are manifesting in the natural weathering of an old tree. Change the time and the location and they become meaningless, just a vague fancy. But Peter, this is a city on the edge of peace. It is a country reuniting itself ready to send ambassadors where there are wars and rumblings of wars. Traditions and myths and martyrdom and history are colliding in some weird energetic way and making a childlike sense of chaos. Hope may be an illusion but there is no mystery, just humanity fumbling forwards and glad to find momentary peace in an otherwise terrifying universe. We grasp at anything that doesn't make us feel small and unimportant. Look at George Bush, money, power, wealth and the biggest job on earth. Deep down he feels just as small and unimportant and mortal as the rest of us."

"How do you know?" Peter asked. "I assume you've never met him."

"No," Kate replied, "and I don't want to met him but how desperate do you have to be to declare a war on terror?"

Kate stood in front of the priest now. She looked directly at him. His averted gaze did not work and he forced himself to look back at her.

"But you had terrorists Kate," Peter pleaded, "here, in Belfast."

"Terrorists," Kate said quietly, "terrorists and freedom fighters and soldiers and suicide bombers, like the rest of us were children once. Maybe," she added, "if we can find meaning in ourselves we can find meaning in the universal." She began to walk further into the graveyard towards the bog meadow.

Peter hesitated, then followed. It was going to be a tough walk and a tougher report. But Kate said little for the rest of the journey. She pointed out the different grasses, the tall bulrushes and the clumps of bog cotton. Then they stopped near one of the smaller paths that criss-crossed the graves. He noticed her eyes following the flight of a small bird as it travelled from one bush to another, settling for a few seconds on a headstone and then taking once more to the air. She pointed to where the bird had rested momentarily and said softly,

"That's where my sister is buried, our Maggie, our beautiful sister Maggie. And sometimes Peter," she whispered, "when I'm alone I can't bear the pain."

Peter fumbled in his coat pocket for a tissue.

"Images on the television of bombs and orphans and wasted unwanted babies make me cry. I look at a two dimensional screen and try to understand anima mundi, the soul of the world, where terrible things can happen. But it is the dry longing to hear her voice, see her coming in to my house for a cup of tea and a smile as she gives me a mild reproof. It is the small, personal, gentled pain that is the worst."

Peter could not reply.

"Why is joy so elusive and grief so tangible Peter? But don't worry," Kate blew her nose and straightened her back. "I think I know what we're supposed to do," she turned to face him, "we are supposed to go on living."

"Yes." Peter said. Then he guided them both, as best he could, back towards the main road.

That night Charlie rang Roisin.

"You'd better come over Roisin. I'm worried. Have you much studying to do?"

Roisin knew her brother was not good when it came to 'woman stuff'.

"Don't worry Charlie," she assured him, "the essay can wait. It's not the end of the world. I'll get a taxi. Will you take some money out of the tin to pay the taxi driver. I've only three pounds and mum won't mind she'll thank me in the morning."

"Ta, big sis." Charlie put the telephone down with a sense of relief. Roisin was right. He was rubbish at this 'woman stuff'

Kate was drunk, really drunk. She had a glass of wine almost every evening to relax and unwind but Roisin knew that Charlie's call meant she had really hit the bottle. When Roisin arrived Kate was already beyond the age of reasoning.

"Nine-eleven, seventy-seven, nineteen-sixteen, seventeen-ninety-eight, nineteen-sixty-nine, the civil rights movement, sixteen-ninety, King Billy, Nineteen-sixty, the year I was born, Nineteen-fifty-six, Maggie was born, nineteen-sixty-four, our Ralph, nineteen-sixty-six, the baby was born and died and so on and so on."

"Come on mum, you need to get to bed."

"I was thinking Roisin," Kate tried to pull herself up on the couch and missed. She was not to be defeated, "I was thinking about time."

"Where you mum?" Roisin sighed and motioned to Charlie to switch the kettle on for a strong cup of coffee.

Kate mumbled "Time you see isn't linear. Time is a resource. Time has depth. Time can't be measured. Time is fictional."

"Come on mum." Roisin almost wailed.

"No let me finish love, let me finish. Time is fictional. Time does not control me. I can be anywhere you see. The past is staring into an Irish famine. The future is abundance without a soul. Reading, I need to read. But reading takes up time. Or uses time. Or measures time. Does it capture time?"

"It's frigging time you went to bed mum. You're drunk."

"I know love. Did you know I liked to curl up with a good book and a glass of wine far more than I ever liked to curl up with you dad. That's sad isn't it?"

"Not really."

"Sometimes I didn't care Roisin. I really didn't care. I didn't care what happened to the characters. Fuck, they don't have to live in the real world. They don't have to get up at fucking seven o'clock in the morning. They don't have to wash out their knickers and tights. They don't have periods. Periods of time."

"Do you want wee cup of coffee mum?"

"Yeah. I think I need a cup of coffee don't you?"

"Yes and you need to go to bed mum. You're exhausted."

"I'm not."

"You are. Turn your head off mum. Please."

"Okay."

The last thing Kate remembered was Roisin tucking the bedclothes around her and kissing her good night.

"Sleep well mum."

"Oh fuck Roisin. That's what I'm supposed to do. I'm supposed to put you to bed, kiss you goodnight. I'm the mammy. That's my job. Help me."

"Help you what mum?"

"I don't know love. Help me to be a good mum."

"You are."

"Why are you putting me to bed? I'm supposed to do that for you."

"You do, you did."

"When?"

"All the time, now go to sleep mum. You're tired."

"All right. I'm sorry love."

"What for?"

"For being stupid."

"Go to sleep mum."

And Kate shut down and slept the untidy sleep of the forlorn, the good, the ordinary and the commonplace.

11

Kate's body surrendered. There are two kinds of dreams, bad dreams and really bad dreams. In all her life Kate had not remembered what she would have called a nice dream. She wondered if anyone ever did dream happy dreams. She doubted it. Sleep usually brought visions of teeth shattering one by one, helpless drownings, earthquakes, prisons and mine shafts none of which she had ever experienced in her life. "Perhaps dreams," she sometimes thought, "are when we actually awaken from the idea of our separateness."

For one night only Kate, nurtured by two bottles of wine, could let the flinching images dance around and tell their stories. The alcohol would ensure a sweaty awakening but no dreaded feeling of collective experience.

Roisin had given Kate a light kiss on her damp cheek, set the alarm on the bedside table for six thirty am and accepted a well-earned cup of tea from Charlie. When the taxi arrived to take her back to her dad's she said a silent thank you to the gods that her brief mothering role was over. She knew her mother would be up as soon as the alarm clanged. She also knew that Kate would probably pretend nothing had happened, go briskly about her chores and laugh later. Her mum suffered the effect of alcohol every so often but binge drinking and addiction were not labels easily applied to someone who could cook five breakfasts the following morning and clock up another eighteen hour day.

"Just hope I have inherited the stamina genes." Roisin said aloud as she fumbled for the key to her Dad's small but neatly proportioned townhouse.

Her dad, unfortunately, was still downstairs in the kitchen brewing a pot of tea.

"Where were you?" he asked.

"Over home. Mum wasn't feeling too well and Charlie was worried."

"What's wrong with her?"

"She's just working too hard."

"She's making plenty of money."

"She deserves it Dad."

"Do you want a cuppa?"

"No thanks I'm going to bed."

"Has she any guests in the house?"

"Yes but they were all in bed asleep." Roisin headed for the stairs.

"Just as well they didn't see her drunk then."

"Just as well she's got balls too dad isn't it?" Roisin closed her bedroom door and closed her eyes. "This is good training," she told herself, "for when I'm on the hospital wards especially the frigging psychiatric unit." She smiled and got ready for bed.

Kate bolted upright exactly two seconds before the alarm clanged. She pulled on her clothes and ran a brush through her hair and a babywipe over her face and under her arms. Morning ablutions finished she closed the bedroom door quietly and headed downstairs. There was no movement from the guests yet and she could detect a faint snoring from Peter's room but the house had not burnt down during the night killing everyone. Apart from the sensation that she had eaten a small woollen jumper which had left an unpleasant coating on her tongue Kate felt fine. One cup of coffee would ensure that she was ready to face whatever the day hurled at her. She went into the kitchen, boiled the kettle, made a pot of tea and a strong coffee. She checked her teeth were still in her mouth then tip-toed into the living room and shook

124

Charlie as gently as she dared. He was cocooned in a green sleeping bag invisible except for his dark eyebrows and brown unruly hair. He murmured something which Kate chose not to hear and then the green caterpillar snuggled slowly again into the comfort of the couch.

"Come on my beautiful butterfly." Kate shook the material a little more roughly. "Time to spread your wings and fly, fly, fly."

"Shut up mum." the muffled voice groaned.

"I could have danced all night, I could have danced all night." Kate's non-melodic voice caught the edge of her son's temper.

"You were swaying all night mum go away."

Kate felt the guilt and swallowed hard.

"Charlie, please," she implored, "the guests will be coming down soon and I have to air the room. Seeing your big hairy legs crawling out of that sleeping bag is not conducive to a boutique breakfast. Please Charlie. I've a wee cup of tea ready for you in the kitchen."

Charlie grunted and began wriggling out of the bag pulling on his religions of the world tee shirt and the jeans he had left hanging on the floor overnight.

"You were daft drunk last night mum," he whispered.

"I was not." Kate replied haughtily.

"Is the pope a Catholic?" Charlie grinned, "Can fish swim? Is George Bush a new age philosopher? Will sick people send for Ian Paisley's mitt?"

"Leave Padre Pio out of this," Kate replied though she too was smiling as she hid the clandestine sleeping arrangements in the cupboard underneath the stairs. Charlie was already in the kitchen looking for a chocolate biscuit. Kate silently composed a prayer. 'Thank God he hasn't inherited early morning ill humour' she said quietly and sent the prayer upwards to any saint who was awake enough to listen. It was Saturday so Patricia would not be over to help. Charlie was paid instead. It was a quiet breakfast, and Kate was grateful. The two Canadians ladies had cereal and toast and headed into the city before nine o'clock and Peter had the common sense to go out to the shops before breakfast and buy a daily newspaper to excuse his non eye-contact and non-existent conversational skills.

The early afternoon brought a visit from a builder whom Kate would not have trusted to thread a needle never mind create a new living space with slates and mortar. He poked around a bit, measured various skirting boards, squinted at the windows, fiddled about with figures in a notebook and finally said,

"Well love how much do you want to spend?"

"How much will it cost?" Kate responded courteously though the endearment hit her like a brick.

"That depends love," he replied, "these old houses," he paused, allowing the phrase to hover threateningly, "never know what problem you might find and as I said it depends on how much you want to spend."

"I have asked you here to price the job." Kate said. "The amount I have to spend is not really the issue. You're the builder. You're the expert on what materials and labour will cost, not me, so if you can give me an estimate."

"Hard to say Missus as I said it depends on how much you want to spend. I'd probably need to talk it over with your husband first just to see what we're up against."

"Thank you." Kate said calmly. "would you mind closing the door on your way out."

"What?"

"I have a budget that's my business. I do not have a husband which is none of your business. I am not your 'love' thank God and I know a cowboy when I meet one. Now get on your bike and as I said close the door on your way out."

"No need to take that tone missus you asked me here to price a job."

"Yes something which you have consistently failed to do. Now stop wasting my time."

The cowboy had not come across many self-composed women in his line of work but he knew one when he saw one. He left loudly leaving the door open. Kate heard him mutter "oul bitch" as he mounted the driver's seat of his white van.

She put another mental notch on the ever expanding belt of life experience and wondered how on earth she was going to solve the problem of her children's ever decreasing living quarters. Charlie could not sleep on the couch for ever and an extra bathroom was now essential. She had also wanted to extend the dining area and build on another bedroom. But that was the third builder who'd yet to come to terms with the suffragette movement. She remembered reading an article in one of the magazines in the gym. The title was 'Post-feminism how far have we travelled'.

"Fuck that" she had thought, "There are still people who believe it's a bad idea to educate girls. Even here some people are trapped in a world where they'd think postillions on a coach was romantic and we're being told that we're careering headlong towards a post-feminist future". She had torn a recipe from the magazine, read her horoscope and left the rest for others to ponder.

"Stupid oul fart." she said now shutting the door. It was going to be a long day. The guests had ordered dinner for seven o'clock and Paddy Joe rang to say he wanted to call in to show her a lovely puppy. Rebel had been stalking the local talent again and the woman whose garden backed onto Paddy Joe's had arrived with a box full of pups. None had the markings of her beloved KC registered spaniel but all had the shaggy, somewhat wayward look of Paddy Joe's mongrel. He thought the pups were lovely, apologised to the neighbours for having spoilt their chances of collecting best of breed at Crufts and accepted the responsibility of rearing them as just payment for Rebel's sins. He was now trying his best to wean them from his wife and onto family, friends and enemies.

Kate had no longer the space for her own daughter never mind a Rebel heir but Paddy Joe was not easily thwarted,

"Rather like his bloody dog" thought Kate.

"Wouldn't you think twenty four hours would be long enough for one day" Kate remarked. "I need about twenty nine hours a day what am I going to do Charlie?"

"Why don't you go to the gym mum?"

"I'd love to for half an hour for a good healthy sweat. It'll clear the alcohol from my blood stream, it must be 90% proof but I have to service the two front rooms."

"I'll do them, you get your bag and go now or you'll not go at all."

"Are you sure?"

"Go on."

Kate stuffed an old pair of red tracksuit bottoms and a faded yellow teeshirt that had once belonged to Charlie into her bag and hurried out before her generous son changed his mind.

As soon as he heard the car reverse out of the driveway Charlie rang Roisin.

"Well, how is she?" Roisin asked. "Any hangover?"

"No, up with the dawn and twiddling about like Maria von Trapp singing into my bloody ear at half past six."

"She's still as daft as a bat"

"I know." Charlie agreed. "Thank God I'm like her. How is la petite maison et le grande papa?"

"Both claustrophobic." Roisin replied. "He keeps asking me where I'm going and telling me what time I should be back."

"Ah," Charlie affected an authoritative tone, "practicing his parenting skills then?"

"Yep," Roisin agreed, "at least mum doesn't go about trying to win parent of the year. He treats me as if I'm eight instead of eighteen."

"Where do the years go?" Charlie tuned into his father's voice. "My little girl. I remember you in pigtails and now you're going off into the big wide world."

"He actually thinks like that Charlie. That's the worrying bit. It wouldn't even occur to him that I've never worn pigtails in my entire life. He just covers his guilt with a glaze of what he believes our childhood must have been like."

"Have you disagreed yet?"

"There's no point. It would be like having an argument with

Pinnochio. I can understand why mum left him. She must have known he was never going to turn into a real boy. Anyway what did you ring for?"

"The dreaded date is well nigh upon us big sis. What are we going to do?"

"Oooh fuck." Roisin's voice wailed across the telephone lines, "It's that time of year again."

"Yep."

"What age is she this year?"

"Forty-five or maybe forty-six. Anyway the birthday girl is somewhere in her early- late forties next Saturday. Any ideas what to buy a mother who hates cards, hates birthdays, hates presents and hates surprises?"

"What did we get her last year?"

"I can't remember."

"Neither can I. Let me think about it. In the meantime listen to see if she drops any hints about what she would like."

"You know mum when we ask she says she doesn't want anything."

"And when we forget she thinks we might not love her."

"Do we?"

"It's a fact of life Charlie. It's compulsory. Anyway we'll think of something. She's fairly easily pleased and that's a blessing."

"You're beginning to sound like her."

"It must be all this co-habiting with dad. Did the builder arrive?"

"She showed him the door."

"Not another one."

"He called her love."

"Ah understandable then but she'll have to move soon on the extension before I fetch an axe to the little wooden boy. He could be firewood by Christmas."

"Patience Roisin, patience. See you later."

Charlie put the telephone down and lifted a leaflet that had come in the morning post which Kate had left on the hall table. It looked like junk mail and he was surprised it had escaped the bin. He began to read it and then began to smile.

"Now there's a little miracle," he thought, "just when we were wondering what we could buy the woman who has everything."

He tucked the leaflet into the back pocket of his jeans and began to whistle as he headed upstairs to fulfil his duties.

At the gym Kate changed hurriedly. She intended spending at least twenty minutes on the treadmill. Funnily enough, given its name it was the only machine in the gym she enjoyed. The rowing apparatus made her feel like a snake trying to shed its skin. The cross-walker still baffled her and the seats on the bikes cut into her backside like haemorrhoids seeking revenge for a life spent in unspoken misery. She had bought the little earphones and was marching along happily across mountain passes with the beat of Woolworth music in her ears. The whole experience would have stopped Einstein from thinking so it practically lulled Kate into trance-like oblivion. A tiny part of her, something akin to an amoeba was aware that she was grinning from ear to ear and her head was moving in a slight rhythm to the beat of the music. Unfortunately the rest of her that was not thinking it was an amoeba was perfectly visible to the rest of the world. Consequently the man on the treadmill next to her was trying desperately not to burst out laughing. He was reminded of those little yellow and red wooden ducks pulled along on a piece of string. He had always thought that particular toy an image of perfect happiness, being pulled by the beak and making a clack clack clacking sound. He could not be absolutely sure whether the woman was singing or not but there was definitely a clacking sound which could vaguely be interpreted as 'climb every mountain'.

His attempts to suppress laughter brought tears to his eyes and he slowed his treadmill down to remove his glasses. The change in movement alerted the non-amoeba red and yellow duck who suddenly realised that she was singing aloud. Kate tried to amend matters. The hoped for sleek and synchronised movements to enable her to remove her headphones, slow her walk, reduce her speed and glide gracefully from the machine did not happen. Instead, she hit the stop button and found herself falling ungraciously off the end of the treadmill with her headphones still attached to the radio unit. She finished up almost strangled and totally bewildered on the floor with a strange man bending over her saying,

"Are you alright, are you alright, you seem to have tripped."

Kate looked up.

"Please tell me I haven't had a heart attack." she said.

"No, I think you stopped the machine too quickly and your earphones stayed connected but you didn't."

If Kate had had the tiny and fortunate chance of being born blonde, beautiful and blue-eyed she would have known to ask quietly for a glass of water. Then she would have paused and rubbed her hand slowly and gently from her thigh to her knee. She would have given a slight but carefully constructed moan. Kate was not born blonde or with the innate intelligence to use moments of acute embarrassment to her advantage.

She scrambled up, still attached to the music unit and said straight into the man's face.

"Thanks, I hope I haven't bloody well wet myself."

Then with every bone in her body wanting to yank itself out of its socket and hit her over the head she took off the earphones and made the heroic climb out of the training room. Inexplicably, the words 'follow every rainbow 'til you find your dream' were circling over the air above her ready, like everything else, to attack.

"Two hundred fucking members" Kate thought as she scrubbed herself wilfully in the shower, "and I have to fall off a frigging machine right next to The Voice-Man."

She dressed hastily scrubbed her teeth to stop her from grinding them to the gums left the changing room and headed as gallantly as she could towards the exit.

"Will you be here tomorrow?" He was standing at the door with her earphones swinging like a pendulum from his right hand. Kate took the earphones and answered as steadily as she could,

"I've no idea, why?"

"I just thought if you were here I could show you the weights room. That's the best training you know. You could walk twenty miles on the treadmill and it will not do you much good."

"I know I've been on it my whole life."

The man smiled.

"The weights are proper training they'll give you muscles."

"I don't want any muscles." Kate replied, shocked.

The man sighed.

"Why do women think that lifting a few weights will suddenly turn them into lethal fighting machines with rippling torsos and muscles like iron. It will only tone your body and it is a healthy exercise."

Kate said, "I've lots of me that needs toning and bits of me that could do with a little less ripple."

"I think you look good for your age."

How do you know my age?"

"Forty-six, forty-seven. It's not difficult."

"What age are you?"

"Fifty but I have the body of a twenty-eight year old."

Kate's eyebrows involuntarily raised themselves.

"Oh," she said meekly and added because she thought she should, "that's interesting."

"Are you going for a cup of coffee?" he asked

"Yes."

"Do you mind if I join you?"

"Not at all." Kate was pleased and thought, " the conversation is a bit weird but at least I'm not making a pigs arse of myself.

She walked towards the small coffee area but life refused to run smoothly,

"Oh shit," she exclaimed, "what time is it?"

"Three o'clock."

"Oh shit, oh shit, I'll have to go. I've got guests for dinner at seven and I haven't even bought it yet."

"Don't worry," the man said, "off you go."

Kate rushed out and threw her bag in the car. She jumped in, started the engine and switched it off again.

"For once," she thought, "business can wait. This is one little servant who isn't going to let a chance slip away."

She went back to the gym. He was sitting sipping his coffee. Kate walked up to the table.

"What time tomorrow?"

"About four."

"Okay, see you then."

"Bye duck."

"What?"

"Sorry, just an expression."

"I'm sorry," Kate said too sharply, while her inner voice screamed for attention, "I don't like being called 'love' or 'duck' or 'missus' or, anything like that."

"Okay see you tomorrow then." The man began sipping at his coffee and lifted the newspaper.

"Or bitch," continued Kate, "well maybe in certain circumstances." Her inner voice was now shouting shut up shut up shut up but she had started so she had to finish. "Bitch could be alright with, you know, low lights, bottle of wine, sexy bed linen."

"I don't drink." He said.

"Oh," Kate paused, "I was lying anyway. I don't like 'bitch' either, under any circumstances. Just as well eh?"

"Yes."

Kate got into car and succumbed to the pleasure of beating herself over the head, "Stupid bitch, stupid bitch, stupid bitch" she repeated all the way to the supermarket.

12

The next morning brought three surprises. First of all the guests were still alive. Kate was positive that the chicken had really needed another half hour in the oven but there they were contentedly munching muesli and buttering toast. The second surprise came from Peter who asked Kate to accompany him to the cemetary. The previous journey, he explained, had caused him some deep thought and he would not mind the opportunity of continuing the conversation.

"What conversation?" thought Kate but agreed to go. Thirdly, Kate was surprised to hear tiny yelps coming from the garage. She sent Charlie to investigate. He came back looking sheepish with a bundle of damp rags tucked in the fold of his arm. Kate stared as the bundle moved.

"Paddy Joe came when you were at the gym mum and I couldn't resist him."

"I'll kill that uncle of yours Charlie. That thing is going straight back."

"Ah mum."

"I mean it. When would I have time to look after a bloody pup. No, no, no, no, no!"

"Can I at least give him some food?"

"Alright, just one meal. There's weetabix in the cupboard and an old saucer under the sink. Mix the cereal with some water."

Charlie prepared the slush and put it on the floor. "He won't eat it mum. Look he keeps tipping over the saucer."

"I bet he's not even weaned properly yet. Here give me the saucer." Kate pushed it under the pup's nose. It yelped and backed away.

"Come on you stupid ragamuffin. Eat or die."

"You're frightening it mum."

"I'm teaching it Charlie. As soon as its fed it's going back to Paddy Joe. And get some kitchen roll it just piddled on the floor."

Charlie quickly wiped away the offending puddle and went outside to put the tissue in the bin and check the garage. When he returned Kate was sitting on the floor with bits of wet weetabix stuck to her fingers simultaneously scolding and feeding the pup.

"You're a natural mum look at it licking. It was starving."

"It's going back tonight."

"Have you thought of a name."

"None of that. It's a dangerous road. Well if I have to sit here like an idiot feeding it the least you can do is clear the dishes from the table."

"Okay mum."

Charlie disappeared but heard Kate tapping her fingers on the saucer and saying softly "Come here Rags, come and finish your breakfast." Rags had a name and consequently a home.

Peter was at the computer typing up his latest document having dutifully put his pound in the tin. Kate picked up the pup and wandered over.

"Have you finished your report Peter?" she asked as innocently as she could.

"It's difficult Kate." he replied, "Hello little fella." he stroked the pup between the ears. "What's his name?"

"He hasn't got one."

Peter continued, "I'm just not sure about this image in the tree business. It's definitely a natural occurrence but the team does need to investigate these matters without public attention. However you seemed to know why I was here."

"Just a lucky guess." Kate replied.

"My problem is that there is nothing to report. People only think they see an image of the Virgin Mary in a tree but we also have a duty to negate rumours before they mushroom and people start claiming miracles."

"Does it matter?"

"Yes in terms of Catholic theology we have to be sure."

"Do you have a special machine?"

"What?"

"How do you measure a miracle?"

"We gather evidence of cures."

"Cures of what?"

"I'm not sure exactly."

"Arthritis, toothache, madness, leprosy, cancer, Aids, depression, pneumonia, starvation, grief, what?" Kate was annoyed.

"That's the problem. How are we supposed to know." The priest suddenly looked too young and too vulnerable. Kate suppressed an urge to pat him between the ears.

"Let's go for that walk Peter."

"Okay."

Peter shut down the computer while Kate hunted for an old piece of blanket for Rags. She told Charlie to go to the supermarket for six empty boxes.

"We only need one mum," he said, "it's a very small dog."

"Believe me," Kate instructed, "we'll need ten before the week is out. Very small dogs have a habit of shitting very large amounts. And get another packet of Weetabix while you're there."

"Can we keep him then mum?"

"We'll see." Kate lifted the ragged bundle and gave it a quick kiss. "You're a wee rascal" she said. And Rags knew in his little doggy heart that he was now officially part of the Lagan empire.

"Solvitur amulando." Peter said as they walked towards the graveyard.

"What?"

"It is solved by walking, St. Augustine, fourth century."

Kate smiled. "I knew an old priest years ago who told how he had been with hundreds of people who were dying. Many of them wished for a little more time just to go for a walk and not one wished for any more time to spend in the office. Most of them were waiting for a miracle I suppose." She added thoughtfully.

"Did the miracles happen?"

"Usually."

"So the priest witnessed many cures."

"That's not what I meant."

"So how did the miracles happen?"

"Naturally, the way most things happen. Some probably wanted to live long enough to see a first grandchild or find the strength for a final walk in a park. Maybe some wanted to watch a fall of snow one last time or see a cherry tree in blossom. If that happened then each would have had their small unbelievably important miracle."

"What about sudden deaths?"

"Miraculously the family go on living, pick up the pieces of their lives and still believe in a god, any god."

"How do you know this Kate? Did you study?"

"All women know these things."

"How?"

"Because we're intermediaries. Women tend to live most of their lives anonymously on the edge of cliffs. We manage the rhythm and the patterns. If we understand the depth of turmoil beneath we can sometimes produce a surface smoothness. You know that miracle when Jesus calmed the storm. It never really impressed me. Any woman with a bit of wit would immediately see what really happened."

"The storm abated for he had the power to calm the sea." Peter said faithfully.

"Typical male perspective." Kate responded, "He did the equivalent of what a woman would do when awakened in a crisis."

"What?"

"Make a cup of tea. That's what Jesus did, metaphorically, made them face their fear by calming the disciples encouraging them to remember their skills as sailors. When they talked about it, years later, it would seem natural for them to think that he calmed the actual storm, not their anxiety.

"How do you explain the wedding feast at Cana?"

"He probably told a few anecdotes and everyone laughed, the same affect as alcohol when a party is dying on its feet. He was a storyteller and not shy of the limelight. His mother knew that. She had reared him."

"Curing people with leprosy."

"Basic hygiene techniques and trying to ensure they did not live in squalid conditions. Rats cause the deformities not the disease"

"Blindness."

"Overcoming society's prejudices about physical disabilities. I imagine he helped them to concentrate on their other senses"

"The man paralysed on the stretcher."

"He was paralysed with guilt Peter. It was manifesting itself physically and he was allowing himself the luxury of victimhood. He had his family catering to him. Jesus saw through that and told him to stop it, to get up off his arse and start living again. I'd like to say the same thing to quite a few people I know."

"He raised Lazarus from the dead."

"Where do you think the Irish wake tradition comes from? People danced and sang and told stories and got drunk for three days when someone died. The idea was literally 'wake' or 'waken' the dead. It was a simple way of ensuring that the person was dead before they were buried. I have a funny feeling Martha and Mary instinctively knew their brother was in some sort of comatose state but they were afraid. Jesus didn't have that fear and was able to work with the so-called dead body and revive it. He had a remarkable understanding of humanity, a mother's understanding."

"Have you any other insights?" Peter asked.

"It always struck me as odd how men in the gospels are identified by their occupation, taxman, debt collector, carpenter, king. The women are usually identified by their suffering. The gospels merged both and became a powerful tool.

"How have you worked all this out Kate?"

"I walk a lot." Kate smiled. "I know men work and think and discover and create and build but women understand the cycles of nature, the dying and rebirth, the despair and hope. It is women, Peter, who choreograph the dance."

"You seem to elevate women."

"How many men do you know who have given birth to anything other than an idea."

They had stopped beside the tree where five or six women were standing saying the rosary.

"I hope this doesn't get out of hand." Kate said. "The last thing we need in west Belfast is a bloody airport."

"Do you want to go to Maggie's grave?"

"No, she's not there."

"How did she die?"

"The same way everyone dies. She gradually left us."

They walked together in silence for a while. Then Kate said. "Her body left her soul."

"Don't you mean the other way around?"

"No."

"I don't understand."

"You really won't go past what you've been taught will you Peter?"

"Help me."

"When we were kids priests and teachers told us our bodies were tabernacles for our souls. It was a load of rubbish."

"What do you believe?"

"Ours souls are not inside our bodies. Our bodies are inside our souls. We are bigger than the tiny space we seem to occupy in this world. Every living thing lives inside its soul. Human consciousness senses it. When we try to understand it and give it a name we use material references and become confused. It is soul. It is pure creative energy. It doesn't die."

"Kate how do you know this?"

"Everyone knows but most people just won't accept it. They like to believe in a power beyond themselves, something bigger, something they can be angry at when things go wrong or plead with in times of despair. They want a gospel or a tablet of stone or a holy book to lead them to paradise."

"What do you want Kate?"

"I think I'll be happy with a rough guide. How many deaths have you witnessed Peter, as a priest?"

"Many, it's part of our training."

"How many births have you seen as a priest?"

"None."

"There's a serious gap in your training then. I've witnessed both and I can't help noticing the similarities." Kate stopped and lit a cigarette and looked at her watch. "I'll have to hurry," she said, "I have an appointment at the gym."

"That's rich."

Kate laughed. I smoke then go to the gym to stay healthy. I'm not scared of death but I am scared of dying. Contradictions. St. Augustine and his great insight, 'it is solved by walking'. But wasn't he the boyo who came up with the idea of original sin too, just to give us a new problem when we are walking about like headless chickens.

"There were two St. Augustines."

"See what I mean, contradictions! Anyway I hope you have a good afternoon Peter."

"I think I'll finish my report."

"What will you say?"

"Leave west Belfast alone they will work it out for themselves. Thanks Kate."

"No problem Peter and there is another saying you might want to heed."

"What's that"

"Sometimes when you need a teacher one comes along."

They had reached the house and Kate went in to collect her bag and car keys. She left her bag in the car and went back to check on Rags. He was sound asleep. Peter gave her the one pound coin to use the computer. She handed it back to him.

"Buy a lottery ticket, this one is on me Peter. I know you'll write what you've seen not what you think you believe. I'm off to meet my fitness freak. Patricia is serving dinner at seven thirty tonight. Hope that's okay."

. . . .

Kate's fitness freak was already warming up in the gym. Kate walked along grinning like an idiot blissfully unaware of the lessons she was about to be taught.

Five minutes later her unearthly groan began in the soles of her feet and worked its way steadily up her body.

"Ahhgggg. I can't do it."

"You can. I'll decrease the weights slightly and then I want you to concentrate and when your mind is focused, push."

"You sound like a bloody mid-wife."

"Stop wittering on and concentrate."

Part of Kate wanted to strangle the fitness fanatic. Another part of her however wanted to prove she could do it. She clenched her teeth and everything else that could be clenched.

"Have you children?" he asked.

"Two, Roisin and Charlie."

"Who is older?"

"Roisin."

"Can you remember Charlie as a baby?"

"Of course I bloody well can."

"Right close you eyes. Now imagine you trapped with your children in a mineshaft and a heavy beam has just fallen trapping little Charlie. There is no-one there to help and you have only three seconds."

Kate focused and immediately lifted the weights high above her shoulders shouting madly "pull him out Roisin pull him out."

Fitness man panicked and eased the weights back down before Kate realised what had happened.

"You have very high attention, haven't you?" he said.

"What's that?"

"The ability to focus. Unfortunately you don't seem to have the ability to keep your mouth shut."

"People have been telling me that all my life."

"Well, silently now, concentrate and lift again. It'll be easier this time because you know you can do it."

141

No-one had ever told Kate she had high attention. She was pleased and subsequently her first lesson in weights went well. Afterwards, in the shower she congratulated herself. Part of it was wonderful and part of the self satisfaction was alien. She began to feel guilty. Putting on her clothes in the changing room she mentally scolded herself.

"Kate," she said sternly, "you've met the man twice. The first time you thought he was going to kill you. Think sensibly and stop wondering now if he would like to have sex with you."

Kate's mind, as with all human minds, no matter what upbringing they receive, could leap from past to present to future in the time it took to take a deep breath. She looked at herself in the mirror and sighed,

"Catch yourself on Kate," she told herself quietly, "this isn't a dream island, you're not a celebrity model, the man is nice but you have to go and wash dishes."

"What do you do for a living then?" the fitness guru asked as they were having coffee before leaving the gym.

"I wash dishes."

"Oh."

"What did you expect?" Kate asked.

"I don't know, something more."

"Well, at least your honest. What do you do?"

"I'm a...I'm in finance."

"Wow."

"It's not very exciting."

"Oh I know it's not very exciting but as it happens your just what I'm looking for."

"Really?"

"Yes. Could I ask you some questions?"

"About finances?"

"Yes and no."

"Alright, ask away. I'll try my best to answer you."

Kate took him at his word.

"Have you a name, are you married, have you children, did

you go to university, have you a hidden disability, are you a home owner, is there a good sense of humour lurking under the surface, would you at some time in the future like to have sex with me." Kate finished her repertoire.

"No, but I admire your subtlety."

"Unlike me, brevity is a quality you obviously possess," Kate replied, " and we must have met because I need someone to teach me more than weight lifting. Do you think that is right, Mr. 'I have no name, abode, partner, heirs, humour or sex drive'."

The man smiled.

"My name is Will," he said, "and I do have sex drive. I'm just not prepared to jump into bed on a first date."

"Old fashioned." Kate said wistfully.

"Just careful." Will replied.

"No, I mean your name William."

"Oh right." Will said relieved.

"You haven't asked me anything yet." Kate continued.

Will smiled again.

"Your name is Kate Lagan, you have two children and live at 72 St. Francis Way. You are divorced, you own your house, you wanted to go to university but did not and have regretted it ever since, you need a new car but will not treat yourself to one. You like people and you are confident but shy. You think you want to meet someone who will fall madly in love with you but if that ever actually happened you would end up throwing dishes at him, probably before you washed them."

"Are you a god?"

"No, your name and address are on your car keys on the table. I saw your car, you asked me about university and the rest was good guesswork. Now what do you want to know about finance?"

Kate took a deep breath. "Everything." she said.

"That's difficult." Will looked at her. "I'm afraid Kate you'll have to be more precise."

Kate sipped her coffee thoughtfully and Will remained silent. Finally Kate formed her question. "I want to know how to get the money out of bricks and mortar. I know it's in there because I've protected that bloody house as if it was a child for nearly twenty years. But, unlike my real children, it now owes me, it owes me big time." she paused, then added, "How do I find the treasure?"

Will laughed. "Good question." he said. "I can help but I need to look at the property. Would some time next week suit"

"What day?"

"Thursday."

"Time?"

"About two."

"Great I'll see you then Will."

"What about the weight training?" Will asked as Kate lifted her bag and car keys.

"Oh, don't worry," Kate said, "I'll keep it up."

She left the remark hanging in the air and walked purposefully out of the gym.

Kate looked at her watch and realised that if she hurried she could pick Roisin up outside the school. She had not seen her daughter for days. She knew Roisin would not mind abandoning her friends for an hour or so and besides Kate could feel a light stirring of excitement, a little glow. It took her ten minutes of careful driving towards the school to give it a name. The word desire slipped its way cautiously into her brain. She would not use the word with Roisin but Kate wondered if her daughter would pick up the feeling intuitively. She was an 'almost woman' now so she would sense it, whereas Charlie would only laugh and probably find the whole thing, if not disgusting, then certainly inedible.

"Oh mum you fancy him don't you?" Roisin giggled and Kate grinned like a school girl.

"Don't be daft Roisin, fancying someone is something you do when you're fourteen, not forty-six."

"Forty-five mum, you're not forty-six til Saturday."

"Oh, I forgot love. It doesn't make much difference though except to note that on Sunday I'll be on the wrong side of forty."

"You look good for your age mum."

144

"Not great."

"No, I wouldn't go that far. You always taught us to be truthful."

"I did not," Kate was shocked, "I used to give you lessons in telling lies. I taught you how to give a good excuse so that the listener feels gratified. That's not lying that's using language creatively. It's a life skill. It should be on the school curriculum."

The girl-woman and the woman-girl sat in the car at the side of the school gates and watched for a while in silence as the uniformed pupils flowed steadily from the school and into the unkown world.

13

Charlie shouted down to Roisin and Kate "Hey hurry up, the view's brilliant." The two females looked at each other.

"Sorry mum," Roisin said, "It was Charlie's idea. We really thought you'd like it." Kate managed against all odds to smile.

"It's lovely darling," she gasped, "a really unexpected treat. In fact," she continued, "if someone had told me I would be climbing Divis mountain at dawn on my forty-sixth birthday I probably would have......" she paused to catch her breath.

"You would have said," Roisin finished her mother's sentence in a helpful tone, "that'll be me, fit as a fiddle, in harmony with nature, at one with the wild mosses and rare birds."

"Close," Kate replied, "I was actually going to say I would have committed suicide."

"Don't exaggerate mum," Roisin chirped, "besides you're not the suicidal type and anyway it's one o'clock in the afternoon, not dawn."

"Oh sorry for losing track of time Roisin. I was in the kitchen getting ready to prepare breakfasts for four guests as dawn was breaking."

"Mum," Roisin had had enough, "you know how you always told us to stop whingeing and get on with things, well stop whingeing and start walking. I promise you'll be really pleased with yourself when we reach the summit."

"Can I have a cigarette?"

"No."

"Okay get behind me and give me a push start before I really do lose the will to live."

Roisin laughed saying "Okay mum, one push and then you're on your own. I'm going to catch up with Charlie. Don't wander off the track in case you meet a big bad wolf."

Roisin strode ahead and was soon a figure in the distance.

Kate stopped again. Her complaints about the walk were dishonest and she scolded herself. She had been delighted when Charlie and Roisin gave her the birthday surprise with their home made card. She had opened the card after the guests had gone out and the leaflet had fallen into her lap.

"Well," Charlie had waited expectantly, "do you like your surprise mum?"

"I don't know what it is." Kate had answered. "unless you've bought me Walton's Mountain."

"No mum," Charlie laughed, "we're going for a walk on the Divis Mountain, you'll love it."

"And here I was thinking it was a twenty-five pound voucher for a beauty parlour." Kate said with what she hoped was not a wistful tone.

"You'd hate that mum." Roisin said immediately. "You used to tell us about walking across the mountain when you were young."

"That's true," Kate had replied thoughtfully, "before the British Army took it over."

"And the IRA." Charlie added.

"And now it's National Trust property," Roisin said, "so it's more or less our mountain again."

"May god look kindly on peace processes everywhere." Kate said, "Young ones used to go up onto the mountain to look for plastic bullets and shotgun cartridges during the Troubles. Fragments of war mixed with fragments of childhood. Let us keep our passion and turn our backs on spent hatred."

"Mum, it's your birthday," Charlie said quickly, "we want you to enjoy it. I'll wash the dishes, Roisin's going to feed Rags. You have a nice long shower and then we'll set off. Okay?"

"Okay." Kate replied. "Thank you both it's a lovely birthday treat."

Here she was, two hours later standing alone on the mountain. She turned slowly in a circle suddenly immersed in a deep pool of time. She began to walk uphill again and heard the singing as it caught in the wind. Children's voices.

"Tra la la la la Tra la la la la. I love to go a wandering along the mountain track. And as I go I love to sing with my knapsack on my back."

Kate sang as the words slipped once again into her memory. Then she saw what she wanted to see. Just ahead of her, on the track Paddy Joe was marching along with Ralph at his side, oldest son and youngest, side by side. Ralph was trying to match his heroe's long strides but would trip and stumble. Each time, and almost before it happened, Paddy Joe would reach out his hand and steady his little brother. In the other hand he carried a sand coloured haversack containing bottles of water, matches, a small parcel of coal and a bottle of milk. Kate watched her two brothers as she climbed. Paddy Joe turned and shouted "Come on you three hurry up." Ralph stopped and echoed "Come on you three hurry up."

Kate waved towards them then, or was it now, and stopped to let her two sisters pass in front of her. Christina was wearing a white dress with big red flowers. Her arms were bare and the dress flowed out from her waist to below her knees. She had abandoned her heeled shoes and wore flat white sandals and ankle socks. She carried one handle of the picnic bag and Maggie held the other handle. Between them the bag swayed with the words of the song. Maggie's beautiful long hair danced with the rhythm of movement and her eyes followed the flight of a small bird.

"You'll break the eggs," Kate shouted as her sisters passed, "you'll break the eggs swinging the bag like that and spoil the picnic."

"Don't be stupid Kate." Christina said. "It's not that heavy between us. And tie your lace or you'll trip and break your leg and spoil the whole day."

"I will not!" Kate shouted. "I can climb just as well as everybody else." She sat down on the grass and hastily retied the lace of her brown shoe then rushed to catch up with the others. Her mother and father would already be at the top. Her daddy would be collecting stones and her mammy would be looking for bits of stick. Kate's nose was dripping. It always did when she was out of breath. She wiped it on the sleeve of her cardigan and followed her family to the top. Kate knew that on the mountain, high above the small city streets they were no longer poor. The fire her father would light to boil the eggs would not be dampened with old newspapers to make it last till evening. The butter would be spread thickly on the slices of plain loaf and they could eat as many eggs as they wished. Kate had helped that morning as her mother packed apples and oranges, tomatoes and scallions, salt and pepper and a battenburg cake neatly into the picnic bag. Kate had wrapped eighteen eggs in newspaper and laid them carefully beside the two loaves and the blue sugar bag. She had felt hungry, just helping. Now she was starving. When she would reach the top the fire would be lit, circled with stones, the smoke drifting across the grass and the flames snatching and blackening the kettle as it boiled. Her mother would cook the eggs in the kettle then leave them to cool on the grass and put tea leaves into the water. The tea would be dark brown and delicious, much nicer than the tea at home. Kate always wondered at this because it was exactly the same water. They would eat like kings and watch the world below them as if they were gods. They owned the mountain on these days and their songs reached heaven, simply because heaven was within their reach.

Kate bent down to rub the grass stain from the hem of her cotton dress and the wind sharpened. A new voice mingled with the others and its clarity reached her mind in time.

"You made it mum good for you." Charlie reached out his hand to congratulate the newly arrived forty—six year old and Kate grabbed his outstretched arm letting the gesture change from greeting to support as he led her towards the circle of cold stones.

"We weren't sure about starting the fire mum before you got here. We were worried that it might be illegal." Charlie said. Kate breathed deeply and looked at her two beautiful children. Within seconds she knew she could trust herself and she began to smile.

"Of course it's illegal," she said, "when did that ever stop anybody doing anything?" She began to issue instructions . "Roisin you gather some sticks and Charlie did you bring firelighters in that rucksack. I thought there was more in it than a raincoat."

"Yep." Charlie replied. "A pot, half a dozen eggs, teabags, crusty rolls, butter and a battenburg cake."

"Matches?" asked Kate.

"Shit, I forgot."

"Don't worry," Kate laughed, "sometimes smokers might be the last to arrive but you can guarantee they'll always bring a light." She tossed the box of matches to Charlie.

The birthday picnic began.

Charlie supervised the fire as men do everywhere once Kate got it to light. He piled on the sticks and brushed the smoke from his eyes. He also had the foresight to bring some coal and as the eggs boiled Roisin went off to look for sphagnum moss. Kate enjoyed a cigarette, the thoughtfulness of her offspring and the reclaimed view of her birth-city. Charlie thought, the scenes, by Northern Irish standards, were quite spectacular. Directly below them Belfast Lough meandered towards the sea. The city looked low and somehow less important. Kate managed to locate the more impressive buildings, Stormont the seat of government, the city hall the seat of disagreement and minor upheaval, the main hospitals and the Harland and Woolfe cranes, Samson and Goliath. It was a city, like many others, built on the swamp of human endeavour. It had been a media hotspot for thirty years, replaced now by Basra and Bali.

"Wars shift" thought Kate, "but mainly because wars are built on sand". She thought of young boys throwing stones at tanks and of armies attacking in defence. Pictures of people caught in dramas beyond their making. Then she saw pictures of a family, sitting on a mountainside hungry for their picnic and unaware of the hunger they would soon experience for justice and peace. They would become tired of the power which tried to dictate the quality of their lives and measure the depth of their fears. She thought of the family, like so many others, wanting to enjoy the ordinariness of their existence. A family, in a house, in a street, in a city, in a country, in a world which had trapped them in a battle beyond their understanding.

Kate's eyes measured Lough Neagh the biggest inland lake in Great Britain. She remembered drawing it, pencilling in the blue lake against the green countryside for an examination in Geography which might help her gain the grades and the empathy from teachers to allow her the privilege of a university place. Now she could see it as it actually was. It was not so terribly imposing now from her elevated view on the mountainside.

"Perhaps," Kate thought, "it's because I'm bigger."

Roisin returned to the camp fire with an enthusiastic intake of breath.

"I've found some mum," she said, "sphagnum moss."

"What is that?" Kate asked.

"We were researching in A-Level biology." Roisin replied. "did you know that sphagnum moss was used in World War One?"

"Tell me about it Roisin." Kate asked simply because she wanted to hear her daughter's voice.

"It was used for bandages isn't that incredible? The moss had a soaking up quality and when young men were injured on the battlefield it was used to stem the flow of blood. It worked really well but because the moss itself had healing qualities. Mum I'd really like to know what it contains. And here it is on our own mountain. When I graduate in medicine I'm going to research natural healing."

Kate looked at the handful of greenery her daughter held up for inspection.

"You are not going to be a good doctor Roisin," she said, "you are going to be a great doctor."

"How do you know that mum. I haven't even got a place at university yet?"

"You think about healing and health before you think about illness and drugs. You have your thoughts the right way round."

"The eggs are cooked mum." Charlie called from the fire. "Are you ready to eat?"

On the way back down the mountain Kate suggested that the Lagan family should take off their shoes and walk the last part barefoot. It was cold and a late sun was struggling to stay alight but they agreed it was a good idea. With their training shoes slung around their necks and their bellies filled, the Lagan's descended the mountain with Kate silently saying thankyou for her journey so far.

In bed alone that night Kate was certain of two things. Her children loved her as much as she loved them and heaven was not, as she had been led to believe, beyond her grasp. It was all around her.

The birthday present taught her that time was a deep precious resource and for Kate time was no longer linear. She was beginning to understand it as another dimension. Maggie and Kate and Christina and Paddy Joe and Ralph singing and shouting as children were still inside her. The child danced because the child knew the secrets of time. In the darkness of her bedroom the child Kate ran back to the mountain and took Maggie's hand. Then they skipped together down through the fields towards home. Meanwhile Kate's body slept for in the other time Kate knew she had work to do.

The sun was already showing its inclination to rise and Kate was out of bed, dressed and downstairs and six thirty am. She woke Charlie who refused to open his eyes until she reminded him that it was Sunday and he could have an extra few hours sleep in her bed. He was out of the sleeping bag and upstairs to Kate's room in five seconds. H crawled into the bed groaning with delight at the treat of Sunday morning sleep ins. He reawakened just enough to swap over the two pillows. The one his mother had slept on felt too damp for comfort. He then stretched his long legs out to the end of the bed and fell sound asleep.

Kate fed Rags his mushy breakfast, mopped up his delight at Kate's inclination for early rising and yelped excitedly as she cuddled and scolded him. Then he was allowed his tour of the back yard. He sniffed at everything until Kate lifted him and he was placed gently back in his box. He would sleep until lunchtime. It was after all a dog's life. Kate's new guests were four young men from Galway. They had their sights on acting careers and were in Belfast with a puppet show to teach community groups about the dangers of religious intolerance. They had explained their show to Kate and she had listened politely. She had had a peep into their van and the sight of a huge ugly puppet with a straggly wool beard and dark clucking eyes had given her quite a nasty turn. She wondered if the young talented puppeteers realised how terrified audiences could be of puppets but decided that their hearts and arts council grants were presumably in the right place. It was no business of hers to suggest that pointing out differences often made people more prejudiced rather than less so.

Community relations was a tricky business usually involving middle class people telling working class people that they should all pull together to make the world a nicer place. Of course if one happened to live in a beautiful suburban avenue one's contribution to community relations was usually stretched to listening to debates on local radio and recycling election pamphlets. Somehow social, religious, political or economic prejudices did not intrude on wealthy communities. Their job, it seemed, was to control the flow of monies into no-hope schemes and build huge walls to separate and divide. The physical walls were then called peace walls and therefore accepted by all. Kate wished they had been called war walls. At least then their removal would have been deemed essential at some stage. The walls of political and economic inequality where the real dividers in Belfast. Until these crumbled active challenging peace was impossible. And Kate thought, it would take more than a couple of amateur actors in a van to help people to understand the necessity and the principles of equality and justice.

153

Kate set the dishes for breakfast and made herself a cup of coffee. The young men had begun their demanding task of their tour with drinks in a local pub. She had heard them come in late so they would not appear for an early breakfast. She hunted out her notebook and pen and began to draw. Flowing backwards in time on the mountain had come to her as naturally as breathing. Today she was going to reverse this newly heightened sense and allow herself to go forward in time. She began by drawing a house. It was a house she had always wanted. It had two big windows on either side of a huge door. It had three windows on the second floor. It had a chimney with smoke curling up to the sky and a long winding path. She drew a tree at the side with bright red apples. She coloured big bright flowers along the edge of the lawn. It was a child's house and she wondered why all children whether they lived in terraced houses or apartments or shacks drew houses exactly the same way.

"Perhaps," Kate thought, "there is a dream in every child to live in a house with solid walls, bright windows and a beautiful garden. She wondered too if there would be room on a planet for each child to occupy a dream house. She knew immediately that there was room enough. Eight million people have lived in Ireland before the famine. In 1846 and for the following ten years men women and children lay on Irish roadsides and starved to death. Their pain still haunted the collective minds of the Irish people. As with all holocausts its roots lay not in the worn out soils of the potato fields but in the political hell of unjust governance which ensured that the bodies of the nation's peasants was kept as dismally as their souls.

"And upon such slavery empires can be built." Kate said, as she drew, "built on a deep foundation of human misery."

Kate wondered if she had any right to communicate with those who died such terrible deaths but human awareness is also what helps define the quality of our souls. And so with her child's drawing on the kitchen shelf in front of her she talked silently to her ancestors.

"I am," she said, "we are…. because of you. We, your great great great great grandchildren have already become wealthy beyond your wildest dreams. Cars, gardens, homes, fridges, supermarkets, aeroplanes, holidays, clothes, jewellery, computers."

"What are these things you talk about?" Silent whispers reached into Kate's mind.

"Material wealth." Kate said.

"And no-one dies of hunger?"

"We are overfed." Kate said, "but often undernourished."

"Where do these things you mention exist?" the voices asked.

"Everywhere, in our homes, in our schools, on our roads."

"That is not possible."

"Why not?"

"The island would sink under the weight. The bogs would soon bury the material wealth, the machines."

"There are few bogs now. Those that are left are protected by law."

"And everyone has a fine house?"

"Some are finer than others," Kate paused and added because she was Kate, "all of them have bathrooms."

"Was it worth dying for?"

"I cannot answer that." Kate said feeling the tears in her eyes, "I am in this time. I'm sorry."

"Was it worth living for then?"

"Yes." Kate said.

"Why?"

"Because one day I will be an ancestor."

"What do you wish for your descendants?"

"What I wish for myself." Kate said.

"What is that?" The voices grew weaker.

"Wisdom."

Kate wrote the date on the page and folded the drawing carefully. She put it in the kitchen drawer and quietly prepared to embrace a new strength as if it moved through her body and circled outwards towards her soul. In the quiet of a Sunday morning with

155

sons and strangers asleep above her Kate surfaced from the time pool, set up the ironing board and began slowly to smooth out the crinkled bed linen. Once again the practical and the ordinary helped.

She smiled remembering her father's words when he had refused to allow them to iron or to sew on Sundays.

"If you sew on a Sunday" he had warned them, "you'll go to hell and then you'll have to pick out the stitches with your nose"

Kate's parents ideas on hell and heaven had been definite. They were places situated miles apart but very often both could be used as moral sticks. Kate now knew they non-existed in exactly the same place. Neither promised eternal happiness or eternal sorrow and she was grateful for that. Eternity she realised, was not a promise, it was a threat. The dead moved towards a universal consciousness. Some, she knew, took longer than others but they had their own work to do and must be left in peace to do it. One day she would become a part of that creative energy. Meanwhile her work here had only just begun. She was not going to wait. She was determined to find heaven wherever she looked. And even more determined to find the energy and resources to enjoy it.

14

During the next few days Kate found time to make two thank-you cards for Roisin and Charlie, take Rags to the vet to be inoculated, take her mother for a short trip to Newcastle and have lunch with Christina. She also began to read a number of leaflets on positive equity, endowment plans, capital repayment schemes and interest only mortgages. When Thursday arrived she set off for her planned meeting with Wil certain of one thing. She was absolutely sure how little she knew.

Will was already sitting at one of the small tables in the café. At first Kate did not recognise him because he was wearing a suit. She realised that he was taller than he thought. He had an awkward way of sitting but perhaps that was due to the persona of the suit. He was twiddling with his mobile phone and staring at the large boat of ice-cream, banana, chocolate chips, fresh cream and two red plastic sails unsure, Kate thought, of where to start.

"Shouldn't you have ordered a café latte?" she asked sitting down opposite him, "to go with the suit?"

"I like ice-cream." Will said, "I thought you wouldn't mind."

"I don't." Kate replied. "Tuck in."

"Okay you can read this while I'm eating." Will handed over a book entitled 'Your Mortgage and Future Peace of Mind'.

Kate flicked through the glossy pages and handed it back.

"I don't want information Will." she said, "I want to know how money works."

"Someone pays you to wash dishes," Will explained, "you get your money, you spend it, you wash dishes the following week and so on and so on."

"I didn't come here to be patronised Will." Kate tried to keep the edge from her voice. "Or to waste my time, or to be told nonsense and you have fresh cream on the side of your lip."

Will wiped his mouth with the paper napkin.

"Do you want the little sails," he asked, "I don't think I'm supposed to eat them."

"I want you to teach me about money." Kate said exasperated.

"I'm not sure if I can." Will carefully removed the sails and placed them on the table. "You see Kate, I don't want any."

"Any what?"

"Any money. I don't need it. My aunt gave me a caravan near Strangford. I do the finance stuff because it interests me. I don't want the cash."

"Your a member of a gym.,"

"I like to keep fit and the steam room is very good."

"What do you do for clothes?"

"I have two suits, a blue one and the dark blue one. The blue one is for business and the dark blue one is for funerals."

"Shoes?"

"Two pairs, a black pair and a brown pair."

"You shouldn't wear brown shoes with a blue suit."

"Nobody really notices at funerals."

"You drive a jeep. I've seen it in the car park at the gym"

"Yes, it came with the caravan and a bicycle."

"What do you use for petrol if you've no money or does your car run on holy water?"

"Food and petrol and ice-cream, I'm a rich man."

"What happens if you get good at this finance stuff?"

"Then I'm a wealthy man but I do not want to be wealthy. I want to be rich."

"Is there a difference?" Kate was intrigued.

"Of course but you have to find out for yourself."

"How?"

"You have to understand financial freedom."

"What's that?"

"It's how much money you need to be free. But before that you have to decide two things."

"What?"

"You have to decide if you want to be free and then you have to decide what you are going to do with your freedom. Most people are under the illusion that more money will bring them happiness. That's why the lottery is so popular. More money if you're greedy can just bring more problems and for many people a great deal of unhappiness. Look at the lives of most so-called celebrities. They have money, mansions and misery. And they are certainly not free."

"Did you know," Kate said, "that you are taller than you think you are?"

"I'm exactly six foot." Will said, "It's just that sometimes it's important to be invisible."

"I know," Kate said, "sometimes I dress invisibly too."

"Like a scullery maid." Will smiled but looked embarrassed. He had not meant the phrase to sound so sharp.

"No-one pays you to wash dishes Kate do they?" He continued, "You own the guest house. I drove past it yesterday."

"Spying?"

"Home working."

"Mmm," Kate said quietly, "deep down I'm a scullery maid."

"I reckon," Will licked some ice-cream off the back of the spoon and then pointed it towards her; "I reckon that Kate Lagan could be anything Kate Lagan wants to be."

"I think you're right Will. Can we talk again?"

"I'll call over to see the property. I need to see it properly before we talk about mortgages. Would tomorrow evening suit you? About eight-thirty?"

"That'll be fine."

Will got up to leave. He reached into his trouser pocket and brought out some coins and looked at them.

159

"It's okay Will," Kate said, "I'll pay for the banana boat. You've given me a lot to think about. I owe you."

"Ta." Will said, "I'll see you tomorrow then." He left as Kate went to the counter to pay the bill. Then she went back to the table, lifted the two little sails and slipped them into her purse with the change. She stopped at the supermarket and bought some flowers. She wanted her home to look particularly pretty the following evening.

....

Kate gasped. "How much do you think it's worth?" she asked again.

Will had returned to the living room with a small tear in the bottom of his trouser leg. Rags was not quite as hospitable as Kate. He treated the intruder with suspicion and the casual enmity seemed mutual.

"That dog needs disciplined." Wil said, his ankle hurt like hell.

"She'll make a good wee guard dog won't you Rags?" Kate said lifting the offending bundle up into her arms. "I didn't know he would nip." she added tapping Rags on the nose.

"Bite," Will said, "not nip. Put that thing in the kitchen will you. I can't concentrate."

Kate left Rags to yelp his protests behind closed doors and asked for the third time.

"How much?"

"I think," Will responded, "it's a rough estimate of course, but I think you could safely put the house on the market for a quarter of a million pounds. How much did you buy it for?"

"I don't want to tell you." Kate said honestly.

"Kate," Will sighed, "will you stop acting like a bloody scullery maid and tell me. It's a business question."

"Okay. Forty-five thousand."

"That's about right then." Wil replied, "Your property went up in value by about 10% in the first years but in the last five years properties in Belfast have risen by 15% annually. And for some

160

reason properties in West Belfast have rocketed to 20% increase. It's a popular area, suddenly. You could put it on the market as a business or for home ownership. It should attract a lot of interest."

"I don't want to sell it."

"Are you mad?"

"Yes.." Kate replied. "It's my business but it's also my home."

"That's it then." Wil said, preparing to leave.

"No." Kate stopped him. "Look Will," she said, "it's a bit like trying to find the money the old granny stuffed into the rocking chair. I want to keep the house but I know I can take the money as well. I've read the glossy brochures and I don't like them. They trick us into believing we are learning something but really they are designed to make us think and act in a certain way. They deny us access to knowledge while spoon-feeding us bits of useless information."

Will was silent and Kate continued,

"You say you don't want wealth but something makes me believe you know how to obtain it. I want you to tell me what you know. I want to learn."

"It's very risky Kate. Why do you want the money?"

"I want to prove to myself that I can do it. Eighteen months ago Will I had no work, no money and very few dreams. Now I have a business which needs to expand because of demand. I'm providing employment. The bank manager calls me by my first name. And I have just found out that my house is worth a small fortune. I have bigger dreams now and I'm prepared to take bigger risks."

"Then don't sell Kate. Use the bricks and mortar as your bank. Re-mortgage and buy a second property with the cash."

"Then what?"

"Re-mortgage that and buy a third property."

"Okay."

"You need to think about it. I'll come back another day."

"No."

"You will be taking on a lot of work."

"Unemployment and poverty is hard work Will. That much I do know and compared to that making money is easy."

"I'll need to sort out the figures and fine detail, contact a mortgage broker and see about a proper valuation then source a lending company. It will take about three months."

"It's November." Kate said. "Do you think I'll be able to find a second property by the new year."

"If you look for it you'll find it." Will said.

"Right." Kate began to dance. "I can't wait to tell the kids and start house-hunting."

"What about this business. Make sure you do not neglect it."

"Don't worry I was thinking of putting Patricia in charge. She could run a medium sized country given the chance, or the inclination."

Kate continued to dance as she spoke and a sudden silly twirl brought her close to Will. She stumbled slightly and he caught her arm. She looked up and into his eyes.

"One more think Kate," Will looked steadily back at her, "whatever you do don't start falling in love with me." He lifted his folder from the breakfast table and walked towards the door.

Kate, possibly for the first time in her life, was speechless. Ten hasty retorts were tripping over themselves trying to be the first to make it to her mouth. Kate beat them back and heard herself saying.

"Thanks Will, see you at the gym maybe. Would this time next week be a good time to work out the details."

"Sure," Wil said, "I'll see myself out."

When the door closed Kate took a deep breath then jumped up and down and clapped her hands. When she finally calmed down she went into the kitchen and opened a bottle of wine. She had guests but Roisin was at her dad's and Charlie was staying with a friend. Group study he called it but Kate knew he needed the break. The house was quiet and Kate needed to celebrate. She lifted a glass, opened the fridge to get the cold bottle of wine and checked to see if there was another bottle still in the cupboard underneath the sink. She poured herself a generous measure. Then she lifted Rags from his box and brought him and her filled glass into the living room. Nights alone had become something of a rarity. Rags cuddled contently at her feet and Kate sipped the wine. Tomorrow she would ask Patricia once again for help to manage but tonight she would enjoy the cool feeling of success tingling through her body to her fingertips. She raised the glass and watched it sparkle in the light of the fire. Tonight Kate Lagan was pleased beyond pleasure.

"I've done it Rags," she said, "all the years I fretted and worried and patched and bargained to pay the mortgage have been worth it. This is my home, this is my business, this is my bank."

She finished the wine, too quickly, and went into the kitchen for a refill. She poured another measure, closed the fridge door and looked across at the opposite wall. She had forgotten the mark and it was more than coincidence that she remembered it again tonight. When Charlie was three he had asked her about it as he sat perched on the kitchen shelf.

"What's that mark on the wall mammy?"

"What mark darling?"

"At the top of the cupboard., if you look up there's a big black line."

"Oh I drew that."

"Why?"

"When you were born I asked your daddy to wash the walls in the kitchen so that everything would be lovely and clean for my darling new baby."

"Did he wash the walls?"

"No, when I came home from the hospital he told me that he had worked out how far I could reach up then he had washed down as far as that. He thought I could finish it once I was back on my feet."

"Did you?"

"Yes, eventually. But I drew that line, just to remind me."

"Remind you of what?"

"Remind me of how far your daddy thought I could reach."

"It's not very high."

163

"I'm not very tall Charlie. But I tell you what. If I hold you in my arms I bet you could draw a line much higher up."

"When?"

"Now."

Kate had hunted in the drawer for a black marker and held her son as high as she dared. He drew a new line, a bit slanted but higher.

Kate raised her glass to her lips glad that both lines could still be seen faintly through various coats of paints. At least she could see them but then she knew they was there.

In the living room Rags yelped aware of the guests coming quietly into the house. Kate stayed in the kitchen but heard them ascending the stairs and finished the second glass as the house and guests settled down for the night. Her third glass brought with it a reflective mood. Kate began to re-mark her emotions. She thought of the anger she had felt as her marriage slowly faded and responsibilities grew. The fiery emotion was now replaced by a comfortable feeling of slight regret. Jealousy had also played its part in her life. Kate always thought that Christina and Paddy Joe were much more intelligent. They seemed to have an innate ability to manage their affairs and their finances. It had taken years to break away from the loving boundaries they set for Kate to follow their example. And it had taken even longer for Kate to understand that the mother and father who had nurtured them had been a loving young couple ready to take on the challenges of a fresh marriage. The parents who had reared her and Ralph were older, tired. The weaknesses of a drier marriage was scaffolded by the older siblings. The rich fertile soil that had given Christina and Paddy Joe a sound sense of who they were had been less promising when Kate was born.

And Maggie had been somewhere in the middle. Kate felt a sudden rush of the swirling unclaimed grief she had known at Maggie's death. Maggie, the in-between child who had held them all together. Shy, beautiful Maggie who knew the names of wild flowers, who fed birds, loved plants and children and poetry and

Ireland with a sweet, quiet, unassuming passion. It had taken the disease four years to claim her and even now each of them could barely whisper her name. But in mysterious ways that huge emotion called grief also changes. Grief can be turned to sorrow or, if it is allowed, it can change to wisdom. Kate could feel the edges of this in her consciousness. But she knew if she tried to grasp it too soon then the very action itself would melt it, as a breath can melt a snowflake. She let it stay where it had landed. She knew a snowflake did not weigh much but it did weigh more than nothing.

Kate sipped slowly at her fourth glass of wine. The room was in darkness and Rags snuffled quietly in his dreams. The fire flickered. Then without warning, Kate came suddenly upon herself. She saw the new born child dark and thin, a few moments into the world and already frightened. She saw the doctor wrap the naked child in a towel and carry it downstairs. She saw him hand the weakling to a childless adult. Kate heard his words,

"You look after this if it survives. The mother may not. It's been a very difficult birth." Kate looked through the glass at the skinny ugly newborn baby and the baby looked back at her across the years.

"Is this what it is all about?" Kate whispered and then she answered her own question.

"Of course it is you daft bat. You were meant to experience all of this because you lived. This is called living. Now finish your wine, get up and set the table for the breakfasts. What do you think your guests are going to eat in the morning, farley's rusks?"

She lifted Rags and put him into his box.

"Good night Rags," she whispered. "you too have been given a little snowflake life, remember that," and Kate began to lay the table for breakfast.

15

Patricia shouted, Roisin screamed and Charlie applauded as Kate told each of them about her good fortune and the value of her property. She had guessed their reactions and waited for the inevitable questions.

"What are you going to do now?" Patricia asked hesitantly.

"What are we going to do with all that money?" Roisin laughed.

"Can we afford a decent car mum?" Charlie requested hopefully.

Kate no longer needed to live in fear of the future but she was learning how to plan for the future. Before she had gone to bed she had taken out her notepad and scribbled down her business plan. It was now five o'clock in the evening and she had announced to a somewhat astonished committee of two almost-reared children and one fully reared friend that she would go through the business plan to see what they could suggest and then they had to agree a way forward.

The four sat down at the table. Kate placed a sheet of paper and a pen in front of each of them. The meeting was delayed slightly. Patricia suddenly needed to go the toilet. Charlie's friend rang to ask about a home work assignment. Then Roisin had to hunt out the kitchen roll to clean up after Rags who was showing evidence of the general mounting excitement in his own puppy way.

When everyone had settled Kate began. "Right," she said, "here's what we're going to do."

"I thought you said we had to suggest ideas." Charlie butted in.

"That was just to get you seated Charlie." Kate replied. "Now listen will you."

"Fuck Kate." It was Patricia's turn, "I never thought I'd be a fully paid up member of a business team. Do you remember when we were at school? It was always two posh girls would be asked to choose the netball teams. The sweat would break on me because I knew I'd be standing there almost last to be picked. Now here I am ready to brainstorm."

"Shut up Patricia," Kate said firmly, "and anyway you were always bloody well picked before I was."

"Shut up both of you." Roisin's voice was clear and precise. "Let's get on with this."

"Okay," Kate began, "now here's the plan."

One hour later Patricia sat back in her chair and sighed.

"I'm going to manage this business then." she said.

"Yes." Kate continued. "I'm going to draw up a contract Patricia. It keeps both of us right and you will be paid properly for a proper job."

"Can you afford it Kate?" Patricia asked.

"Can we both afford it Patricia?" Kate asked.

The two friends looked at each other. It was a difficult question for each of them.

"I'll try." Patricia promised.

"So will I." Kate said.

"It will bring a lot of changes." Patricia needed to push thing further than she really wanted to.

"I know Patricia." Kate moved the pages out of the way and took her friends hand. "I've no idea where all this will lead us but I am sure of one thing I'm not going back."

Patricia pressed gently on the hand. "Neither am I Kate." she said. "But there is one thing I need to know."

"What's that?" Kate was prepared to answer most things.

"This Will Roberts guy?"

"You're going to ask me is he trustworthy Patricia. The only answer is… I think so." Kate replied.

"No," Patricia grinned, "I was going to ask you if he was sexy."

Kate laughed, "Not in front of the children please."

Charlie and Roisin groaned and the meeting ended with a cup of tea and Kate's promises to update the team after her meeting with Will. Patricia left saying that Jimmy would be annoyed because his dinner would not be ready at the usual time. Kate made a tiny footnote in her mind to buy a property with a self-contained flat, gave Patricia a hug at the front door and went back to her children.

Then the three of them danced round the living room yelling and cheering as daft as three bats.

"You did it mum, you did it!" Roisin shouted.

"We're rich, we're rich." Charlie shouted.

"We're alive and happy and hopeful" Kate hugged her children and added. "And we're on our way kids."

"Where to?"

"Heaven." Kate replied. She stopped dancing suddenly and held their hands.

"Oh mum," Charlie wailed, "don't go all philosophical on us, not now."

"I wont Charlie," was Kate's earnest reply, "but I just want to say one more thing. Can I?"

"Go ahead mum." Roisin's firm voice led Kate to her statement.

Kate took a deep breath. "This is it kids and I just want you to know something very very important."

Charlie and Roisin waited and Kate continued.

"We are already rich," she said, "we always have been, I know that now, but we can become wealthy as well. I want us to do it on one condition. We must learn to understand the difference."

"We will" Roisin and Charlie spoke together, then Charlie added, "mum, I want to be a lawyer for human rights."

Roisin said, "mum, I want to be a doctor who treats people not patients."

And Kate said, "kids I want to be a warrior for 'the republic of heaven'."

And then they danced again.

It is a truly wonderful thing to have dreams for children. It is miraculous for children to have dreams for their parents. Within the dance Kate knew that if parenting had been a game they she had just been picked for the 'a' team. Kate had known that being poor was hard work. She had no idea that being rich would stretch her to the edges of her soul.

Her meetings over the following weeks with Will taught her the benefits of positive equity and the discipline of patience. A valuation of her house brought setbacks. The garage was leaking, the chimney needed repointing, guttering replaced and wiring upgraded.

"Minor works," Will said as he read the valuation report, "nothing major. Do you want to go ahead with the remortgage?"

"Yes." and Kate offered a silent prayer to the gods of minor works. She signed the forms Will took from his folder and asked what happened next. Wil explained that further delays might be possible but suggested she arrange to have the repairs carried out as soon as possible. Rain, frost, a fall in the number of guests and the grinding oversell of a fattening Christmas dampened Kate's will but not her spirit.

The minor repairs were carried out before Christmas and Kate covered the sign for a week's holiday. On Christmas Eve her former husband arrived with money for Charlie and Roisin and a bouquet of flowers for Kate. She was not sure whether she was pleased or alarmed at the gesture. He was duly thanked and duly warmed with two glasses of mulled wine and a plate of chocolate truffles. Though Kate hated the blatant advertising of the season she did enjoy the smells. She decorated the house with holly and candles and hid sachets of spicy granules behind the radiators. For years the Lagans could not afford to succumb to the virtual need for presents by the sleighful. They had decided this year that extra money did not necessarily have to mean extra waste. Consequently their presents for each other were small, thoughtful, appreciated and more expensive that in previous years. In addition, the turkey was organic, the cranberry sauce rich, the Black Forest Gateau fresh not frozen and the salmon wild, not farmed. Kate realised that money did make a difference but the pleasure was in the detail. The new year came exactly one week later as it had done for the two thousand years of the Christian calendar.

Roisin went back to stay with her father and study for exams. Charlie tried his best to balance homework with internet chat and googling. Patricia began work as full time manager in the guest house. Kate paid the usual attention to her gym workouts and a great deal more attention to the local property market. In the third week of January Will arrived with more paperwork.

"I haven't seen you at the gym lately." Kate's voice greeted him lightly as she opened the door. She added "happy Christmas by the way."

"It's a bit late for that greeting isn't it?" Will replied.

"Okay," Kate was undeterred, "happy January then." Kate said.

"It's nearly over."

"Happy February then," Kate said.

Rags was barking furiously in the kitchen.

"Shut up Rags," Kate called.

"Any guests?"

"Four young lads from Dundalk." Kate said and led Will through to the living room. "They're trying to break into the music scene in Belfast. I didn't even know there was one."

"Can you turn on the light?" Will asked. "We can't very well go over paperwork in the dark."

"Oh." Kate tried to sound chirpy. "I just thought the candles would be enough. They were left over from Christmas. I didn't want to throw them away half used. And storing them is no good. They just seem to get damp and the wick won't burn."

"Like people." Will said switching on the electric light.

Kate began blowing out the candles asking between gritted blows.

"How was your Christmas anyway?"

"Cold." Will opened the folder and took out various documents which he laid on the table.

170

"Caravans must be freezing in the winter." Kate gave another blow.

"No, just damp. If you want proper cold you have to go to Lapland."

"How do you go there," Kate blew again, "by sleigh?"

"Helicopter."

"Lovely idea isn't it," Kate said, "Lapland in the winter Strangford in the summer."

"Or the Bahamas." Will replied.

Kate blew out the last candle and laughed. "You'd need to find a lot of loose change down the side of the couch for that lifestyle Will."

"Let's get started Kate. I only have thirty minutes."

"Right." Kate tried her best to be business like and brief but there was definitely an annoying little ache. It positively refused to be blown out. She watched as Wil rubbed his glasses on a handkerchief and began methodically to sort out the papers. She liked his hands. She liked the way he held the pen poised over the paperwork. She pulled a chair from the other side of the table and set it nearer Will's with the words, "easier for both of us if I sit here."

"You don't give up easily do you?" Will tried to dampen his smile.

"No," Kate replied, "now what do I sign?"

"Any questions?" Will asked handing her the pen.

"What happens if my house goes down in value?"

"Why would your house go down in value when everyone else's house in Belfast is going up in value?"

"Can I afford the repayments?"

"What are you doing with the extra money now?"

"Putting it into the bank."

"Do you think the bank is going to give you five times more than the amount you deposit?"

"No."

"Are you going to sign or not?"

"Yes." Kate signed various documents.

"When do I get the money?"

"In about five weeks."

"How much commission will you receive?"

"Enough."

"Can I have a kiss to seal the contract?"

"No."

"Okley dokley." Kate said. "Now can I just run through everything again with you. Then I'll understand it all better and be able to explain it to the rest of the family.

"Leave your family out of it." Will said sternly.

"I can't. Christina and Paddy Joe and my mother would be really annoyed. Ralph doesn't much care."

"Have you told them what you're doing?"

"Not yet."

"Why?"

"They would try to talk me out of it, tell me I was crazy and suffocate me with advice."

"The answers were already inside you Kate. Now don't tell your family."

"What about Roisin and Charlie?"

"What have they suggested so far?"

"Nothing really. Roisin said I need a decent winter coat and Charlie said I need a new car."

"They're both right and that is good advice. You should tell them everything. They won't try to talk you out of doing what you want to do."

"They're good kids."

"They seem to be by all accounts. Now take your time and explain to me slowly what you have done."

Kate began,

"I've revalued my home in line with current prices. The equity is a staggering two hundred thousand pounds. I remortgage my property at its present value taking into account fees, costs and my ability to make monthly repayments."

"How much can you remortgage for?" Will enquired.

"Eighty per cent."

"Good girl, what kind of mortgage are you applying for?"

"Interest only."

"Why?"

"Repayments are not as high and the property is still going up in value. I may change later to a capital repayment mortgage. Now I bloody well know the difference." she added.

"Go on."

"Eighty percent of two hundred thousand is one hundred and sixty thousand pounds."

"Are you going to take that much?"

"No."

"Why?"

"Too risky, too greedy."

"Good girl, go on."

"I'm remortgaging the house at one hundred and fifty thousand pounds. That gives me one hundred thousand pounds."

"What are you going to do with that?"

"Put a sixty thousand pounds deposit on another property and put twenty thousand pounds in the bank and keep ten thousand pounds to refurbish the new property. Then I need ten thousand pounds to meet repayments and bills until the second property starts to pay for itself."

"How?"

"Lagan's Guesthouse No. 2."

"What does that leave you?"

"Nothing."

"Put fifteen thousand in the bank Kate, put three thousand towards a new car and spend two thousand on a holiday."

"Seriously?"

"Seriously. You have to take care of yourself. Oh and buy a new coat."

"Am I doing the right thing Will?"

"The answers are inside you already Kate." Will put the signed papers back into his folder and stood up to leave.

Kate followed him to the door. "Thanks Will." she said sheepishly.

"Stop talking like a besotted school girl Kate," he said. "You're a business woman." Kate felt a rush of anger but he added quickly. "Don't worry I think you're doing the right thing." He lifted his hand and she thought he was going to run his fingers along her cheek. She waited expectantly.

He patted the top of her head and murmured again "Good girl."

There was an awkward silence.

"I've got to go Kate." he said, "I'll telephone you with a progress report okay?"

"Okay." Kate was just about to retreat into the hall when he suddenly bent down and kissed her lightly on the cheek. Then he turned and headed towards his car.

"Shit, shit, shit." Kate said as she closed the door. But the moment melted. She telephoned Roisin.

"Are you studying Roisin?"

"Sort of mum. What do you want?"

"Oh Roisin, I have to talk to someone."

"Can it wait until the morning mum?"

"Yes love, don't worry"

Roisin arrived in a taxi twenty minutes later.

"Thank you darling. How did you know I needed you?"

"Never mind that mum. Can you pay the taxi driver?"

"Of course. Here's five pounds."

Roisin took the money paid the taxi driver and asked him to come back in an hour.

"Are you sure love?" he said.

"Quite sure," she answered, "and by the way I'm not your love."

"It's only an expression."

"Well yeah," Roisin conceded, "but I've had a hard day. Sorry."

"See you in an hour then Miss."

"Okay. Thanks."

Roisin went straight into the kitchen and switched on the kettle asking "Any guests?"

"Four lads but they won't be back till dawn." Kate replied. "They'll be famous one day."

"How do you know?"

"They call themselves 'Thoughtless Giraffe'. They are really good at keeping their rooms tidy and very courteous all steps in the right direction."

"What's the panic mum? I thought everything was going well and according to plan."

"It is!"

"So what's wrong?"

"I think I'm falling in love with Will."

"Mum, I'm a bit too old to have a step-father."

"Roisin I'm a bit old to have adolescent dreams."

· "What are you going to do?"

"I'm going to break the code."

"What code?"

"Eve's code. That way I can move beyond this nonsense."

"What's Eve's code. I've never heard of it."

"It's just a name I've given something."

"Mum, not another revelation." Roisin glanced at the cold candles then back at Kate with an expression of sympathy. "Where you having a business meeting with Will or trying to seduce him?"

"Both. That's why I want to talk to you. I promised myself I would never let it happen to me again.

"I thought you decided to choose a different route with no bumps in the road and no black holes." Roisin was concerned and she also had an essay to prepare. "I haven't much time mum." Kate gave herself a mental slap. This was no heart-to-heart. This was confessional.

"Remember a few years ago I had a sort of fling with a man Roisin." She began. Roisin was going to sound an opinion but Kate was already there. "I know you and Charlie really disliked him when you eventually met him ."

"At least you listened to what we had to say," Roisin conceded, "and told him to move on to his next victim."

"Thank goodness for intelligent children," Kate sighed, "that's why I wanted to talk to you tonight. When that ridiculous affair was a secret I thought I had power."

"That's stupid mum."

"I know that now, I didn't then. I thought the secret made me different from everyone else. I thought it made my life more interesting and it gave me control. It didn't. It just kept me confused and guilty and hurt. It was the idea that had the power. I thought that a secret affair made me special but it made me vulnerable and weak. It had control over me not the other way around."

"Why do you call it Eve's code?"

"Because I think it may only happen to women."

"Why?"

"Men have learnt to manipulate us. They encourage us to keep secrets. In my experience men aren't very bright in a general sort of way, probably why they don't like candles." She mused and paused.

"Go on mum."

"Well the code must be strong, almost visible to them. They can twist it around in their heads to make themselves feel innocent but worse than that they can twist it around in our heads to make us feel guilty."

"Emotional blackmail." Roisin said quietly and added, "conditional love."

"Yes," Kate agreed, "That's what I found myself doing tonight with Will. Acting like some God forsaken Eve offering him an apple."

"I thought you were stronger than that mum."

"So did I Roisin. Do you think it's a chemical reaction?"

"It's just the way you were taught mum. All those fifteen mysteries of the Rosary and God being a 'he' and all these women in the gospels running after Jesus with their complaints. No wonder he thought he was God. What man wouldn't?"

"That's awful Roisin."

"Mum," Roisin was exasperated, "you were brought up to feel guilty. But you brought us up to feel free. You have taught us well but you need to take heed of your own lessons."

"I knew you would help me." Kate gave her daughter a quick

unconditional kiss on the cheek.

Roisin wiped it with her hand saying, "Remember how you explained it to us. You said there were at least four labels, romance, love, sex and procreation. You told us that we had to learn to recognise the differences."

Kate smiled, "half the time I don't think you're even listening to me Roisin. Charlie renamed the procreation one, he calls it sex with intent"

Roisin smiled too,

"No more candles mum and no more sentimental rubbish. Charlie and I would like to see you in a good relationship with someone. But it has to be on level ground. Surely two adults can love each other without one ending up as a doormat. Kick the romance habit mum and understand what you taught us to understand."

"What's that Roisin?"

"Love is bloody hard work. And the man who made up that Adam and Eve rubbish needs a good kick up the backside."

Kate laughed and knew she had been right to reveal her little growing secret to her daughter before she did lose control. And Kate would be there, perhaps with softer counselling, when Roisin was experiencing romance in all its masculine guile. She cleared the candles from the room while Roisin hunted in the fridge for a snack. The silence they were sharing was broken when Charlie came through the front door and announced there was a taxi waiting to transport some woman to Valhalla.

"Fancy a taxi driver calling me a woman." Roisin laughed then quickly frowned at the idea.

"See you tomorrow Mum. I want to hear about the business side of things as well."

"What else were you two talking about then?" Charlie asked innocently.

Roisin looked at her mother. Kate smiled. "Nothing that would interest you Charlie." she said. "I'm afraid the evolutionary process is slower in males. It'll take a few generations for your lot to understand but don't worry," she looked at Roisin, "I'm working on it."

"Anything to eat?" Charlie said, "I'm starving."

"Welsh rarebit or salmon et croute." Kate replied.

"What's that?"

"Cheese on toast or salmon sandwiches." Kate laughed, waved to Roisin in the taxi and thought that it might take longer than a few generations for equal rights to harmonise. The rest of the evening was spent explaining her newly acquired knowledge of the mortgage market to her son. He listened intently much to Kate's surprise. When he had repeated the information back to her with a clear understanding of the risks and opportunities Kate knew that the risks were worth taking. In the process Charlie had a better understanding of how money actually worked than any business studies course would ever teach him.

16

Words in the singular are powerful. Love, sin, hate, beauty, child, father, home, country. Words put together for their sounds, their rhythms, their music and their meaning can create poetry, passion, or war. We remembers the jingles the sound bites the commandments, the nursery rhymes. We believe love has something to do with an internal organ. Imagine someone seriously saying 'follow your kidneys not your head, or whisper on a moonlit night into a tender ear 'I love you with all my liver." Humanity is tricked with clauses of no meaning and no reality. The mind however, is not an organ. It is not made up of cells or tissues. It does not make the body work the brain has that function. When a brain is damaged the body is crippled. When a mind is damaged or not fully functional then humanity is crippled. We are left tottering at the beginning of our evolutionary journey. Until we learn to love with the mind not the head or heart we are merely at the nursery-rhyme stage of our existence and our understanding. Creation gives us access to our own minds, the poorest, the weakest, the least academic, the most learned. Some of us are aware and believe this is a good thing. Others are also aware and believe it is a dangerous way forward. A free mind is naturally creative, naturally inquisitive. It seeks challenges, forms questions, searches for knowledge. Some powerful people deem it necessary to fill these minds as early as possible with trifles. Kate was no longer going to allow her mind to be crippled. "Intelligence is the ability to learn," she thought.

"Extelligence is the learning within us, as a bird knows how to build a nest, extratelligence is what we can experience beyond our own minds. Intratelligence is what we gain by using all senses." Kate put them together. She gave her new awareness a name. She named it 'omnitelligence'.

A free market she realised was for the few and for personal gain. A free world was for the multitudes and humanity's gain. She understood at a sub-conscious level that humanity could not respond until it freed itself from a poverty of self, a poverty of mind and a poverty of spirit. Kate, alone with her thoughts in the garden, shouted loudly,

"We are programmed not to see." and then repeated the words that had become so important to her, " Heaven is to see. Hell is not to see."

Those edges of her consciousness she had struggled to free were beginning at last to grasp new realities. She had no idea where the ideas would lead her. Her mind was untangling itself from all the mental toxins she had absorbed in her life. She was not a genius. She would never discover the theory of everything but at least her quest for freedom was also guiding her to dismiss all she had been programmed to receive, an artificial intelligence at its most menacing.

She would learn anew. She realised that the fundamental idea of a supreme being, manifested now and again in the form of a male prophet, was a clever excuse for starting wars, creating divisions and silhouetting differences. No-one would convince her now that a priest wearing his shirt collar back to front was any closer to 'goodness' to omnitelligence than a child standing naked on the Nile. Belief in supremacy whether it was dressed up as a god or a culture or a religion or an empire was wrong. Scientists carried out orders to make weapons that could maim and kill. Pilots carried out orders to drop bombs that could maim and kill. Presidents carried out orders and gave orders to maim and kill. The only difference Kate decided between the man who dropped bombs from a height and the man who strapped them around his waist was that one went home to his family and the other did not.

The latter was referred to as a 'suicide bomber'. Could the former then be referred to as a 'salaried bomber'?

"Words" Kate thought, "can make us fearful."

But she was learning not to be afraid of money. She was also learning not to be afraid of thinking . Kate wanted the thoughts of a child. When a child's voice asked who made the world the answer was dressed up as 'god'. Children knew this was a lie because their response was always 'why cant I see god then'.

Children knew a heaven until a hell was imposed upon them. Kate wanted her mind to return to a child-like state. She wanted to learn again to be amazed at the beauty of the world. She wanted to be freed from the ugliness that some humans had painted on it's natural surface. She shouted again,

"The emperor isn't wearing any clothes", and she knew now that she was not the only person who could see. Someday she would find others who would share her kind of heaven.

Kate smiled. She thought of the romantic nonsense she had tried to conjure with Will. It was another toxin recognised and released without harm. But she did need to contact him. She returned inside and rang his mobile to tell him the good news. He did not answer and she left a message,

"Hi Will, Kate here. Just to let you know that I've found the property I want. Lagan's Guesthouse Number Two is on its way'

Kate had noticed the 'for sale' sign almost by accident. She had brought her mother over to north Belfast to visit a distant relative. Kate had left her mother at the gate of the old terraced house with the promise to collect her in exactly one hour. There was no time to go home and she drove around to find a quiet coffee shop which still permitted smoking. She finally found one of those rare establishments and sat at a table by the window stirring a substance which was presumably coffee because that was what she had ordered. The café was in a row of shops on the main road. As Kate went to light her cigarette she looked out of the window and there was the house on the opposite side of the road. It was the house she had drawn. Detached, double fronted with a Georgian style door and fanlight. It was on an elevated site with a curving path to the front and an old tree struggling in an overgrown garden. The only thing missing was a curl of smoke from the chimney. She left the coffee, stubbed out her cigarette and crossed the road to have a closer look. The paint on the sills was peeling badly. The path was mossy and the old net curtains looked as if they could stand without help from a rail.

"All good signs," she thought "it's a bit distressed so perhaps there is a need to sell, a lack of interest and I hope a realistic price."

Until that moment Kate had not thought of looking beyond her own area of the city. She told herself quickly that if west Belfast had needed a guesthouse then north Belfast deserved one. The north of the city still harboured pockets of so-called tribal tensions. There were some residents still holding onto big ideas as to how 'the Troubles' would end. These thinkers were existing somewhere around 1992. There were people and politicians who had not quite grasped the concept of how good it might be to talk to someone with a different point of view, regardless of whether that person had an Irish, Scottish, Welsh, English, Polish, Hebrew, Indian or Mandarin name.

This ignorance manifested in sporadic violence. Consequently properties were not sought or marketed to the same rising extent as other areas of the city. Kate learnt with one telephone call that the house price was within her budget if slightly outside a visionary location. There was no other interested party. The house had been inherited by three cousins on the death of an elderly aunt and they were anxious to sell. Within a week Kate's offer was accepted. With the paperwork and finances in place Kate signed the contract and took possession in just under twelve weeks and she put the extension to her west house on hold.

The 'north' house was gutted, rewired, and redecorated. The application to open as a guesthouse was processed simultaneously. Kate loved every minute of the chaos. She bargained, pleaded, threatened and cooked for various groups of workmen. She paid at the completion of each stage and allowed herself between food courses and damp courses a little pat on the back. She was busy and challenged and happy. Roisin and Charlie on their frequent visits to 'the site' romped about like kids in a playground. Patricia was impressed without a hint of envy. Everyone else sat back and waited for the disaster they were sure would happen. Kate later regretted only one thing. In this crazy time she did not heed the appointment of a new bishop for the diocese, announced in the local media. He arrived in Belfast the day she was supervising the erection of the guesthouse sign at the bottom of a now moss-free and well manicured lawn. Lagan's northside was open and ready for business. She had decided to supervise personally and Patricia had agreed to train two girls studying for initial qualifications in the hospitality industry. The local enterprise agency in west Belfast had asked could they place some students at the guesthouse. Patricia was nurturing the trainees rather hidden talents with a complex mixture of mothering, scolding, bribery and instruction. It seemed to work. Their standards were gradually rising under the ever-watchful eye of their manager. The week the north guest-house opened Kate and Patricia met for a business lunch. Patricia loved her new management and training roles but was exasper-ated at what she thought was slow progress.

"Have they dispensed with the huge earrings and nose jewel-lery?" Kate asked.

"Not a sparkle in sight" Patricia had expressed her fear that a silver plated stud might end up in the scrambled eggs and had put a blanket ban on anything that could dangle, distract or choke.

"Have they stopped teaching in school?" she asked Kate.

"Why?"

Kate appreciated Patricia's views on the learning outcomes of young people within an expensive and over-rated education system.

"It took me three weeks to teach them that windows are rect-angular and thus have corners. I had to point out how clean they had made the circle in the middle but how dirty the corners were by comparison. They iron as if they have cloven hooves. One asked me what a housemaid's pillowcase was and the other one asked, "If Mrs Lagan poached eggs does that mean she steals them."

"What did you say to that?" Kate laughed

"I said never, ever call her Mrs. Lagan! I've shown them how to scramble, fry, boil and poach eggs and how to iron and clean. I have also taught them ways to greet guests on arrival. She sighed.

"What did they say?" Kate asked, smiling

"Hiya! Come on in!" Patricia toughened her accent.

"They're young" Kate responded, "they'll learn. We were probably just as bad at their age."

'I'm not so sure about that Kate. I was twelve years old when I began cooking for everybody in the house. I was the eldest. I took it for granted it was my job. I don't even remember how I learnt. My ma would tell me to throw a handful of this into a pot or a bit of that and not to forget the onion. When I asked how long things needed to cook she'd say 'have it ready for your da coming in from work love'. Then she'd hitch one of the younger ones under her arm and stand rocking the pram to get the baby to sleep. It never occurred to me that I was calculating how much I would need, how long it would take to cook and then subtracting that from the time my da would be in from work and remembering if it was his night for the confraternity, the pigeon club, the bookies or the pub. And I thought I was no good at maths when I was at school, or anything else. Thanks Kate" she added thoughtfully.

"What for?" Kate was surprised at her friend's sudden change of tone.

"For teaching me that I had the skills to manage."

"I wasn't teaching you to manage Patricia" Kate said quickly "I was teaching you to fish."

"What?"

"Give someone a fish and you feed them for a day. Teach them to fish and you feed them for life. It's a bit overcooked that expression and it doesn't tell you how to get to the River Jordan but its helpful in its way."

She looked at Patricia.

"That's what I want you to do with the apprentices Patricia. Teach them self-employment. Teach them to think for themselves and not to wait on orders. Let them learn how good they really can be if they want it. It has taken us nearly fifty years. Lets hope they do it in five."

The two women enjoyed their lunch and then began to look at the forward guest bookings, weekly budgets and monthly accounts. When coffee arrived Kate made her request,

"Patricia, I was wondering," she began then paused,

"Ask away Kate. I can only say yes no or maybe."

"I was wondering about your Susan. The twins are starting school all day soon. Do you think she would have some spare time?"

"Maybe"

"Would she be interested in part-time work?"

"Yes."

'Great! I need a team that I know and trust. Especially when I buy a third property."

"Wow, you're not serious Kate?"

"Yes I am. If Susan could eventually take over running the west house I was thinking that you might consider running the north house. That would leave me free to look at other properties. And you know Patricia there's a self-contained apartment in the north house. You might consider moving in the future." Kate waited.

"It might be that or jail Kate."

"Jimmy?"

Patricia's laugh turned to a sigh.

"Yes. I don't think I have the enthusiasm for a crime of passion but I'm seriously considering undetectable traces of powdered glass in his soup, or failing that, soap on the back steps."

"Neither would work Patricia. Your Jimmy has the constitution of a donkey and he'd only slip on the step, break a leg and you would have ten times the burden you have now. Will you ever leave him?"

"Yes. No. Maybe"

Patricia looked at Kate who wisely said,

"I can't help you there. That's your decision entirely. All I'm offering in the future is a place of refuge and a place to think."

"I will think about it Kate," Patricia was earnest, "I have no space to read never mind clear my head to think. I still feel responsible for the old goat. He'd be lost without me."

"I wouldn't be too sure about that Patricia. Men have an uncanny way of surviving. We delude ourselves into thinking that they can't live without us. We discover, usually by accident, that we can live without them. They kick up a terrible fuss but it usually takes them only a few weeks to find a shop that sells floury potatoes and tablets for the washing machine."

"I'd love time and space to read Kate. I finish a book I think I'm full then I realise it has just made me hungry for more. I was going to do another course. There's an exam at the end of it. Imagine me sitting an exam Kate even wanting to study for an exam. Jimmy thinks I'm wasting my time."

"You are Patricia," Kate replied, "on him"

"If I moved to the apartment I'd really miss the twins."

Patricia loved her grandchildren with the patience and zeal that had not been available to her in the early years of her own motherhood. She was trying to make up for lost time. Kate was exasperated.

"Patricia I'm offering you a place to live in the future and fifteen minutes drive from Susan and the twins. I'm not suggesting forced deportation to Australia."

Then Kate added thoughtfully, "Mind you, it might be a good idea to keep the image in front of you when you do suggest moving because that's the circle of argument with which your family will attack. I'm not saying they don't love you Patricia and want the best for you but it's their idea of what's good for you. They want to keep you where they feel most comfortable."

Patricia slowly stirred her coffee, now cold.

"I know what you mean Kate," she said looking at the cup.

"It seemed as if I had just taken down Susan's school photograph when I was using the frame for one of her wedding photos.

It was on the wall and before I knew it the twins photos were on either side, all balanced and correct."

"And all nailed onto a wall above your head." Kate's voice was quiet but steady.

"I know it sounds selfish Kate but sometimes the responsibility wears me down I love them all. I adore the twins but everywhere I turn I see love and no escape."

"Take the photographs down Patricia. Put them on a low shelf where you can lift them and kiss them but not be ruled by them. Susan might be annoyed at first. She doesn't even realise what she is doing, but it is your house and your life."

"It sounds harsh."

"It is harsh Patricia. Birds don't build nests for their offspring and neither should we. You can sit in your rocking chair and nurse your great grandchildren but that's twenty years away. Until then you have a lot of living to do. And no-one has ever managed to live in the future. We only have now Patricia. We have to make the most of it. Two years ago we were both stumbling from one bloody crisis to another. When I think about it I believe women of our age just might enjoy creating our worries. It's a way of assuring ourselves that we are still alive. We really have to move away from that and grow."

Kate beckoned to the waiter for the bill and the two women prepared to leave. Patricia was not going to let Kate have the last word however. She had grown in many ways but she was determined to keep a mischievous humour when it suited her.

"Have you seen yer man Will lately Kate?" She asked as innocently as she could.

"He dealt with all the paperwork for the house," Kate replied "until the lawyer took over. He telephoned a couple of times to ask how the work was progressing but I haven't seen him for a while."

"Miss him?"

"Yes, no, maybe," Kate was unsure, "he said I could stand on my own two feet"

"I thought you had managed that fairly well before he appeared on the scene."

"Oh I know Patricia. But sometimes it's pleasant to be told now and again. He said he'd bring me to see his caravan sometime."

As soon as she said it Kate wanted to bite her tongue.

"Well!" Patricia lifted her bag, "I've heard it called a lot of things in my time Kate but never would you like to see my caravan."

The women laughed and parted, Patricia to telephone Susan about a job and Kate to wonder if she should telephone Will. She coaxed her car back to north Belfast.

When Charlie came home from school to the new and private apartment Kate was waiting for advice on a more practical subject. In spite of her change in fortune she had resisted buying a new car. Some of the old make-ends-meet habits persisted. She still enjoyed rent-free driving and filling her petrol tank with the cheapest deals she could find. Charlie referred to it as her 'thrift shop toxin'. He said it ran through his mother as if she was a stick of holiday rock. Kate insisted that it was not meanness but environmental responsibility and if she had a vein of anything running through her it was solid gold. They had laughed but now Charlie's joking and the spluttering car were reaching the finishing line.

"Okay Jeremy Clarkson," Kate announced when her son had disrobed himself of his school uniform,

"I know you've done the research so what car will suit Kate Lagan and Kate Lagan's new purse?"

Charlie had known that the day would come when his mother could safely collect him from school without the jeers of 'oul wreck' ringing in his ears. He had not been quite sure if the taunts referred to the car or his mother. He glanced at Kate now. She was certainly fitter and she looked more prosperous. He was very proud of her really but it was something he would not confess aloud to anyone. He sat down at the computer with Rags cuddling down in his usual position at his feet. Rags loved Charlie with something approaching doggy idolatry and was not afraid to display the affection. He licked Charlie's sneakers and growled contentedly. Charlie lent down and absentmindedly rubbed Rags between the ears. Rags drooled and licked his master's hand as Charlie announced his decision.

"A Mazda RX8 mum," his voice was confident and he added to impress,

"It has suicide doors and a wankel engine."

"Sounds like a teenager on drugs," Kate mused

Charlie ignored the remark and continued,

"Top speed of 148mph, brake horsepower is 250 and 0 to 60 in 5.9 seconds. The engine has rotary pistons," he waved his hand in a circular motion.

"You know how pistons go up and down mum, well because of the advanced technology the camshaft uses direct motion which is much better."

"Does it have a wheel on each corner and a nice badge on the front?" Kate asked.

"Mum! It's a cross between a sports car and a family saloon, very enviable."

"I don't want people to be jealous of me Charlie. I want them to be proud of me. What colour?"

Charlie could already see the car at the school gates.

"Blue" he replied.

"I fancy silver."

"Definitely blue."

"Price?"

"I'll have to work out the figures. I'm not sure yet."

"Price?"

"Twenty three thousand"

"No."

Charlie had vision but he also had sense.

"Second-hand mum? There are some real bargains out there."

"Price?"

"About fifteen thousand, maybe fourteen on ebay."

"Okay."

Charlie grinned broadly. He was just about to throw a compliment of 'cool mum' after Kate's retreating figure when he heard her singing drifting towards him from the kitchen.

"Lord won't you buy me a Mercedes Benz, my friends all drive

Porches I must make amends."

He knew his mother well. He got up and followed her doggedly into the kitchen, Rags at his heels.

"You know something Charlie," Kate had halted her tuneless singing, "I've always fancied a Mercedes."

"Mum! Why?" He knew she had to be stopped with caution.

"I like the song."

Charlie groaned,

"That's not a very good basis to decide on a car."

"People like love songs," Kate remarked "that's not a very good basis to decide on a marriage. Don't worry though I'll leave the nuts and bolts to you. A Mazda…?"

"RX8, blue." Charlie leaned down and gave his mum a quick kiss on the cheek.

"Cool mum" he said.

....

"It has a wankel engine," Kate was explaining to her mother the day after the car was purchased. They were proceeding royally along the Antrim Coast Road. It was a rare treat. Kate had carefully packed a picnic. Lunch in the open air was preferable to lunch at the 'new' house. Kate's mother had not made the required mental leap to accept her daughter's move to north Belfast She had announced grandly on her first visit to the property the house was lovely as houses go, but that she did not like it.

"I don't know why you wanted to move off your own road Catherine," she had said several times when Kate had finally revealed her purchase and some of her plans to the family.

"Are you taking up that lovely blue carpet in the hall?" Her mother had asked on her first visit to the house.

"I believe it would be just the right size for my back bedroom. That carpet would last a lifetime."

"It already has," Kate responded and had personally supervised the carpet's final journey to the council dump.

"Your father had a bit of trouble like that." Kate's mother now announced as the Coast Road stretched appealing before them.

Kate's foot went quickly to the brake pedal as her voice squeaked, "what?"

"When he got a bit older," her mother continued, "he had a bit of engine trouble. Not that I said a word to any of you about it. In our day we dealt with private matters privately. We didn't go about announcing it in every magazine like they do these days, disgusting."

"Will we stop and have something to eat soon?" Kate asked.

"Sure we're miles away from that new house of yours," her mother replied, "besides I'm not very keen on that kitchen. It's not half as cosy as your own."

"I've brought a picnic. We can stop at the next lay-by and enjoy the view."

The two drove on for awhile in silence.

"It's a lovely car Catherine," her mother finally conceded, "we'll both enjoy it. As a matter of fact I was just saying to Paddy Joe the other day that I haven't seen your father's niece for years. She lives in Fermanagh somewhere. I'm sure I have the address on the back of an old photograph. You know that box in the wardrobe where I keep all the certificates. I must look the address up soon. She'll get a big surprise when she sees us at the door. It'll be a lovely day out in a this car."

Kate glanced resignedly at her mother." Maybe Christina will come with us," she said.

"Maggie would have loved it as well." Kate's mother replied and then, for every reason, she quietly began to cry.

"I miss her so much Catherine," she said.

"So do I mum." The two women regained silence for a time careful not to reveal the closeness of their thoughts, each sensitively guarding the depth of pain. Kate, trusting the new power steering reached over and held her mother's hand.

The outing though was a success. When Kate left her mother home at twilight the old guilt surfaced to her mind. She knew the necessity of keeping her family at a safe distance as her plans evolved. They believed she was being reckless with money just as they had believed she had been reckless without it. She knew they loved her enough to be concerned when things were going wrong but was not certain if she could depend on them when things were going right. As with most families they were always on hand to help with failure but unsure of what support was needed when they witnessed success.

There is a deep Irish inhibition to give sincere compliments, only matched by the inability to receive compliments graciously and without excuse. Even the young beautiful people at the gym displayed cultural twist of character and could turn a praise belly-up in micro-seconds.

"That's a lovely crop top," Kate had overheard one sun kissed girl say to her companion adding without pause for breath "unusual shade of red isn't it. I always think of blue as your colour."

Kate had stopped exercising and stared at them thinking,

"Those two would look good in bin bags. Why is she doing that to her friend?"

Kate need not have worried for as she pulled her long green tee-shirt further over her hips the companion had rallied with,

"Are those shorts you're wearing a size smaller than usual? You should be careful they don't expose that skin irritation."

Habitual, sly, powerful put-downs seeped their way through all aspects of life. 'Could do better' was proclaimed from every billboard, newspaper and television screen, then neatly disguised by a celebrity failure story which assured the passive masses that 'they could do worse'.

Kate was learning how to-out manoeuvre the media emperors. She was cultivating the art of self-reference and trying to avoid self-reverence. She was delighted when she saw evidence of Roisin and Charlie using the same principles, guiding each other. Kate no longer believed she had good children. She knew she had incredible children. She had no moral right to impose her beliefs on her children but she understood she had a responsibility to share her ideas and accept their opinions. As she headed towards north

Belfast and a welcoming glass of chilled sauvignon blanc she knew they were turning their dreams into joy. It had required a mental clearout, quiet determination, a renewed sense of worth and a belief that if one acted fairly and justly in all transactions then one had a right to be rich. She reached the house and turned the car into the driveway ready to meet the guests whom Charlie had greeted and settled two hours earlier.

"And," she thought opening the door, "if being rich brings with it new responsibilities and clearer thoughts then so be it...Amen."

17

The new business in north Belfast grew steadily, despite the absence of a nearby shrine. People appreciated honesty and value. Word spread that Lagan's Guesthouses were a good place to stay. The young priest Padre Peter emailed Kate informing her that his report had been written. He had stressed his belief that the tree image was just as they had discussed, a natural occurrence. His superiors had read and filed his report and decided that no further action was necessary. There had been another sighting of Mary on a hillside in Poland which could not be ignored in case John Paul 11 appeared as well. Peter was already making preparations for the journey, though reasonable accommodation was fifteen miles away. It was going to be a tough assignment. Kate had replied to the email, advising the young priest to wrap up warmly and to make sure he brought sturdy walking shoes. She added a invitation to call for a cup of tea if he ever found himself back in Belfast. What else could she say?

The fear of thousands of pilgrims sailing, flying or flocking up Belfast Lough duly sank as no newsworthy miracle occurred. The world had bigger things on its mind. There was fear about Bush and his presidency, continuing conflict in the Middle East, North Korea's energy supplements and the ill-defined axis of evil. There was anxiety about the international community's response to coups, earthquakes, famines, weaponry, political scandals and bird flu.

Against that backdrop, Mary the Mother of God was of little consequence. Kate wondered if anyone, even the mother of god could give an exact definition of an international community. She had no idea of her next door neighbour's favourite colour so how could anyone know the will and wishes of six billion people?

The women who had faithfully gathered to say the rosary around the tree were gradually disheartened by the cold, the odd scurrying of an unholy rat across their path and the lack of an immediate and miraculous response to their prayers and petitions. They returned to the warmth of the churches and the sermons of intermediaries. This gave them wholesome council and the general sense of security they had been seeking in the first place. Though they did not realise it their real prayers had been duly answered.

One day in late spring Kate made time again to walk again in Milltown Cemetery. As soon as she arrived a part of her, as always, reverted to an old familiar state. She walked briskly to her father's grave, sat down on the stone surround and smoked a cigarette in loving memory. Then she walked past the section where Maggie's body had been laid to rest reminding herself that three years had passed. Kate looked up at the sky following the flight of birds . She knew now that souls were far beyond the small space allotted to them by those who knew no better. She thought of her father and her sister and her little brown brother. All three were beyond the human sense of living and they faced the unparalleled challenges of a universal sense of being. She had recently thought of the little brother she had not known and had asked Charlie if he had heard of limbo in religious lessons in school.

"It's a sort of dance," he replied, "isn't there a pole and some scantily dressed women who bend their backs and waddle underneath?"

Kate was exasperated,

"Not that Charlie. I mean Limbo, the place, the dimension, the concept."

"Never heard of it mum. Is it in Africa or possibly Asia?"

195

"Neither. We were told in school that it was the place dead babies went to if they were not baptised."

"Where was it then?"

"Not quite heaven and not quite hell or so we were taught."

"Must be pretty full then." Charlie replied. "Why could the dead babies not go to heaven?"

"They were still marked with original sin."

"You were taught some crap mum weren't you?"

"Yes. Eve didn't tempt Adam," Kate's voice had risen in annoyance at the stupidity of it all, "even if that particular fairy tale was true Eve would surely have had the wit to rescue the poor man."

"From what?" Charlie asked.

"From the garden of Eden. If it existed at all it wasn't a paradise. It was a prison. I've always tried to guide you to ask questions and make choices Charlie. If a child is told not to eat an apple a parent should be glad if the child questions. Eve searched for knowledge and ended up being labelled like a naughty child with original sin."

Now as Kate walked alone through the grasses and rushes and bog cotton and hawthorn she thought of St. Augustine. His thesis on original sin had earned him a sainthood nine centuries after his death. He was acknowledged as patron saint of brewers, printers, sore eyes and theologians. Kate thought the mixture appropriate. Heaven according to catholic belief systems was littered with saints and Kate traced her mistrust of the system right back to St Paul, the first writer of internal memos to the faithful. She maintained a guarded suspicion of anyone who could switch so dramatically from fundamental persecution to fundamental evangelicism in the space of a blinding flash of light. She knew what other disciples had done when Jesus died. They went back home to their families and began fishing again. They were scared. They picked up the threads of their abandoned lives and trades, someone had to put food on the table. Months later they returned to Jerusalem and talked about shared experiences. It was only then that they began to realise they might just have witnessed something worthwhile. For Kate those actions were so natural and so sacredly human. As

196

the versions of their experiences were related, years later, to scribes they were indeed divine stories in many ways.

Paul's conversion was rather too obviously miraculous to be truly believable. He followed this with a swift pro-active use of scribes, soldiers, servants, messengers and secretaries many of whom would have helped in his previous crusade. They were used to taking his orders and copying memos and Kate presumed they did so again with the same zeal but differently headed notepaper. This was a story changed in the telling, characters moulded to suit the writer's turn of phrase rather than the word made flesh by human actions. It became the story of a life re-sequenced and refined to suit Paul, a god-author.

Kate arrived at the tree on the main path. She stopped and looked at the image. It was wrong of course. She was certain now. The face she saw was young and caucasian. Two thousand years ago a middle aged woman with at least three sons, Jude, James and Jesus would look much older, possibly quite haggard and certainly with a brown skin which showed the natural aging of a hot climate and a hard life. Kate doubted the rich flowing garments and thought of the saints and artists and bishops who had taken this woman, stripped her of her identity and clothed her again in pale blue raiment. They had taken away her actual living and replaced it with a life better suited to their ideas. Kate looked at the tree. Then she said,

"It took me years to realise you must have bled after the birth. The journey back to Nazareth couldn't have been pleasant."

"Terrible, but my son was healthy and beautiful and that kept me going."

"Why do you come back?"

"I don't. People believe what they see. Or in your case Kate, what they hear."

"Are you always asked questions?"

"Yes"

"Do you give answers?"

"No." Kate was undeterred, as usual.

"What was the secret of Fatima, the one only the pope is supposed to know?"

"There is no secret, no messiah, no man-god or god-man."

"I thought so. No supreme being then, no mystery?"

"No"

"No second coming, no eternal heaven?"

"No"

"Good! I'm inclined to think that eternity is merely a distraction. Why do you have a Belfast accent?"

"Can you speak Hebrew Kate?"

"No"

"Then don't ask daft questions."

"Why did Jesus say to the thief today you will be with me in heaven?"

"Did he?"

"I thought you were there?"

"I was at the bottom of an eight foot cross, crying my eyes out. I didn't hear what he said. What did he say to the other thief?"

"Ignored him by all accounts, gospel truth seemingly."

"My son would never do a thing like that, ignore someone suffering right beside him."

"I don't think my Charlie would either. Three men dying in excruciating pain, two for stealing and one for telling people it might be a good idea to love each other. What's heaven?"

"Could you live in a place of eternal static peace, no room for thoughts or emotions or creation and the endless plucking of harp strings?"

"Sounds like hell. Personally I like a challenge."

"You'll enjoy it then."

"What?"

"Your heaven."

"I'm enjoying it now."

"That's what I mean."

"Will I have a body, later?"

"What sort of body would you like?"

"An eighteen year old one with long legs and startling blue eyes."

"Sometimes a body can shape a mind and a soul. Which would you prefer a beautiful body or a beautiful soul? The choice is yours."

"Can I keep my mind?"

"Yes. It's still very young."

"Mind and soul it is then. Though I'll keep going to the gym anyway. Can I ask something else because you do seem to be answering my questions?"

"You're answering them yourself but never mind. What is the question?"

"Was it a virgin birth?"

"The Hebrew word is almah. It doesn't technically mean a virgiń. It simply denotes an unmarried young woman. May I ask you a question?"

"Yes" Kate answered vaguely wondering how she knew an obscure Hebrew word.

"Who is the better person. Is it someone who does something good because religion says this is how it should be or is it the person who does good without any sense of religion or god?"

"It doesn't matter really. Some people believe a candle gives light. Others believe it shows how much darkness there is. It's a matter of perspective. Patricia's neighbours put these great white pillars at either side of their front door. Everyone calls it the White House now. The owners think it's a compliment. But life isn't about comparisons. Life, like creation is a deeply personal activity. I have a long journey ahead." Kate touched the image and said goodbye.

Looking further up the tree Kate noticed a small bird as it rested on a branch. The new leaves on the tree rustled and wind rushed through the branches. Kate turned to leave and was not quite sure if what she heard was the wind in the branches or her own thoughts.

She had over the past year faced most of the fears that had shaped her life. She had said goodbye to the fear of change, loneliness, injury, sickness, addiction, money, managers and cats. It was time to listen to another voice just once more. Once more, time opened.

"You're very quiet Maggie," Kate said "are you praying?"

Maggie's voice, though barely audible, swept into Kate's mind, a rush of wind bringing burning heat to her head and her eyes. Time passed.

Silence, slow careful breathing. Then the gentler breeze of other words.

"I wasn't praying Kate. I was shouting."

"Who were you shouting at?"

"God. I thought he would make me well again but he didn't. I'm angry with him." Kate was back in a quiet room.

In that peaceful place she was witnessing a silent anger overwhelmingly greater than anything she had ever experienced and greater than anything she would ever have to face. The two sisters breathed for a space of time within which time no longer existed. Later as the day faded they broke the surface of that deep universe and Kate asked with a softness which burned her throat,

"Are you still angry Maggie?"

Maggie's voice reached Kate slowly and gently through woven layers of living,

"No Kate. At first I thought if I was brave I could climb to the top of the mountain and I would be free. We can't be free if we are full of anger only if we are full of love. I'm going with only love. That's what I'm thinking about now."

Kate again felt the words on her cheek as soft as an angel kiss and she remembered with love as Maggie said,

"Will you pull the curtains across Kate so that I can see the moon. Then I'll sleep for a while. I'm so very very tired."

They had watched until dawn as Maggie slept and the sun rose on her last day.

As Kate the cemetary she knew that the actions of hatred and anger caused untold misery and death. But she also knew that it is love that holds the true power for humanity. Love was the mantle for healing and creation. And love could not die. Kate was now sure of Maggie's new challenges in a greater universe, for Maggie had given her a final generous gift. Kate's fear of dying and equal fear of living were gone forever.

....

Two weeks later Kate arranged to meet Will. She had not seen him since the north Belfast business had opened. There had been an infrequent exchange of text messages which had included a vague invitation to visit the caravan. Kate's sympathetic enquiries about damp conditions on a caravan site had been met with a hesitant response from Will.

'Not on a site, looks over a lake, v. isolated'

Kate had responded in text language, her latest skill.

'Must b lonely luv 2 c it nice views?'

The simple answer had come back 'yes'. Kate hated texts. She didn't know whether that meant yes there were lovely views or yes I will take you to see it. When she telephoned him for advice on a third property she asked about the caravan. Will told her that if she intended visiting then she had to bring marigolds. He had added rather hastily that he meant the gloves not the flowers as the place needed a woman's touch. Kate had interpreted this as an invitation to clean and promptly put the chauvinist remark, the man and the bloody caravan out of her thoughts. However she knew she needed objective advice on her third business idea. Now she was driving her car along a small road in west Belfast. The road was flanked on each side by rows of terraced houses. Will was already waiting and she pulled her car close to the kerb behind his jeep. He saw her in the rear view mirror, left his car and joined her in the Mazda.

"Well?" Kate asked

"Well what?"

"Do you like my car?"

"It's fine."

"Don't you think it suits me?"

"You shouldn't get too obsessed with image Kate. It can be very misleading."

Kate sighed, sensing defeat and a short if appropriate scolding. She conceded.

"I suppose you are right though it does get me across town without a fuss. Well what do you think of the property?"

Kate pointed towards the house on the other side of the street.

"Price, specifications, repayments?" Will asked abruptly.

Kate was annoyed at his usual brevity but she knew it also helped her to focus and she replied promptly,

"One hundred and five thousand pounds, three bedrooms, good kitchen, serviceable bathroom on ground floor, small garden at rear. It needs a quick makeover but no huge improvements, twenty-five thousand pounds deposit and the rental income of about four hundred and fifty pounds a month should cover mortgage repayments."

She was pleased and for an obscure mammal-second wanted someone to rub her between the ears. She shook off the image and prepared to answer the next question.

"Who would rent it?"

"It's within walking distance of the hospital so nurses or young doctors might show an interest. There is also part of the university college close by and students could be an option. It is near the main transport system, shops and good schools. It might be a good rental opportunity for a young family."

Kate had learnt to do her homework and continued,

"Most of the houses in the street are privately owned by families, well maintained and prices are rising by 10% annually. There are a few other rentals in the immediate area and all are occupied. I found out that there is a good degree of networking and support between the landlords instead of competition. I think that is a good sign of responsible ownership. It keeps the other residents happy, no wild parties or street fights."

"The asking price is too high." Will concluded "You could get the same property twenty thousand pounds cheaper half a mile away. Leave this and look a bit further."

"No" Kate said rather too quickly. Will looked at her as she plunged into her bag for a cigarette.

"Kate," he said slowly "you don't need a cigarette. Now what's the real reason you want to buy this property. And before you answer remember the first rule of business is objectivity."

Kate looked steadily at Will as she lit a cigarette,

"It's a rule I've never much cared about."

"You haven't answered my question Kate." Will said rolling down the passenger window.

Kate looked at him with a steady eye. Then she looked past him at the house for sale. It was small and neat with an emerald green door which led directly into the living space. Three small bedrooms and an attic which could possibly be converted to a study. The yard, the tin bath and the scullery were gone for ever. The modernisation had happened and was indeed beneficial. Kate smiled.

"It's the house where I was born" she said proudly and waited patiently for Will's response, momentarily unsure of herself or her ability.

"If you've already decided to buy and I think you have, then I'd advise you to set up a limited company. If you intend keeping your head in the clouds then that will help to keep your feet on the ground."

"Okay" Kate smiled again. "When the sale goes through it will need a good cleaning. I'll let you know and you can call in with your marigolds. How do I set up a limited company?"

Will went to his jeep and came back with a file which he handed to her through the open window,

"Read this and let me know when and what you want to sign. Keep in touch."

"Don't you want to see inside?" She asked.

"Not really". Will walked back to his car as Kate switched on her engine. As soon as his jeep swept out of the street she switched the engine off and lit another cigarette.

For a few moments Kate was going nowhere.

There were certain times when she had the ability to stand outside herself, a quality that she felt was much more beneficial that objectivity. Objectivity meant developing a certain coldness towards others and worse, a certain emptiness within one's self. If she thought objectively she could hear the emptiness fill with the clink of heavy coins. In that direction lay despair. She was learning to embrace a new seventh sense of being outside her body. She watched, in sometimes quiet astonishment, as the physical side of her bartered and bantered, ordered and pleaded, cooked and cleaned and swept. She would use this new sense with confidence.

When the sale was completed in early summer the 'inside'Kate sweated with the usual burden of completing a new task. The 'outside' Kate painted and smiled and encouraged. She tallied accounts and met collective family memories with a growing ease. At times she wanted her two selves to blend back together in a comforting embrace but that celebration would have to wait until the business was completed. She knew then that the fusion could happen. Setbacks, misunderstandings delays and minor failures were discouraging but not self-defeating. With the house almost ready for occupancy Kate again contacted her adviser.

She had read and understood all the necessary requirements for setting up a limited company. Charlie and Roisin had agreed to become directors under strict instructions that they were not to use the titles as boasting javelins in any dealings with friends or relatives. Kate had explained,

"This is not a jousting competition kids. It is part of the responsibility of being rich."

Charlie had left his seat at the table and cantered around the room with Rags at his heels shouting,

"Come hither oh knight. I'll challenge ye to a dual."

As Rags barked and Roisin laughed Kate realised with a rush of joy that her children understood exactly what she meant and would even excuse her imagery. Rags had settled again at Charlie's feet as he sat down to add his signature to the forms. Lagan Properties Ltd. was born. The company could enter into contracts, sue and be sued but the holding trustees, Kate, Roisin and Charlie were not individually responsible or liable. The company had perpetual succession [Kate thought of this as a modern alternative to perpetual succour]. It had a corporate structure with its trustees having both rights and responsibilities. The governing document, its memorandum and articles of association had been drafted and costed. Charlie had enjoyed designing the headed stationery as part of the legal requirements. The company was, Kate had held her breath before reading this section aloud, exempt from audit until its turnover exceeded one million pounds per annum and its accounts would be returned to the official bodies each year for inspection and public scrutiny. Roisin had agreed to take minutes of each meeting and present an annual report in consultation with the accountant, honestly, fairly and in good faith, after one year of trading. Will had helped. He told Kate he had drawn a few favours from former friends or colleagues to provide the costing, contracts and accurate details of all legal responsibilities. He had then, to Kate's surprise, offered to drive her to the offices in the city centre where she had to lodge all legal documents.

And so it was that the director of Lagan Properties Limited watched herself emerge from the city office with a briefcase in one hand and an unlit cigarette in the other hand aware of the living which stretched before her. She put the cigarette back into the packet and perched herself in the passenger seat of Will's jeep with a 'Phew!' There was nothing else she could think of saying. Will pulled the car from the kerb and drove out of the city along the shores of Belfast Lough.

"Where are we going?" Kate finally asked when she had recovered the skill of speaking.

"It's a lovely afternoon. I thought you would like to see the caravan."

The couple drove for twenty miles in silence. Will did not see the need to speak and Kate could not trust herself to speak. Eventually he turned the car from the coast and drove for a few miles along a minor road turning finally onto a track and then into a hidden laneway. The lane weaved in a ragged fashion for half a mile or so and the jeep was driven steadily up a small hill. At the top Will braked and the car came to a halt. Kate looked out of the windscreen towards a small lake, still and silent as ice. To the left was a small copse of trees and to the right what looked like a mid-west American cabin. Will started the car again and made a right curve towards the homestead.

"I thought you said you lived in a caravan?" Kate's voice had returned at last.

"It's the easiest thing to say. The word cabin has connotations. It's the same idea anyway, isolated, free, simple."

"Lonely?"

"Alone, which is completely different. Would you like a cup of tea?"

He parked the jeep on a patch of hardened earth near the cabin.
"Who owns the land?"

"Freehold."

"Who owns the lake?"

"The fish."

Will took a key from his pocket and opened the door. Kate noticed it was latched not locked but Will headed over to a small cupboard and used the key to open it. The cabin was cosy or seemed so on a warm afternoon. It housed a small gas stove, a couch, a table and a room beyond which Kate presumed held a bed, a wardrobe and bathroom facilities. Will lit the stove and took some water from a bucket explaining that the water came from an old well in a nearby field. As the kettle warmed he informed Kate that the water was delicious.

'It's really pure, free from additives once you remove the frogspawn and weeds"

He was right. Five minutes later Kate was sitting on the couch sipping the most delicious tea she had tasted since she had been a child on a mountain. Will went into the other room and came back with an old wooden chair. He placed it near the stove and sat down. Kate recognised it as a gesture which said no candles and no cuddling but she had found her voice.

"Do you like me Will?" She took a sip of the hot tea and burned her tongue.

"Yes"

"Why?"

"You're not flimsy. You do twitter on a bit but you are solid, real."

Kate was not sure whether to feel pleased or insulted but she realised that she did not mind either way.

"I don't meet many real people anymore." Will continued "I have to look for them."

"Did you look for me?"

"No. I tripped over you. Funny that. You made me laugh."

Kate got up and looked out of the window at the lake. This was important. This place, this moment. She suddenly knew how careful she had to be. Will's words reached her as she knew they would.

"Do you want me to take you to bed?"

And Kate surprised herself because she knew what to say,

"No."

"Why?"

"I don't want to be a Mrs. Rochester."

"The first or the second?"

"Neither of them."

Kate had made her choice and she continued in what she hoped was not a shaky voice.

"Both were mad you know. The first wife because her husband lost interest in her sexually. There is such a condition. We see it all around us. Years ago doctors would perform hysterectomies to bring on early menopause. It was believed that this cutting out would cure the illness, the yearning to be female. It didn't work of course but women were inclined to trust male doctors and sometimes it was done against their wishes." Kate paused aware of the rising tension in her voice. Will remained silent so she continued,

"The second Mrs. Rochester was mad because she believed that having a maimed husband would make her life complete. Metaphorically she castrated them both by thinking that the union meant happy ever after."

Kate turned from the view of the lake and looked at Will waiting for some sort of response.

"You do twitter on don't you" he said. "here give me your cup and we'll head back to Belfast."

"I'd like to go for a walk." Kate said quietly and gave herself the luxury of a smile as Will answered,

"There isn't time for that."

He lifted the latch and Kate slipped underneath his arm and out into the open air. She did not hear the words "some other day maybe" as he closed the door.

They drove back towards Belfast through numerous small villages. Eventually Will broke the silence,

"Are you rich now Kate?"

"Yes"

"Be careful then" he said. "You know inside every fat person is a thin one and lots of chocolate?"

Kate smiled and he continued,

"Well, inside every wealthy person there is a victim and lots of ego."

"That's okay" Kate replied "Because I think I know what's inside a rich person."

"A knowledge of who you really are, mind body and spirit, a deep sense of gratitude and a burning desire to inspire others." Will said.

"I hadn't quite worked all that out yet" Kate replied. "But isn't there a flaw. People who set out to inspire others can end up starting wars"

Kate's voice had a sudden nervous edge and Will caught the tone. He slowed the jeep, lifted his hand and touched her gently on the cheek.

"Inspiration only works when it is passed on one-to-one-to-one. Remember that."

Kate smiled at the touch of the words but she did not shut up,

"That could start a war too Will."

"No" he replied firmly. "But it could start a revolution. There is a remarkable difference."

He paused then repeated his question,

"Are you rich Kate?"

"Yes" Kate replied confidently. "Would you stop here Will?"

"You're not going to kiss me in public." Will's voice was suddenly full of alarm.

"Don't be daft. I want an ice-cream. That shop has a big plastic cone outside. Do you want a slider or a ninety-nine?"

Will stopped the car in the narrow village street and Kate went into the dark little shop. She ordered two huge ninety-nines from one of the two old ladies guarding their wares and hunted in her bag for some change. Will, as usual, had not proposed to pay. She emerged a moment later, climbed awkwardly into the car and with one hand on the steering wheel and the other clasping his ice-cream Will drove her safely home.

In late summer Kate's short advertisement in a local paper describing the fully furnished rental accommodation brought several enquiries. She interviewed fourteen perspective residents and finally chose two post-graduate students. Their income as research assistants at the university meant they had the capacity to meet the rent. Their keenness during the interview to discuss their doctoral theses suggested a limit on wild parties and their joint arrival on bicycles clinched the decision. On a lovely bright morning the two young men met Kate at the house to sign the nine month contact, hand over their deposit and collect the keys. She had wandered around the house before their arrival idly examining the curtains and the rugs, the two couches and the kitchen utensils. Everything was clean and easily maintained. She looked out of the kitchen window at the wooden decking. The city was changing and Kate said aloud,

"For better or worse, for richer or poorer. It isn't for me to judge but it is for me to be part of it."

She also knew that where childhood is remembered with love and joy and no regrets then that was the place where the soul began. The doorbell rang and she went to greet her students.

Before evening two other things would happen and Kate would feel the echoes for quite some time...

The new bishop who had been appointed for the diocese of Down and Connor was modern, moderate and black. He was a man who appreciated clear lines of communication and new technologies. He also felt he had a gift of listening to his flock. His promotion to bishop had not come as a surprise for he was aware of his skills. The location however had been a bit of a shock. He had expected a diocese near Soweto where the Franciscan fathers had originally accepted him as a novice for the priesthood. He had excelled in academic studies and had proved his ability to think out of the box a somewhat new requirement in the training colleges. He had risen quickly through the churches cumbersome hierocracy. His posting to Ireland was, he eventually believed, at least a step closer to Rome.

His initial impression had been that the people were rather backward in their thinking but they were slowly accepting their identity as Europeans and that indeed was progress. He had paid short and private visits to many places on his arrival, including Milltown Cemetery. In this respect the people were right. The place was a disgrace. Despite the turmoil of his first few weeks in office he had found time to arrange a scheme for local unemployed youths. He was not a man to let a parish committee get in the way of democracy and he had heard the voice of the people. Under his innovative scheme the main path in the cemetery was to be widened, the area drenched with weed killer and all obstacles removed which prevented his flock to pray in comfort to their dead. Bishop Francis [he liked to be called by his first name] was above all a practical man. He knew that if things looked neat and tidy then people generally behaved in a neat and tidy way. Strong clear messages on the ground and from the altar would soon have the chapels as full as they were in the townships back home. Clearing cluttered paths gave clear vision and in his zeal he had no idea that Mary the Mother of God would be the first to go. For Bishop Francis there was little grey in the world. He thought simply, in black and white. As Kate left her third property in the hands of the two young students and drove back to the north of the city he sent in the bulldozers and the tree crashed across the path. Kate did not hear it fall...

that he may just make it as a lawyer who was also popular at parties, a rare combination.

Charlie and Roisin had a surprise for their mother at the end of the meal. They were sure she would hate it but they knew they had to convince her it was necessary. Kate felt incredibly happy. At the end of the meal she was deliciously full but realised she was also absolutely exhausted. The wine had been excellent but it was beginning to mist their collective memory and all three were enjoying a pleasant disagreement about sleeping bags.

"I bought those sleeping bags" Kate insisted as Charlie refilled her glass. "I scraped the money together for weeks."

"You didn't mum." Roisin knew the conversation was turning to her advantage. 'I borrowed them from Aunt Christina. I remember lying about some school trip. You sound like Nana. Next thing you'll be telling us about holes in your shoes and stale bread."

"I remember my grandfather, your great grandfather, telling me about watching a child kick a crust of bread along the street until he reached his own house then the child picked it up and ate it. Terrible poverty in those days."

"Mum!"

"I know kids, I know. Just don't forget will you?"

"No", they responded quietly.

"It's the wine." Kate explained "It always makes me sentimental and and …."

Charlie butted in "I couldn't sleep in mine for ages. The bloody sleeping bag. I kept thinking about Uncle Harry using it. Kept thinking I could smell his feet."

"I doubt it" Kate laughed. "Christina would have made sure they were spotless."

"She used them in Italy." Roisin chimed in glancing at Charlie. "I remember you were jealous of her mum."

"I was never jealous of Christina Roisin. She needed that holiday. I was scared of her sometimes. She's always so capable. She has done well though. I'm glad her and Paddy Joe decided to invest in that cottage in Donegal. It will do them good to get away at the weekends."

"That's where you should go mum." Roisin was determined.

"To Donegal? What would I do in Donegal?"

"To Italy mum. You should take a holiday in Italy."

Kate looked at her daughter in horror.

"Roisin I'd hate it. I don't like travelling. I can't speak Italian. I'd get that itchy rash on my legs and I'd look like a lost soul sitting by myself on a beach trying to hold in my tummy."

"We thought Patricia might go with you." Charlie suggested. "You need a proper rest mum. You haven't had a day off in eighteen months."

Kate was defensive. "There's nobody to look after things."

But even as she said the words she realised how weak they sounded. Sometimes being good at something has its rewards and its penalties. Roisin seized the opportunity, just as her mother would have done.

"We've already thought of that. Richard and Susan are going to look after the west house and Charlie and Melanie will look after here and before you interrupt mum, if you go in the last week of October Charlie will be on mid-term break. I'll come back from Galway that weekend as well just to supervise."

"It's too much responsibility for you kids."

Kate knew she had lost the argument. Her children could run a minor planet if they were so inclined. Charlie laughed and sealed the deal by telling his mother that he could handle anything, including her. The only thing they needed, he informed his mum, was her credit card. Kate finally agreed knowing she did need a break and trusting her children to make a sensible choice.

Five weeks later Kate and Patricia were on a plane heading for Milan. After the hustle and bustle of shopping, the excitement of the adventure, the fuss about passports and travellers cheques and the science of packing twice as many things as would naturally fit into a suitcase, the two fell silent when they had boarded the plane in Dublin. They ordered a taxi at Milan airport which brought them to the small village of Trarego. Twenty minutes further they found the hotel built closely and serenely into the foothills of the

Alps. They settled into their separate rooms but a reserve had come between them. Kate wondered if Patricia resented the fact the Kate had paid for the entire holiday. Patricia wondered if Kate had asked her to go as an employee or a friend. She was not quite sure how to act now they had both journeyed so far from familiar zones. She needed time to consider many things and decided not to eat in the restaurant that evening. They both went to bed early and without supper. It could be a long fortnight. Rest, isolation and relaxation did not come easily to either of them.

At breakfast next morning Kate suggested a walk around the village. It had an old church with a famous stained-glass window according to the guidebook. Patricia agreed suggesting a look around the three or four shops as well where they could practice their phrase-book Italian. They set off in silence. The church was duly visited, the window inspected and the shops picked over. The two friends began their walk back up the steep twisting road to the hotel passing a few elderly couples who nodded politely to them. Kate broke the silence,

"Do you think we should have gone to one of those seaside resorts Patricia. It's a bit quiet here isn't it. Nothing but the hills and walks and panoramic views. We might be bored."

Patricia shrugged. Roisin had put some thought and research into the holiday destination. She knew her mother needed a retreat and Charlie had agreed with the choice. It was a small, exclusive, family-owned hotel offering good food, excellent wine and massage therapies. On arrival Kate had strolled around and could not help thinking 'monastic'. She was delighted. There were no bikini-clad women in the small indoor pool and no groups of young tourists. The balconies offered magnificent views and there were additional small alcoves allowing guests to read or contemplate or daydream. Kate had fallen in love with the surroundings. Patricia had not commentated on anything so far and this was Kate's only anxiety. They returned to the hotel, had a beautiful lunch and separated. Patricia said she wanted to read. Kate slept and then went to swim. As the evening drew close she telephoned Patricia's room to agree a time to dine. Patricia answered the telephone and Kate realised at once that tears not books had been her afternoon's occupation.

"Is there something wrong Patricia?" she asked, immediately concerned.

"No." Patricia sniffed and Kate heard a healthy nose-blow at the other end of the line.

"Do you want to talk about it over dinner?"

"No" another sniff and the rustle of tissues. "Kate, if you don't mind I'll skip dinner tonight. I really need to be by myself. I'll see you at breakfast in the morning. Is that okay?"

"You shouldn't even ask Patricia. This holiday is for both of us to relax. Try to sleep and I'll see you in the morning."

Kate put down the hotel telephone and slowly began to get ready for dinner. She wondered again if the holiday had been a mistake then shook the idea from her mind. After all they were both grown women in a sophisticated situation. They did not need to hold each others hands for ever. She would find out what was wrong soon enough. Tonight she was going to enjoy her meal. She was not disappointed. It was delicious. She glanced at the other tables where middle-aged couples were quietly conversing and Kate realised that she was quite contented dining alone. She thanked the waiter in her virgin Italian and retired to her room.

She undressed, slipped into the beautiful cream pyjamas her children had bought as a surprise gift and climbed into the king-sized bed. Knowing sleep was at least an hour away she allowed herself to drift into a favourite pastime. At home she had little energy or inclination to listen to radio. The local broadcasts verged on democratic madness and Radio Four, especially Woman's Hour made her grind her teeth. But one programme did help her to sleep and she found the activity more interesting than counting sheep. She lay back on four of the six pillows and began to choose her records, her book and her luxury for her own desert island.

"Well Kirsty, my first record is...."

Kate's mind drifted tunelessly through old ballads, seventies

Kate had left messages for Will to update him on the progress of the house. He had not returned her calls and then his mobile number was disconnected. Kate had thought it strange and had rummaged through files to find the name and number of the firm who seemed to employ him at irregular intervals. She had not contacted him at work before. There had been no need. He had said he was rarely at the office and preferred taking calls to his mobile. Kate imagined he would not mind if she telephoned the office with the news of her latest enterprise successfully up and running. She let herself into the apartment, called down to Melanie that she could head home early, gave Rags a biscuit and lifted the telephone. She had scribbled the number down on the back of a used envelope. Her request to speak to Will Roberts was met with silence. Then a voice came back on the line.

· "I'm sorry. This is the switchboard I'll put you through to one of the secretaries now. They may be able to help. Please hold."

Kate listened to the secretary, held her breath for a second and then repeated,

"Pardon!"

The secretary gave an audible sigh and repeated the information.

"Mr. Roberts is at this moment on a private plane making its way to Cape Verde."

Kate composed herself but failed to keep the astonished questioning tone from her voice.

"Mr. Roberts. Mr. William Roberts?"

"There might be some misunderstanding I'm afraid Mrs. Lagan." The secretary's tone was light but firm as she continued,

"The switchboard told me you had asked to speak to Mr. Roberts. I assumed you meant Mr. Wilson Roberts who, as I said, is currently on a private jet. Obviously there has been some confusion. You may have made a mistake."

"Yes" Kate replied "It seems I have. By the way it's Ms. Lagan. I wonder could you tell me who Will, I mean, Mr. Roberts is travelling with?"

"Members of his family I believe. I'm sorry. I'm really not at liberty to give any more information. You may have the wrong man and Mr. Roberts is very private about his personal affairs."

"Yes, so I see."

Kate's voice seemed distant even to herself as the secretary said a polite but abrupt goodbye. The line went dead. Even so Kate heard herself say thank you to no-one listening. She crossed over to the window, opened it wide and shouted at the top of her voice at the passing but indifferent clouds,

"Goodbye Will Roberts. Wherever you are, whoever you are!"

She closed the window and turned to Rags,

"Come on Rags, lets go for a walk in the park. Wife, kids, private plane! Two blue suits my backside!"

She began to laugh and Rags understanding all the words he needed to understand dived under the table to retrieve his ball for a romp with Kate.

The secretary took another telephone call and when she had replaced the receiver remembered to ask her colleague sitting across the room for confirmation. She did not like untidiness.

"Mr. Roberts is travelling with his family isn't he?"

"Yes" her colleague looked up from a keyboard adding,

"His sister I believe and his elderly aunt. I heard him informing the other directors when I brought their coffee into the board room last week. Why?"

"Just someone enquiring about him. I don't know why the switchboard put the call through to me. She may have had the wrong name, I can't imagine anyone calling Mr. Roberts 'Will' It's not important anyway."

In the long air-conditioned corridor one door quietly closed and another, equally quietly, opened.

212

18

Summer was slowing down. The bright twilights changed colours as sunsets were gradually replaced by a wise and insistent moon. Kate loved this exchange of seasons and the subtle compliance of natural birth rest and rebirth. On a cool September evening the three Lagans stood at the window of the apartment. Kate and Roisin curtsied to the harvest moon. Behind them Charlie bowed partly to the moon and partly to the great universe which had shown them such generosity. If anyone asked he would have said he was humouring his mother. A moment later as he joined Roisin in the kitchen to put the finishing touches to the celebration meal they heard Kate's voice trying to keep to tune as she sang,

"You saw the crescent, I saw the whole of the moon."

Roisin laughed, "She has both wrong this time, the words and the tune."

"I know." Charlie lifted the salmon fillets from the oven as Roisin put the dressing on the herb salad. '

"She's still as daft as a bat you know. The guests will be thinking we have a werewolf instead of a dog. I hope Melanie has shut the doors to keep out the noise."

Melanie was the younger of Patricia's protégées. She had blossomed and was now duty manager in north Belfast. The other trainee had decided that the hospitality industry was not in her blood. She had opted for a media course at the technical college dreaming of future celebrity status. Kate had willingly let her follow her dreams. She had then employed a young man called Richard. He had left his job as trainee-stylist in a city branch of a famous hairdressing chain. When Kate interviewed him he said honestly that he knew nothing about guesthouses. He also explained that he had left his previous post under a cloud.

"I was totally exasperated" he told Kate, "So I just announced to everyone, staff and customers, that snipping a few hairs from the top of an ego-sized head and then charging eighty-five quid for something a child with a pair of plastic scissors could do, was at best a rip-off and at worst a sin!"

Kate envisaged difficulties but recognised potential when she met it. She enjoyed his preachy humour. The guests adored him and Patricia's first informal assessment glowed. She told Kate that he ironed like a young god and cleaned as if he meant it. He had also added omelettes and crepes to the breakfast menu which he cooked and served with a flourish and a false French accent. Kate knew these were sound indications of future management responsibilities and a great deal of laughter before he would, no doubt set up his own business. Susan was also enjoying the part-time work and fervently hoped that she could match her mother's gift of making others feel instantly at home.

The Lagan's had planned this particular evening meal all summer but each had been too busy. It was early Autumn hailing their success rather than high summer. Roisin had excelled in her examinations and won a place at medical school in University College Galway. She would begin 'fresher week' with a list of 'do's 'don'ts' and 'definitely nots' from her mother. Charlie had prepared little for his examinations and had achieved the highest grades in ten subjects. Kate realised that he would either become a top lawyer or a tramp. She had been delighted with their accomplishments and wanted to treat them both. Roisin had opted for new clothes and an end to matronly advise. Kate had complied with both requests knowing in her heart that her daughter would soar and Kate would often ache for her company. Charlie opted for driving lessons and a guitar. Kate duly revised her future vision for her son deciding that he may just make it as a lawyer who was also popular at parties, a rare combination.

Charlie and Roisin had a surprise for their mother at the end of the meal. They were sure she would hate it but they knew they had to convince her it was necessary. Kate felt incredibly happy. At the end of the meal she was deliciously full but realised she was also absolutely exhausted. The wine had been excellent but it was beginning to mist their collective memory and all three were enjoying a pleasant disagreement about sleeping bags.

"I bought those sleeping bags" Kate insisted as Charlie refilled her glass. "I scraped the money together for weeks."

"You didn't mum." Roisin knew the conversation was turning to her advantage. 'I borrowed them from Aunt Christina. I remember lying about some school trip. You sound like Nana. Next thing you'll be telling us about holes in your shoes and stale bread."

"I remember my grandfather, your great grandfather, telling me about watching a child kick a crust of bread along the street until he reached his own house then the child picked it up and ate it. Terrible poverty in those days."

"Mum!"

"I know kids, I know. Just don't forget will you?"

"No", they responded quietly.

"It's the wine." Kate explained "It always makes me sentimental and and ...."

Charlie butted in "I couldn't sleep in mine for ages. The bloody sleeping bag. I kept thinking about Uncle Harry using it. Kept thinking I could smell his feet."

"I doubt it" Kate laughed. "Christina would have made sure they were spotless."

"She used them in Italy." Roisin chimed in glancing at Charlie. "I remember you were jealous of her mum."

"I was never jealous of Christina Roisin. She needed that holiday. I was scared of her sometimes. She's always so capable. She has done well though. I'm glad her and Paddy Joe decided to invest in that cottage in Donegal. It will do them good to get away at the weekends."

215

"That's where you should go mum." Roisin was determined.
"To Donegal? What would I do in Donegal?"
"To Italy mum. You should take a holiday in Italy."
Kate looked at her daughter in horror.
"Roisin I'd hate it. I don't like travelling. I can't speak Italian. I'd get that itchy rash on my legs and I'd look like a lost soul sitting by myself on a beach trying to hold in my tummy."
"We thought Patricia might go with you." Charlie suggested. "You need a proper rest mum. You haven't had a day off in eighteen months."

Kate was defensive. "There's nobody to look after things."

But even as she said the words she realised how weak they sounded. Sometimes being good at something has its rewards and its penalties. Roisin seized the opportunity, just as her mother would have done.

"We've already thought of that. Richard and Susan are going to look after the west house and Charlie and Melanie will look after here and before you interrupt mum, if you go in the last week of October Charlie will be on mid-term break. I'll come back from Galway that weekend as well just to supervise."

"It's too much responsibility for you kids."

Kate knew she had lost the argument. Her children could run a minor planet if they were so inclined. Charlie laughed and sealed the deal by telling his mother that he could handle anything, including her. The only thing they needed, he informed his mum, was her credit card. Kate finally agreed knowing she did need a break and trusting her children to make a sensible choice.

Five weeks later Kate and Patricia were on a plane heading for Milan. After the hustle and bustle of shopping, the excitement of the adventure, the fuss about passports and travellers cheques and the science of packing twice as many things as would naturally fit into a suitcase, the two fell silent when they had boarded the plane in Dublin. They ordered a taxi at Milan airport which brought them to the small village of Trarego. Twenty minutes further they found the hotel built closely and serenely into the foothills of the

Alps. They settled into their separate rooms but a reserve had come between them. Kate wondered if Patricia resented the fact the Kate had paid for the entire holiday. Patricia wondered if Kate had asked her to go as an employee or a friend. She was not quite sure how to act now they had both journeyed so far from familiar zones. She needed time to consider many things and decided not to eat in the restaurant that evening. They both went to bed early and without supper. It could be a long fortnight. Rest, isolation and relaxation did not come easily to either of them.

At breakfast next morning Kate suggested a walk around the village. It had an old church with a famous stained-glass window according to the guidebook. Patricia agreed suggesting a look around the three or four shops as well where they could practice their phrase-book Italian. They set off in silence. The church was duly visited, the window inspected and the shops picked over. The two friends began their walk back up the steep twisting road to the hotel passing a few elderly couples who nodded politely to them. Kate broke the silence,

"Do you think we should have gone to one of those seaside resorts Patricia. It's a bit quiet here isn't it. Nothing but the hills and walks and panoramic views. We might be bored."

Patricia shrugged. Roisin had put some thought and research into the holiday destination. She knew her mother needed a retreat and Charlie had agreed with the choice. It was a small, exclusive, family-owned hotel offering good food, excellent wine and massage therapies. On arrival Kate had strolled around and could not help thinking 'monastic'. She was delighted. There were no bikini-clad women in the small indoor pool and no groups of young tourists. The balconies offered magnificent views and there were additional small alcoves allowing guests to read or contemplate or daydream. Kate had fallen in love with the surroundings. Patricia had not commentated on anything so far and this was Kate's only anxiety. They returned to the hotel, had a beautiful lunch and separated. Patricia said she wanted to read. Kate slept and then went to swim. As the evening drew close she telephoned Patricia's room to agree a time to dine. Patricia answered the telephone and Kate realised at once that tears not books had been her afternoon's occupation.

"Is there something wrong Patricia?" she asked, immediately concerned.

"No." Patricia sniffed and Kate heard a healthy nose-blow at the other end of the line.

"Do you want to talk about it over dinner?"

"No" another sniff and the rustle of tissues. "Kate, if you don't mind I'll skip dinner tonight. I really need to be by myself. I'll see you at breakfast in the morning. Is that okay?"

"You shouldn't even ask Patricia. This holiday is for both of us to relax. Try to sleep and I'll see you in the morning."

Kate put down the hotel telephone and slowly began to get ready for dinner. She wondered again if the holiday had been a mistake then shook the idea from her mind. After all they were both grown women in a sophisticated situation. They did not need to hold each others hands for ever. She would find out what was wrong soon enough. Tonight she was going to enjoy her meal. She was not disappointed. It was delicious. She glanced at the other tables where middle-aged couples were quietly conversing and Kate realised that she was quite contented dining alone. She thanked the waiter in her virgin Italian and retired to her room.

She undressed, slipped into the beautiful cream pyjamas her children had bought as a surprise gift and climbed into the king-sized bed. Knowing sleep was at least an hour away she allowed herself to drift into a favourite pastime. At home she had little energy or inclination to listen to radio. The local broadcasts verged on democratic madness and Radio Four, especially Woman's Hour made her grind her teeth. But one programme did help her to sleep and she found the activity more interesting than counting sheep. She lay back on four of the six pillows and began to choose her records, her book and her luxury for her own desert island.

"Well Kirsty, my first record is…."

Kate's mind drifted tunelessly through old ballads, seventies rock classics, rebel songs and hymns. The second record she would dedicate to her parents, the third to her children and so on, until the final question,

"And what Kate would you say has been your biggest difficulty in Belfast over the years?"

Kate threw one of the pillows down to the bottom of the bed. There was such a thing as too much comfort. She wondered idly if her answer would be an analysis of political, racial, religious or social tensions but decided that would not be in her terms of reference. As her head sank slowly on the remaining pillows she realised that the answer she would give was obvious.

"Well, Kirsty, my biggest difficulty is getting a window cleaner. You can't get a window cleaner in Belfast for love or money. You can get doctors, chemists, researchers, economists, Indian head massage, tapas, titanic tours, romance, Thai salads, ice cream in winter and ice hockey in summer but not somebody brave enough to clean the windows and help us see out. We've been looking through dirty glass for over thirty years."

"And your luxury Kate?"

"Creamy silk..."

Kate fell sound asleep. The morning brought a warm and steady rainfall. Kate was already sitting in the dining room with fruit juice and cereal when Patricia glided in. She walked straight to the self service area and Kate heard her voice ringing with confidence as she "bon-journo....d" and "gracia....d" to the waiter, the manager and the couple waiting patiently behind her for their cereal and prunes. Armed with the beginnings of breakfast she sat down opposite Kate saying dramatically,

"Well! This is the life isn't it. Happy, happy days Kate Lagan. Bon journo, bon journo!"

"I thought you were going to come down to breakfast and announce that you were heading home." Kate said

"You must be joking Kate."

"You were crying last night Patricia."

"Oh that." Patricia gulped down the fruit juice and poured

milk and a generous helping of sugar over her cornflakes. "I needed a good healthy cry. I was saying goodbye to old friends."

"Me?" Kate was anxious but Patricia smiled.

"To be honest Kate, at first, I couldn't get away from the fact that you have paid for everything. For forty-eight hours I kept thinking of myself as some sort of Victorian travelling companion, especially when I saw the hotel and the location."

"I'm sorry Patricia. I didn't mean it to be like this. I'm sorry for embarrassing you."

Patricia grinned and looked directly at Kate.

"Don't worry Kate. And definitely don't apologise. I realised I was acting and thinking stupidly. If you can pay then I'm delighted that you are rich enough and if we can relax and grow and feel comfortable in these surroundings then I know I've come a long way. Patricia Bernadette Veronica Mary Kinnaird is going to enjoy every bloody minute of this!"

Patricia took a spoonful of cereal. Kate watched her and waited.

"The friends I said goodbye to last night have no importance to me now Kate."

"And I wasn't one of them?"

"No. I thought I was jealous then I realised how important it was for both us to be here."

"To relax?"

"Yes, but for time to think as well, to reconsider. Remember the day you told me that you thought your mind was getting bigger?"

"You thought I was mad."

"I know. But now I really know what you meant. It's happening to me Kate. I tried to shut it out at home in Belfast. But yesterday I decided to empty out all the rubbish I've been gathering for years. I imagined they were bosom thoughts and bosom buddies but they are really just barriers. It's a big decision."

"I know. What or who did you start with?"

"Jimmy."

"Why?"

"He laughs at the books I read. He wants to keep me and my

mind where he can find us. He thinks his name is stamped on me the way it was stamped on the marriage and the mortgage. He still says my wife, my house, but it's always 'our' bills."

"Pronouns are slippery. I try to avoid them if I can." Kate waited for Patricia to continue.

"Shall we order the rest of our breakfast first Kate I'm famished?"

"Okay. Tea or coffee?"

"Both, then croissants and crepes and honey and butter and yoghurt."

"And ambrosia."

"Yep, that too." Patricia said her eyes twinkling, "I love creamed rice!"

The women ordered and Kate said,

"You know Jimmy has to give you half the value of the house whether or not your name is on the deeds."

"Yes" Patricia was elated. "It wasn't only fiction I was reading at night. There's going to be some tough negotiating when I get back to Belfast. Either he moves or I do. We bought that house for twenty-five thousand pounds Kate. It must be worth three times that now."

"More like five times Patricia."

"I don't want the money for the sake of the cash, though that's important too. I want time to plan a future for myself Kate. Do you think Will could advise me?"

"He's gone Patricia."

"Gone where?"

"I don't know really. Perhaps to where the grass is greener. I don't mind and I know plenty of people now who can give you good advice about selling or remortgaging. Don't worry."

"I won't" Patricia said as their breakfast arrived on two shimmering trays.

"I thought he was in love with you Kate. Do you mean to say he just walked away without saying goodbye?"

"He said I was solid and real. That was enough. Anyway I

might see him again some day, you never know."

"When he wants sex?"

"No Patricia." Kate smiled and added purposefully, "When he wants warriors."

"You're too far ahead of me Kate"

"I thought we were at the end Patricia. Do you know something, I think we're only at the beginning."

"I know" Patricia said quietly, "that's why I said goodbye."

The two friends finished breakfast and decided to walk in the morning rain. Feeling brave and light hearted they headed up towards the mountains rather than down towards the village. Roisin had explained that the hotel was built on ley lines. Kate and Patricia had not heard of this. Now they were experiencing it. There was a natural serenity in the area. It was giving them both a connection to each other and to something greater than themselves. The rain washed over their heads and faces as they climbed and they felt as if they were walking through a host of clouds rather than walking below them.

"So many days" Patricia said as they paused at a bend in the road to look back at how far they had climbed, "so many days I woke thinking every silver lining had a cloud. When good things happened to me I tried to get them over with as quickly as possible to give me time to prepare for the bad thing that would inevitably follow. What a way to live a life Kate."

A car passed them speeding up the narrow road.

"I suppose he thinks he is going fast" Kate said "He only has the illusion of speed. I have discovered that walking is the natural heartbeat. Walking to the edge of oneself in the rain is primitive and timeless Patricia. And anyway I think we need the clouds and the lining. Both can be beautiful, both help us to know why we are here."

At the next curve of the road they came across one of many little shrines. It was a statue of the virgin Mary, locked in her little glass case with plastic flowers at her feet, set neatly and securely into a niche in the wall to protect her from the rain and the sun. Kate and Patricia looked down at the little monument.

"It was a pity about the tree wasn't it Kate" Patricia said, wiping the raindrops from the end of her nose.

"There are people who want everything to be neat and tidy Patricia. They are happy enough with the bishop's sense of purpose. People seem to like him now they are comfortable with his, mmmm, accent." Anyway I reckon somebody will write a story about it one day. They'll hear the bare facts and no doubt invent the rest. Probably throw in a few miracles just for good measure.

"Did you know there are only seven stories in the world Kate?" Patricia began to list them as the rain softened,

"Love and hate, birth and death, success and failure, poverty and riches, bravery and cowardice, good and evil, darkness and light. You can mix them up of course, take a bit of one and add a bit of another but you end up with the same stories."

"And the difference in the mixture" Kate added thoughtfully, "is whether you get heaven or hell. Will we turn around now and head back to the hotel?"

"On one condition Kate."

"What's that?"

"Let's not walk." Patricia linked her arm through Kate's. They looked at each other and knew what they had to do. They began at once. A cyclist stopping to admire the view, turned his eyes from the mountains and watched in amazement two middle-aged women arm-in-arm skipping down the winding Italian road singing above the rain in pure Belfast voices,

"On the hillside stands a lady, who she is we do not know.

All she wants is gold and silver, all she wants is a nice young man."

They had all the time in the world before night fall.

....

"That was delicious."

Patricia sat back wiping the crumbs from the side of the table just as the waiter came quietly forward to remove the plates.

"Force of habit." she added looking up at him and grinning as he replenished the empty wine glasses. They had decided to have their last evening meal on the balcony. The rain had gone and the warm low sun shone across at them. They smiled back.

"What are you thinking?" Patricia asked.

"You're not going to believe this" Kate replied taking a sip of wine, "I was thinking of Divis Tower."

Patricia kept her eyes towards the sun though a vision of the bare concrete tower block, the gateway to west Belfast, nudged its peculiar way into her vision."

"My granddad used to live there in the seventies," she said "twenty-first floor, the lift didn't work, the walls were covered with graffiti and he had a bad leg."

"Tough times." Kate mused.

"He was always tripping over a soldier pointing a gun every time he went out to buy a loaf. He would shout and make a fuss and blame his clumsiness on his gammy leg. It was as good a warning as any to the boys who might have had a weapon or two about them as well," she added thoughtfully.

"I hated the place" she continued "no-one could see out because the windows were so dirty. Who was going to climb up the side of Divis Tower to clean a bloody window? They wouldn't have felt the wind rushing past, just a hail of bullets"

"The British Army have moved from the top floor haven't they Patricia?"

"Yep! It was part of the peace processing deal. Why?"

"I'm going to buy the top floor Patricia. Turn it into a studio apartment. It's two minutes walk from the city centre. It's a great investment."

"Will you rent it to someone?'

"Not for a while. If you take the apartment in the north house and if Charlie heads off to university then I think I might live there. I'll get the windows cleaned." Kate smiled,

"and I would finally have a clear view of the place I was born."

Her mobile phone beeped on the table. It was a message from Charlie,

'Luv u mum: evrythg here fine: shine on'

Kate smiled, set the phone back on the table and walked the few steps to the edge of the balcony. She looked up at the mountains. She looked through the clouds to the sky. She smelt the sweet freshness of the earlier rain and felt the evening sun boast its warmth on her skin.

"I know why I'm here Patricia" she said without turning around. Her voice drifting upwards.

"I have nested too long. Now I am going to fly!"

Her friend smiled, tasting the wine on her lips. She slipped her notebook and pen out of her bag and put them on the table.

"I'm happy too Kate" she said, "I finally know what I want to do."

· Patricia lifted both glasses and joined Kate at the very edge of the balcony. They raised their glasses to salute the universe.

"For the second time in our lives Patricia" Kate proclaimed to her friend, "We're a knicker-day ahead of ourselves!"

They clinked glasses and both women burst into laughter.

ISBN 141209592-1